THE FINAL STAND

JAMES HUNT

❀ Created with Vellum

PROLOGUE

*S*hell casings and bullets littered the rocky dirt, but Katy Thorton wasn't finished with her target practice. She laid on her stomach, her eye pressed against the scope as she aligned the crosshairs over her target one hundred yards downrange.

The metal circle hanging from a tree branch between a pair of rocks was only three inches in diameter. It was what she called the perfect bullseye. She hadn't been able to consistently hit it since she hung the small medallion three months ago. Her goal was to hit three in a row. She had just hit two.

Dozens of other targets rested between Katy and her penultimate challenge. Every piece of metal was dented from the thousands of rounds that she had emptied over the past few years. Living off-grid didn't provide much recreational time, but the few free moments she did have were spent here.

The wind had kicked back up, and the metal circle swung precariously from side to side. She had always struggled to hit moving targets.

Katy relaxed the tension in her body and controlled her breathing as she placed her finger on the trigger. She closed her left eye, her right focused on the metal pendulum passing over the crosshairs of her scope, waiting. Finally, she squeezed the trigger.

The long rifle recoiled sharply against her arm. The sound of the gunshot echoed through the mountain air, and she smiled when she heard the familiar metal ping of the bullet striking her target. Katy removed her eye from the scope and rested her chin on the stock of the rifle, admiring her skilled shot. She had woken up before dawn to finish her chores so she could come out here to relax and practice. She was glad she did.

Today was going to be hard. Katy knew that the moment she received the call from her brother last week. She hadn't called him back even though he had called her over a dozen times since then. She was sure he would call today as well. She had come out here for a distraction.

But now, with her bullets dispensed and no more ammunition for practice, the distraction was over, and her mind wandered to the funeral happening in Charlotte.

Katy quickly pushed the thought from her head and stood. She dusted the dirt and bits of rock from her stomach and legs. Her attire was the same as every day. Long cargo pants, a long-sleeve performance shirt, sunglasses, and ball cap.

The clothes were old but clean. What her wardrobe lacked in variety, it compensated for with its functionality. And she didn't have anyone to impress out here. She lived alone. She enjoyed being alone.

Katy picked up her gear and departed her homemade

range on the mountainside and walked back through the forest to her cabin.

The area had good hunting grounds, fresh water, and was far away from any large metropolitan area. The nearest town was three miles away, and it held a population of fewer than one hundred people. She had bought her patch of paradise with cash, but the view from the mountain top was priceless.

Katy was one hundred miles east of Charlotte, where her family lived. One hundred miles away from the choking congestion that plagued the city daily. One hundred miles away from the crime-infested streets, away from the people who would rather look at their phones than talk to one another. One hundred miles away from people who had forgotten what life was really about.

Living.

Of course, isolation had its downsides. Katy hadn't seen her family in years, and her absence had put a strain on their relationship. It had been hard to leave them, but at the time she didn't see any other way.

A lot had changed since then, and she had grown so used to being alone; she no longer remembered what it was like to need someone. She was self-sufficient now, prepared to face anything. She was a survivor.

After years of solitude, Katy noticed the cracks in society. She saw the vulnerability in law and order and how easy it could collapse. She believed a catastrophic event, either man-made or brought on by the wrath of nature, would trigger nationwide panic. It was the kind of event that would claim the lives of millions.

But Katy refused to be a victim. She had spent the past five years preparing, honing her skills, bracing for the inevitable. When the time came, she would be ready.

However, the thought of society's collapse turned Katy's thoughts back to her family, and she stopped walking. She lifted her gaze to the sky and studied the position of the sun. It was nearly nine o'clock in the morning now. In a few hours, her family would be gathered around her father's casket in the old Baptist church where they had gone to services on Sunday when she was a child. And even though her father was dead, Katy couldn't manage to find an ounce of grief.

Mike, Katy's brother, wanted her to attend the funeral. And for his sake, she almost did. But every time she considered going, Katy remembered the last conversation she had with her father, and her anger overrode her sympathy. Just like now.

It was a twenty-minute walk from her range to the cabin, and Katy was glad to see her small home nestled in the shade of the mountainside, surrounded by trees.

A few hides hung from lines on the porch. She had hunted deer last week, and the skin she peeled from the buck would provide good leather for clothes and packs. When she hunted, she wasted nothing of the animal. Every part was used.

Survival was more than just knowing how to take care of yourself, it was maximizing the efficiency of resources. And Katy had grown very efficient.

Katy entered the cabin and removed her gear, setting her weapon and her pack by the door. The inside of the cabin was bare bones. The kitchen consisted of a potbelly stove, a fireplace, and a dry freezer, along with cabinets where she stored the food that she used daily. There was a living room with a small table where she ate her meals, which provided a scenic view of the surrounding mountains.

Past the living room was the hallway, which led to the bedrooms. She had two rooms, but since she never received visitors, the spare bedroom was used as storage space.

Katy entered her own bedroom, which mimicked the minimalistic style of the rest of the cabin. She had her bed, a dresser, and a chest at the foot of her bed which held all of her personal items. She also had a mirror on the wall, but she tended to avoid it if she could.

Katy walked to the chest at the foot of her bed and entered the combination for the lock. She waited for the click when the correct sequence of numbers had been entered, then opened the lid.

Inside were mementos from her past. Some were from her childhood, others from her time in the military, but what she wanted was beneath those personal items.

The satellite phone Katy removed from the trunk was her one link to the outside world aside from the CB radio she used to check the weather reports.

The weather could change on a dime up in the mountains, and it was important to know what was coming so she could properly prepare.

Katy gripped the phone in her hand, and then sat on the edge of the bed. She knew Mike would be hurting today, and if she couldn't be there physically, she thought a quick call might help.

But when Katy pressed the power button on the phone, nothing happened. She frowned, pressing it again. Nothing. She couldn't remember the last time she charged it, so she retrieved the cable and then walked over to her solar-powered battery charger. She plugged in the device and then pressed the power button again.

Still nothing.

Katy stared at the satellite phone for a moment longer, wondering if she had done something wrong, but then a thought caused the hair on the back of her neck to stiffen. She quickly set the phone down and hurried to her CB radio in the living room.

Katy flicked the power dial once, then twice, but received no response. Two of her most reliable electronic devices were no longer working. It wasn't likely that both of them would quit working at the same time unless—

Katy rushed back into her room and grabbed a fresh go-bag, along with her concealed 9mm Ruger, which was her favorite handgun. She hurried toward the door, picking up her rifle along the way. She reloaded the weapon with a fresh magazine, packing a few extras, and then hurried out the door.

Armed and with her go-bag, Katy hurried to the old 1975 Jeep Wrangler and tossed her gear in the backseat. She had purchased the vehicle from an auction and fixed it up herself. She stripped it down to the bare necessities. It didn't even have A/C, but it could get her anywhere she needed to go, on nearly any terrain.

The old Jeep started up like Katy thought it would, and she backed out of the cabin and followed the single dirt path off of her property. It was slow going until she reached the first paved road, and then she was able to pick up speed as she headed toward the town.

Katy had both hands on the wheel, the sun beating down from above and not a cloud in the sky. She never understood why the weather was so nice on a bad day.

The paved road reached the bending curve at the base of the mountain, and it wouldn't be long before she spied the little town that she would have to pass through before she could turn onto the highway. But as she drew closer, she saw a truck had broken down and she slowed, recognizing the vehicle. It belonged to Waylon Hart, a local farmer who sold his produce in town. He had some of the best apples she'd ever tasted.

Katy parked the Jeep at a distance and retrieved her rifle. She approached slowly, her senses heightened by the situation. Both truck doors were left open, and the front of the engine was steaming. Busted radiator.

If the car had broken down, it wouldn't have made sense for Waylon to leave the doors open. Sure, they were in a small town, but when Katy saw the keys still dangling from the ignition, she knew that something was wrong.

Both hands still on her rifle, Katy stepped back from the truck and noticed the bullet holes on the back right tire well, and a smear of blood by the door frame.

Gunfire, distant but clear, echoed down the road. Katy instinctively raised her rifle despite the threat's proximity.

Not wanting anyone to hear her coming in her Jeep, Katy proceeded on foot, hugging the mountainside, and keeping her guard up for any more surprises that she might uncover along the way.

But when Katy finally cleared the side of the mountain and saw the town up ahead, she froze for a second, thinking that her mind was playing tricks on her.

A blockade had been erected on both sides of the town. There was no way of going through it unless you had a tank or some kind of armored vehicle because the machine gun nest that was perched with a man guarding it was meant to mow down anyone that got close.

Katy was too far away from the rest of the town to see

anything else, and if she approached from the road, then Mr. Machine Gun would have a clear line of sight on her.

Masked men corralled the townspeople by gunpoint, herding them into the library in the center of town.

And while Katy had no idea who might have taken over the town, she now understood what was happening. No electronics. Broken-down vehicles on the road. The country had been attacked by an EMP.

1

Mike Thorton was dressed in his black suit and tie, with a white shirt, and the reflection he caught in the bathroom mirror reminded him of the waiter at the steakhouse Lisa took him to on their fifteenth wedding anniversary last month. His parents watched the kids, and they spent the night in the city, eating, drinking, and catching up on some much-needed romance. It was a good night.

Mike stared down at the phone on the bathroom counter. He had been battling calling his sister one last time. She hadn't answered him all week. He didn't know why he thought today would be different.

Mike sighed and shifted his weight from his right foot to his left and crossed his arms. He knew he shouldn't have gotten his hopes up. He was asking too much of her to come down for the funeral. He knew she and Dad had their differences, but he never understood what started their feud.

And now Mike was dressed in the only black suit he owned, which Lisa had thankfully cleaned for him, wearing a tie that was choking him to death, and waiting for the rest of the family to get ready.

Even now, he heard the echoes of his family through the walls, and their muffled voices made him smile. He couldn't imagine Kelly, his oldest and only daughter, hating him the way that Katy hated their dad. His heart ached at just the thought of it. And while their relationship wasn't at its best right now because Kelly was in the tumultuous throes of puberty, he knew they didn't hate each other. The only time they really argued was when Kelly dressed for school like she was going to the beach.

The phone buzzed, and Mike's heart jumped, hoping that it was his sister. It wasn't.

"Hey, Kev," Mike said, trying not to sound disappointed.

"Hey, Mikey." Kevin MacDonald was Mike's partner at the Charlotte PD. The pair had been together ever since both of them passed the detectives' exam eight years prior. They had become close over the years, and both men thought of each other as brothers more than colleagues. "How are you holding up?"

Mike shifted the weight on his feet again and cleared his throat. "I'm all right. How are things going with the transfer?"

"We're putting him in the van now," Kevin answered.

"Good," Mike said. "Any problems?"

"No," Kevin answered. "And don't worry about this. You have enough on your plate."

Three months ago, Mike and Kevin were part of a massive statewide investigation involving the FBI to capture a serial killer who had tormented their state for eight months. Mike and Kevin worked the case day and night until they caught their man.

Melvin Harris was a thirty-two-year-old Caucasian male who had murdered twenty-eight people, terrorizing the Charlotte area and surrounding small-town Appalachia. In the seventeen years that Mike had been a police officer, Melvin Harris was the most violent, perverse, and intelligent criminal that he had ever apprehended.

"We'll get this man boarded on his flight, and then I'm off to pick up my cycle from the shop," Kevin said. "It's a beautiful day for a ride."

Kevin was a ride-or-die Harley aficionado. At the start of every shift, he always drove by McClellan's Motorcycle shop so Kevin could look at the vintage, fully-restored 1960 Panhead. He'd even gotten Mike to ride with him a few times. It was fun.

"Listen, I'll have my phone off for the procession, but don't be afraid to keep sending me text updates," Mike said. "It'll be nice to have some good news once today is over."

"You got it, buddy," Kevin said. "And give my best to the family."

"I will," Mike said. "Thanks, partner."

The call ended, and Mike kept both arms straight at his side. He really would have rather been helping his partner transfer Harris over to the federal holding facility where he would be awaiting trial. Even though Mike and Charlotte PD were technically the ones who had arrested him, because of the violent nature of his crimes and the fact that he killed people in three different states, they had to turn the creature over to the Feds, but Mike didn't mind. The less time spent with that monster, the better.

It was Melvin's eyes that were so unsettling. The way that they studied you like a person would study an animal at the zoo. He didn't believe people were his equals. He only thought of them as games to be played, instruments of his pleasure to satisfy his darkest desires. The man was a psychopath, and it was only a matter of time before he was executed by lethal injection.

Mike rubbed his eyes and saw a cup of coffee in his future. He needed to be awake for the drive into the city to pick up his mother. He pocketed his phone and then exited the bedroom, listening to Lisa help their son, Casey, with his outfit. Some coffee was still left in the carafe from breakfast, and he poured the remaining caffeine into his mug. He sipped from it slowly, hoping the extra caffeine would help his mood.

"Sweetheart?" Lisa called from upstairs. "Can you check to see if I left my purse in the car?"

"Sure!" Mike gulped the rest of the lukewarm coffee and set the mug down. He entered the garage, flicking on a light, and opened the passenger side door of their Honda Accord. Mike spied the purse on the floorboard and picked it up.

But before Mike turned back for the door into the house, he stopped as the blue tarp covering his father's pickup caught his eye.

Two years ago, his parents had decided to downsize and move into an apartment in the city. His father had said that he was too old and too tired to keep fixing everything around the house and taking care of the yard.

"I just want to be able to call someone and have them come and fix what's broken," Tim Thorton had said. "And I never want to mow another damn lawn for the rest of my life."

But downsizing the house also meant downsizing the car collection that his father had accumulated over the past forty years.

And while Mike thought that his father was going to sell all of them, he was surprised when his dad drove over to the house in his 1972 Ford 150. It was brilliant cherry red with an eight-inch suspension kit, chrome wheels, and twenty-six inch big tires.

Growing up, it had always been Mike's favorite vehicle, and when his father told him that he was giving him the keys, Mike's jaw hit the floor.

Tim Thorton had never been a man of charity, but his father's words surprised him.

"I know how much you liked this truck. I should have let you drive it more, instead of just letting it collect dust in the garage," his father said. "I know I was strict with you growing up. But it was the way that my father raised me, and it was the only way I knew how to raise you. Sometimes I wonder if I hadn't been so hard, then maybe Katy wouldn't have distanced herself from the family."

Mike remembered how his father looked away in that moment, wiping something from his eyes, though the old man never admitted to crying, Mike knew his father had teared up.

"Anyway," Tim said, handing Mike the keys. "I want you to have it. I don't know if Kelly is into trucks, but after you have your fun with it, I thought Casey might like it when he's older. It could become a family heirloom, you know?"

The door to the garage opened, and Lisa stood in the doorway. She had one earring on her left ear and the other in her hand. She wore a black dress that hugged the curves of her body, and even in the dim fluorescent lighting of the garage, the only thing that Mike could think of at that moment was how much he wanted to whisk her to the bedroom.

"Hey." Lisa stepped down into the garage, her heels clicking as she walked to him, and planted a warm kiss on his lips. "Did you get lost?"

"No," Mike said, then gestured to the phone. "Kevin just called. They're loading Melvin in the van right now."

Lisa shivered. "What that man did was despicable." She took a breath and then reached for his hand. "How are you doing? You didn't say much this morning. And I didn't see you eat any breakfast."

"I had some toast," Mike said.

Lisa arched both eyebrows. "Breakfast of champions."

Mike smiled and then handed his wife her purse. "Katy still hasn't called."

Lisa hugged him. "Oh, honey. I'm sorry."

Mike kissed his wife's forehead. "It's fine. She hasn't been a part of our family for a long time. I don't know why I thought she'd want to start now." He took Lisa's hand, and the pair walked to the door, but Mike caught himself glancing at the truck one last time.

Once back in the house, the quiet morning suddenly erupted in a chorus of sibling squabbling upstairs.

"Casey, you little turd!"

The scream preceded Mike's son, Casey, the "little turd" running down the stairs with a big grin on his face, already dressed in his matching black suit and tie. Lisa had bought it for him, though Mike thought it was a waste of money since the kid was nine and would grow out of it by this same time next year.

"Whoa, whoa, whoa." Mike caught Casey before he sprinted past him and then lifted him up off the ground and set him on the kitchen table. "What are you doing?"

Casey used both hands to cover his mouth and muffle the

laughter building up inside of him. But Mike didn't have to wait long before he realized what happened.

Kelly, Mike's fifteen-year-old daughter, stomped down the stairs, stopping at the halfway mark and bending over the rail, pointing at Casey. "You are dead!"

Lisa moved toward Kelly and blocked her path at the stairs. "Kelly, what is going on?"

Kelly took a finger and wiped some of the white cream that covered her face, then let it rest on her fingertip. "It's icing."

Casey giggled.

"It's not funny!" Kelly flung her arm down, the motion sending the white frosting onto the carpet.

"Okay, that's enough." Lisa pointed to their daughter and then back up the stairs. "Just wipe it off and finish getting ready."

"Mom, do you know how many pimples this is going to give me? And he dumped out all of my facial cleansers to fill it up with that fucking icing!"

"Language!" Lisa said, raising her voice. "Upstairs now, and finish getting ready. We will deal with this later."

Kelly grunted in frustration, then stomped back up to the second floor. Mike slowly turned back to his son, and the moment he saw Casey's grin, he couldn't help but smile himself. Thankfully, Lisa didn't share their humor.

"That wasn't nice, young man," Lisa said.

Casey finally dropped his hands from his mouth. "I don't know why she's so mad. I've seen her eat tubs of icing whenever she gets moody." He shrugged, his voice rising one octave. "I thought she'd like it."

"Yeah, I'm sure bringing your sister joy was the only thing that crossed your mind when you decided to replace her face

15

cream with icing," Mike said, then moved his son from the table to the floor. "I'd give her some space, okay? And I think it goes without saying that you lost your computer privileges for the weekend."

"Yeah," Casey said, grinning again. "But it was worth it."

This time even Lisa laughed. But the laughter was cut short with the familiar drone of a power outage, and the house grew eerily quiet.

2

"*D*ad! The power is out!" Kelly screamed from upstairs.

"We can see that, honey." Mike walked over to the nearest light switch and did the ceremonious flip up and down, which did nothing. "It might just be the breakers. I'll go and check." He left his wife and son in the kitchen and then returned to the garage.

It was pitch black inside, and when Mike reached for his phone to use the flashlight application, he found that his phone was also dead. He frowned. It had just been at eighty-five percent. He kept the doorway between the house and the garage propped open, using what limited light he had as he carefully navigated the front of the garage toward the fuse box and popped it open.

Mimicking his ceremonious flick of the light switch in the house, Mike saw the breakers hadn't been tripped. It was a blackout.

Mike stepped back inside the house where his daughter

had already come downstairs, half of the icing still on her face, her anger transformed into a poutier glare.

"Dad, even the water won't run," Kelly said, then gestured to her face. "I need to get this off."

"Just wipe it off with a towel," Mike said, and then turned to his wife. "Can I use your phone?"

Confused, Lisa retrieved her phone from her purse, but it never made it into Mike's hands. "It's not working. It must have died overnight."

Mike paused and reached deep into the back of his mind where he retrieved a conversation that had been played between himself and his sister a long time ago. Something he always thought was crazy.

Mike walked to their front door and stopped before he opened it, turning back to his daughter. "Kelly, go upstairs and see if your phone is working."

Kelly frowned. "Why—"

"Do it now, please." Mike's tone was stern, so his daughter dropped her protest and returned up the stairs.

"Mike," Lisa said, catching her husband before he stepped outside. "What is going on? You're starting to scare me."

"I'm not sure yet." Mike stepped outside, squinting from the sunshine, and walked down his driveway until he was at his mailbox by the road.

Their house was located in a small cul-de-sac in one of the many suburbs outside of Charlotte. It was a nice neighborhood, middle class, most everyone in the area married with kids, though there were a few exceptions. But it was a good place to live, a safe place to raise a family.

However, what Mike saw as he looked down the road didn't make any sense. Cars were stopped in the middle of the street, their drivers out of the vehicles and checking the engines.

Lisa joined him by the mailbox, noticing the stalled cars. "What do you think is wrong with them?"

Mike opened his mouth to speak, but when he was unable to find his voice, he closed it again and shook his head.

"Mike, Lisa!" The voice came from their right, and both of them turned to find their neighbor, Jason Fuller, walking across his yard and onto the Thortons' property. "Is your power out too?"

"Yeah, we just lost it about a minute ago," Lisa answered.

"Us too," Jason said, shaking Mike's hand as he joined the pair by the mailbox. He pointed down the road toward the cars that they saw disabled in the street. "What's going on down there?"

"Hey!" Nasir Ashkani, their neighbor from across the street, walked down his driveway, waving his hand to catch their attention. "Did your power go out?"

"Yeah!" Jason said. "Looks like it's the whole block!"

Mike turned to Jason, noticing that the man was still in his pajamas, his crown of brown hair that circled the bald spot on the top of his head disheveled. "Jason, do you have your phone on you?"

"What? Oh, I think so." Jason reached into his pajama pockets and removed his phone, but Mike had his question answered before he even asked. "I can't get the damn thing to turn on. It must have not charged last night. But what's crazy is Melanie's phone isn't working either. I heard her complaining about it right before I walked out the door."

Mike staggered back from the mailbox, and both Lisa and Jason reached for his arms as if he might fall, but Mike caught himself.

"Mike, are you all right?" Jason asked. "You're white as a ghost."

"Honey, what's wrong?" Lisa grabbed his arm and squeezed.

During most of the conversations Mike had with his sister during those first years after she moved from the city and into the wilderness to live off-grid, she would talk about all the different ways that society could collapse, and there was one particular event that mirrored what Mike saw now.

"Just think about it," Katy said as they sat in Mike's living room, sipping whiskey after the kids had gone to sleep. "Everything runs off of computers these days. Cars, phones, even our power grid and most of our utilities. Everything is automated and controlled by a few pieces of metal and plastic. But what if all of those devices stopped working?" She snapped her fingers. "Just like that. All at the same time. All of a sudden, three hundred million people no longer have power or running water. They can't call anyone for help. They can't go anywhere because their cars won't start. And even if they did start, they wouldn't be able to drive on the roads because they would be clogged with other broken-down vehicles. And no power means no refrigeration. Food would spoil. People would be rioting in the streets in less than a day. Maybe even hours. It would be like the earth itself had stopped spinning."

Mike remembered taking a sip of whiskey after that, trying not to dismiss his sister's conspiracy theories so quickly. "But how would something like that even happen? How do you shut down an entire nation?"

Katy leaned forward. "It's called an EMP."

"Mike?" Lisa shook his arm, tightening her grip. "Mike, what's wrong?"

Mike blinked, coming out of the memory, and saw the concerned expressions on both his wife's face and his neighbors'. "I need to check on something." He retreated toward the house. "I'll be right back. I promise." He jogged back into the house and then bypassed both his son and daughter, who were now watching the world outside through the front living room window.

"Dad?" Kelly asked. "What's going on?"

"Just stay inside the house, okay?" Mike disappeared into the garage again and opened the driver door to the Honda. They had bought it last year brand new, and it came with all of the bells and whistles. The keys were already inside the vehicle, and Mike inserted the car key into the engine and turned it over, hearing nothing but a click.

"No." Mike turned the key back and then turned it forward again, disheartened by another click. He took his hands off the keys and then leaned back. He shut his eyes, shaking his head. "This can't be happening. This can't be real."

But after years of thinking that his sister was crazy for wanting to get away from civilization and live a life of solitude, the unthinkable had happened. And now, Katy was ready while millions of others were caught unprepared.

Mike opened his eyes, starting to sweat in his suit. It was summertime, and it wouldn't be long before temperatures rose. And with no A/C, Mike knew that it wouldn't be long before tempers rose along with the heat.

He tilted his head toward the truck, remembering something else that Katy had told him about an EMP.

"It should only affect machinery that uses a microprocessor computer chip," Katy said. "So, newer cars that have computerized fuel injection wouldn't work, but most older cars, probably pre-1975 models, most of them would still work since they don't have any computer systems in them."

Mike leaned forward again, knowing that his father's truck was an early seventies model. He got out of the Honda and climbed into the truck's cab. Like the sedan, the keys were already inside, and Mike shut his eyes and held his breath as he placed the keys into the ignition.

Mike turned the key, and the engine started without hesitation. Mike exhaled at the sound of the truck's V8 rumbling softly in the garage and smiled as he rested his forehead on the crest of the steering wheel.

His family still had a way out.

Not wanting to choke to death on the exhaust, Mike checked the fuel gauge and found that it was full, and then he killed the engine. He took a moment to think about his next moves, then finally climbed out of the truck and returned to the house, where his wife and kids were waiting for him in the living room.

"Mike, what is going on?" Lisa asked, flanked on either side by their children.

Mike knew that it was going to be difficult to explain, but it was better if Lisa was on the same page as him before things started to rapidly deteriorate.

"Lisa, kids, I need you to listen to me very carefully because we don't have a lot of time." Mike walked over to them and grabbed his wife's hand, leading them all to the couch where they sat down. He crouched on his knees, keeping eye contact with them. "Something happened. I'm not sure exactly how, but... it did."

"Dad, what are you talking about?" Casey asked, his voice quiet and scared as he leaned into his mother's side.

"We're going to be okay, buddy." Mike placed his hand on

his son's leg. "All I need you to do is go upstairs and pack all the clothes that you can fit into your backpack, okay?" He looked at Kelly. "Same for you, sweetie."

"Dad, this doesn't make any sense," Kelly said, trying not to act scared. "The power just went out. It's going to come back on." She looked at her mother. "Right?"

Lisa was quiet for a moment, her attention focused on Mike, studying his eyes. "Go upstairs and do what your father says." She gave each of her children an encouraging shove off the couch. "Go on. I'll be up to help you in a minute."

The kids hesitated, but eventually slid off the couch and walked to the stairs, Kelly taking her younger brother's hand as they ascended to the second floor together.

Mike smiled at the sight of Kelly comforting her younger brother. That's what older siblings were for. The younger ones might drive you crazy, but you felt a need to protect them when they were scared. He wasn't sure if he did that enough with Katy.

"Mike," Lisa said, pulling his attention back to her. "Are you going to tell me what's going on? Or are you going to make me guess?"

Mike cleared his throat and decided that the best way for him to go into this was to just tell her everything up front. "I think we were hit with an EMP. It's a kind of device that, if detonated in the atmosphere, has the poten-tial to destroy any electronic device powered by a micro-processor."

Lisa was quiet for a moment, letting the words sink in before she slowly, and carefully, spoke. "And how would something like that happen?"

"I'm not sure," Mike answered. "Katy told me that a

nuclear device detonated at a high altitude would be enough to—"

"Jesus, are you saying that our country was attacked with a nuclear weapon?" Lisa moved about anxiously on the couch but kept her voice quiet. "Are we in danger?"

Mike held her hands in his own, and she calmed. "We don't have to worry about fallout." At least he didn't think so. "Right now, our biggest enemy is other people. The power isn't coming back on. We need to get out of Charlotte before things take a turn for the worse."

"How?" Lisa answered. "You said that nothing is working."

"My dad's truck still runs. It doesn't have any computer components to run the engine." Mike kept a firm grip on Lisa's hands, making sure that she didn't look away. "I need you to pack us both a bag of clothes. Try and fit a week's worth if you can. And make sure the kids have their hiking boots on. Then I need you to pack as much water and non-perishable food—"

"—Mike, this is crazy—"

"—that you can find in the house, and load it all into the truck. Honey." Mike kissed her forehead and stayed close. "I know this sounds crazy, but we need to do this before things get worse. Because if my sister was right, and I can't believe I'm saying this, then we need to get out of the city and head to her cabin in the mountains."

"You want us to go and stay with your sister?" Lisa asked, and then leaned back. "Mike, she wouldn't even call you back to talk to you about your father. What makes you think she's going to want the four of us crashing at her cabin?"

"Five," Mike answered. "I'm going into the city to get my mom." He stood and then headed for the bedroom, loosening his tie. If he was going to be on the move, then he needed to change into something more comfortable for the journey.

Lisa followed him into the bedroom. "Mike, I think we just need to slow down and think about this a little more. I mean, you want us to just leave the house? Our home?"

Mike tossed his shirt and jacket on the bed and then grabbed one of his Charlotte PD polos from the closet. He figured if he dressed like a cop, it would be easier for him to move about the city. "I know it sounds extreme, but just look around, Lisa. Nothing works. No power. No water. How long do you think that food in the fridge is going to last?" He pulled the polo over his head, then kicked off his dress shoes and pants and put on a pair of jeans and his running shoes. "People are going to start to panic, and the faster we can get out of here, the better off we'll be in avoiding pandemonium." He tied the laces and then moved to the small safe where he stored his weapon. He grabbed both his service pistol and his backup revolver, which he wore around his ankle, along with spare ammunition for each, which he wore around his belt. "The best thing for us to do right now is to get ready to leave. If I'm wrong, then we stay. But—" He grabbed his badge off the top of the dresser and clipped it to his belt, completing his ensemble. "I need you to trust me."

Mike knew that she was still worried, and he didn't expect her to not have doubts, but he needed her to get on board with the plan.

"It might seem odd now, but I know that this is the best play for our family," Mike said. "And that's what I'm concerned about most. Okay?"

Lisa took a deep breath and then finally nodded. "Okay."

Mike walked to his wife and hugged her tight. "We're

going to be fine. I'm going to head into the city, grab my mom, and be back before you know it."

Lisa squeezed him tight before she let him go. "So are you taking the truck?"

Mike shook his head. "The fewer people know that we have a working vehicle, the better. I don't want to draw attention to us by parading around in the bright red truck. And with the number of cars that are probably broken down in the city, I don't think I'd be able to drive very far. I'll take my bicycle. It'll be easier to navigate through the city, and it'll be quicker than walking." But how he was going to get his mother back on his bicycle he wasn't sure yet.

"Be careful out there," Lisa said.

"I will."

The pair kissed and then Mike called down his kids one more time to give them a hug and kiss goodbye, both of whom were still freaked out by their sudden change in plans.

"You'll come back?" Casey asked.

"Of course," Mike answered.

"You promise?" Kelly asked.

Mike kissed the top of her head and hugged her. "I promise."

It was hard letting go of his children, but Mike knew that time wasn't on his side. He grabbed his bicycle from the garage and pedaled down the street. Along the way, he saw his neighbors step out from their homes, grouping together and huddling around their cell phones, murmuring over what could be happening.

Mike saw all of those people and thought about his detective shield. He realized now maybe he shouldn't have brought it because people would be looking for answers, and the sight of the badge would attract attention. And his mission to retrieve his mother would require an element of stealth and anonymity.

Life was quiet and still right now, but Mike felt something coming. It was something that he couldn't name or see, but he knew that it was there on the horizon. He hoped it wouldn't be as bad as he thought, but he had always put too much faith in people.

etective Kevin MacDonald rubbed his forehead, which was still throbbing from the impact of the crash. A high-pitched whine deafened his hearing, and his vision was blurred. He was worried that he might have a concussion, but when his vision cleared and he saw Melvin Harris staring at him, Kevin sobered up very quickly.

Melvin had moved as close to Kevin as the restraints allowed, the chains taut. But the moment that Kevin placed his hand on the Taser, Melvin slowly inched back to his seat, and before Kevin had a chance to do anything else, the driver opened the panel from the front seat.

"Everyone all right back there?" It was Officer Jimenez, peering through the grated holes of the cage.

"We're fine," Kevin answered. "What happened up there?"

"Not sure," Jimenez said, his voice a little shaky. "The engine shut off and then all of the traffic on the road stopped. We smacked into the car in front of us, and someone sideswiped us on the left."

Kevin looked to the back doors. From his position, they

appeared to be fine. "I don't think we got rear-ended. I'm going to step out and have a look." He tossed a final glare to Melvin, the man still staring at him with those dead, black eyes. "Don't you worry about making your flight. Even if we miss it, I'll drive you to Quantico myself."

Melvin smiled. "I'd look forward to the alone time with you, Detective. Though I'm not sure you and I would have the same taste in music for the road trip."

Even the man's voice made Kevin's skin crawl, and rather than go tit for tat with a man that had a one-way ticket to death row, Kevin opened the back door, flooding the inside of the van with sunlight, and stepped out onto the asphalt.

It took a few seconds for Kevin's eyes to adjust to the light, but when he was finally able to see the highway, he stood slack-jawed. "Oh my god."

The entire four-lane highway running in and out of Charlotte was completely gridlocked. Not a single vehicle was moving, and there were more collisions than he could count.

Kevin reached for his cell phone and tried to dial the precinct, but his phone gave him nothing but a black screen. He frowned and moved up toward the front of the van, having to go up the right side because the car that smacked into the left couldn't move.

Officer Jimenez was already out of the vehicle, his partner and driver, Officer Kershaw, struggling to climb over the seats before he landed awkwardly on the pavement. He straightened out, catching his breath. He was a big man, and Kevin was surprised to see him able to perform that little maneuver.

"You two all right?" Kevin asked.

"We're fine," Jimenez answered.

JAMES HUNT

"Yeah, all good." Kershaw offered a thumbs-up, still catching his breath.

Kevin glanced around at the car wrecks, shocked by the standstill. "What is going on?" He turned back to the officers. "Can you reach anyone on the radio? My phone's dead."

"Radio isn't working," Kershaw answered. "Van won't start either."

"What about your cell phones?" Kevin asked.

"I left mine back at the station," Jimenez answered.

"I've got mine." Kershaw pulled the device from his pocket, but like Kevin's phone, and every phone in the city, it was dead. "What do you want to do, Detective?"

Kevin looked up and down the road, getting his bearings. They were already too far away from the city to head back to the precinct, but the airport couldn't have been more than fifteen or twenty miles. It'd be a hell of a walk. And while he might have been up for the trip, he wasn't sure how his compadres would feel about the journey.

"We need to get him to the airport," Kevin said, trying his best to sound as authoritative as possible. "It'll take us a few hours on foot, but if we keep a steady pace, we should make it before they take off. Not that I think they'd leave without their star passenger."

Surprisingly, it wasn't Kershaw who threw out the objection as Jimenez wiped the sweat from his brow. "Detective, I don't know if that's a good idea. The forecast said there was a high of ninety-five today. Dressed down in gear like this, we might get a heat stroke from walking that distance. Plus, there's no shade on the highway. You really want to walk him all the way there?"

"Want doesn't have anything to do with it," Kevin

answered. "But we need to get him there, and we need to move sooner rather than later. It's only going to get hotter."

Jimenez rolled his eyes, and Kershaw reached back inside the van. "I'll bring us some water, make sure that we're hydrated for the trip. I always keep some in the cooler."

"Good idea," Kevin said, keeping an eye on the road. The collisions he saw around him didn't spawn any serious injuries, but nearly every single motorist had stepped out of their vehicle to inspect the damage. And the growing murmurs over the road sounded like thunder from storm clouds in the distance.

Kevin rounded the corner of the van, finding Melvin in the same place where he left him.

"Calling Triple-A, Detective?" Melvin kept his tone innocent. The guy was slick. Even though he and Mike had caught the bastard red-handed, he still refused to enter a plea of guilty. The man was content with dragging out a trial for as long as possible. Melvin knew all roads led to lethal injection.

"You'll be walking," Kevin answered.

Melvin glanced down to his shackles and then looked back up at Kevin with a smirk on his face. "Detective, I don't think we'll make good time with these chains around my feet. Will you be allowing me to stretch my legs?"

Kevin moved closer to the bastard, shoving a finger in his face. "The only thing that I'm going to be giving you will be a solid foot up your ass if you slow us down."

The smile never left Melvin's face. "A simple no would have been fine."

Kevin waited for Jimenez to join him in the back of the van. There were always at least two officers to handle unchaining a criminal like Melvin. The man was slippery and smart, and Kevin refused to give the man any wiggle room.

Once Jimenez unhooked the bar from the bottom of the van, Kevin stepped out, gun on his holster, as Jimenez led the convict out into the daylight.

"My, my, my, what do we have here?" Melvin smiled at the wreckage that surrounded them along the highway, but Kevin didn't want to stay idle for very long. With Melvin's blue jumpsuit and handcuffs around both his feet and ankles, Kevin knew that they were bound to attract some attention from the rest of the crowds.

"All right, listen up," Kevin said, addressing both officers and their prisoner. "We move quickly, and we move with purpose through the crowd. We don't stop, and we don't let anyone get close. Got it?"

"Yes, sir." Melvin was the first to reply, and the other two officers rolled their eyes.

"All right, let's move." Kevin led the charge, clearing the path while the other two officers kept a firm hold on Melvin.

Like Kevin expected, the sight of the cops and the prisoner pulled everyone's focus away from their vehicles, and people rushed toward them, bombarding Kevin with questions.

"Do you know what's happening?"

"Why did all the cars stop?"

"I've talked to seven different people, and no one has a phone that is working."

"My kids are in the car, and I have a baby that needs to get home, now!"

"My mother is sick."

"My brother needs me to come and pick him up."

It was too many people for Kevin to handle, but he stuck

to the plan, quickly cutting through the crowd with purpose. But people continued to close in, shrinking Melvin's buffer of empty space.

"I said, get back!" Kevin shouted above the nervous buzz of the droning crowd. He kept one hand on his pistol, but the crowd was unfazed by the act. Their instincts of survival and curiosity were overriding the orders of a man in a uniform. Crowd control wasn't working. He needed to find a way out.

Kevin turned back to the officers to tell them to try and find a hole in the crowd, but amidst the chaos of the moment, Kevin only saw Melvin Harris's black, beady eyes. Melvin formed a wry smile which grew wider the longer the pair held eye contact. It wasn't until Melvin's laughter rose into the air, mixing with the crowd's unanswered questions, that Kevin snapped out of his daze.

Hearing Melvin's laughter made Kevin consider putting a bullet between Melvin's peepers and be done with it, save the world and judicial system a hell of a lot of trouble.

But he couldn't do that. Because he was a cop. A man of the law. Instead, he leaned into Kershaw's ear, shouting above the noise of the crowd.

"We'll switch places," Kevin said, his voice nearly vanishing into thin air the moment the words left his lips. "I need you to help clear a path."

Kevin wasn't sure if the big man would be offended, but Kevin was glad to have Kershaw chuckle as he slapped his own belly and winked.

"I'll be like a snowplow out there," Kershaw said, and then passed the baton that was Melvin's arm to Kevin and took the lead.

"All right, people, move!" Kershaw's voice boomed over the worrisome requests, and Kevin was surprised to see the mob of people actually listen to him as a hole opened up and he moved away from the center of the road and toward the sidewalk.

All they had to do was make it off the highway and onto a side road. He knew Charlotte well enough to be able to travel the back roads without having to worry about navigation. While he wasn't a native, he had lived here since college.

Kershaw finally cleared a path to the side of the road, leaving most of the horde behind them, though there was another patch of people that they'd have to go through up ahead.

"Is this your big plan, Detective?" Melvin asked, his feet shuffling against the pavement in quick strides as he struggled to keep pace with everyone else. "You're going to walk me through all of these people who need your help?"

"They need me to make sure that you get the hell out of this city more than they need me to check their cars," Kevin answered.

"I suppose that's true." Melvin was still smirking. "But what happens when you come across something that you can't ignore? Are you willing to let me go?"

"I'm not letting you go anywhere," Kevin answered, an edge to his voice that he hadn't intended. He hated that this serial killer could get under his skin. He knew when it came to intellect that Melvin was leagues ahead of his own mind. But his acceptance of that fact didn't make that pill any easier to swallow.

"I think you're underestimating your moral compass," Melvin said. "I happen to love the fact that people have a moral compass. It's a trait that I don't possess, of course, but that doesn't mean I can't pretend to have it every once in a while."

"Stop talking." Kevin tightened his grip on Melvin's arm. They were getting closer to the second patch of people, and this one looked denser than the first one. More restless too.

"You see, it's all about watching and studying," Melvin said. "Because I never had the instinct for real emotion, I had to learn to fake it, like most psychopaths."

Kevin kept his eyes forward. He didn't want to engage with Melvin any more than necessary.

"It's all about the details," Melvin said. "You have to have a motivation, and root source of emotion to latch onto, but it also has to be relatable. You want to trigger empathy, which makes the victim want to help you more than they want to help themselves. It makes them willing to put themselves in a dangerous situation, putting their own lives at risk." He laughed. "I have to tell you, Detective, when you're able to trick someone like that, it's thrilling."

"I doubt that," Kevin said.

Kershaw approached the crowd, already shouting for the people to let them pass, but this time no hole formed. Instead, the people met Kershaw head-on, this group more aggressive.

"What the hell is going on?"

"You want to tell me why my car won't start?"

"And why my phone is shut off?"

"Are we under some kind of attack?"

The dissent of the group compounded into angrier sentiments with every question that was hurled from the horde. And Kershaw could do little but turn around and glance back at Kevin with a look of bewilderment about what to do next.

Kevin knew that they wouldn't be able to push through this group of people without triggering a riot. A mob was like a wildfire. It was impossible to control, hard to contain, and didn't stop until it burned itself out.

"Kershaw!" Kevin shouted, motioning for the officer to trade places, and he waited until Kershaw had a firm grip on Melvin before he stepped forward to address the growing crowd. He held up his hands, showing the badge in his left. From his position, he counted at least fifty people. And that was only the number of folks that he was able to see. "I know everyone has questions, but right now the best thing for you to do is return to your homes while all of this gets sorted out."

"And who is sorting it out?" The voice from somewhere in the back triggered a ripple effect of agreement throughout the crowd, and the pulse of anger forced Kevin back a step.

"And we're just supposed to leave our cars out here on the highway?"

"I live twenty miles away. How the hell am I supposed to walk that far in this heat?"

"I've got medication at home. I need to take it soon. Why can't you call someone to come and help us?"

Kevin didn't want to reveal that he didn't know what was going on, and he didn't want them to know he couldn't call for backup. The only factor keeping the crowd from rioting was the belief that the authorities could still do something to help them. To provide answers to their questions.

"I have a prisoner that I need to transport, but I can assure you that an emergency crew is working on the situation right now," Kevin said.

"He's lying."

Kevin spun around, and the rest of the crowd focused on Melvin.

"He doesn't know what's happening," Melvin said. "And

he can't call for help or backup because he doesn't have any communication either."

More ripples of dissent pulsed through the crowd, and Kevin's face turned a bright shade of red.

"Cover the prisoner's mouth! I don't want him saying another word!" Kevin pointed his finger at Melvin, but when he turned to the crowd, the damage had already been done.

The thin veil of authority that Kevin held was torn to shreds. The mob charged at Kevin and the officers like a tidal wave.

Kevin retreated back to the other officers as the bodies swarmed him, but by the time he turned around, he saw the first few people reach the officers and what was worse, Melvin.

Kevin reached for his pistol, but when he tried to remove it from the holster, his elbow remained pinned down from the bum rush of pedestrians.

"Everyone back!" Kevin shouted above the crowd, but the mob mentality had taken over. He was powerless. "Kershaw! Jimenez!" He searched for the officers in the crowd, but he had lost the patrolmen.

Unable to locate the officers or Melvin, Kevin elbowed the civilians around him, creating enough space for him to unholster his weapon. He didn't want to do what he was about to, but the mob had left him no choice.

Kevin raised the pistol high into the air, and squeezed the trigger.

The gunshot thundered above the rumble of the crowd, which grew silent and ducked the moment that Kevin fired. "Everyone, step aside!" Kevin barked his order loudly.

People cleared a path for him as he marched forward. Kevin searched rapidly for any signs of Melvin and the officers, but the longer that he walked without seeing either of them, the more worried he became that something terrible had happened.

"Detective…"

Kevin turned to his left and saw Kershaw on his back, clutching a bloody wound on his stomach. "Kershaw!" Kevin hurried to the officer's side and helped apply pressure on the wound. "Just hang on." But as Kevin reached for his phone to call for backup, he suddenly remembered that they were alone.

Kershaw must have known his fate too, because the big officer shook his head as blood filled his mouth, staining his teeth a dark crimson. He reached his bloodied hand for Kevin's and squeezed. It was warm and slick, and Kershaw struggled to keep a good grip, but he held on all the same.

"He's gone," Kershaw said. "I saw Jimenez go after him, but I don't know where they took off."

"How did this happen?" Kevin asked, knowing while he couldn't save the officer's life, he could figure out what went wrong.

"There were so many people," Kershaw said, his voice straining from the wound in his stomach. "Melvin got loose, and he grabbed my pistol."

Kevin looked down and saw that the man's weapon was gone. But Kevin frowned. "I only heard my own gunshot."

Kershaw shook his head, and then coughed, spitting blood onto his chin and the front of the uniform. "The cuffs. He got… the cuffs." Kershaw struggled to catch his breath now, and his eyes bulged from his skull.

Kevin placed his hand over the wound on Kershaw's stomach, realizing now that the officer hadn't been shot, but stabbed. Kevin looked to the cuff key that should have been on Kershaw's belt, finding it was gone.

Melvin Harris was one of the most dangerous men that Kevin had ever come across. Now he was not only free, he was armed. And the killer was now loose in a city without law and order.

ike was drenched in sweat as he drew closer to Charlotte. He had chosen to stay off the main roads, avoiding the crippling congestion and panicked crowds.

Even now on his bike, he could hear the growing murmur of dissent as he approached the city. He had already seen several cases of looting along his journey.

Mike's instincts as a detective had wanted him to stop the lawlessness, but he knew that he was running low on time.

The city would continue to deteriorate the longer the effects of the EMP lingered. It had only been a few hours, and people were already starting to lose their minds. He couldn't imagine what people would do once all of the food in their fridge spoiled, or their kids didn't have the medicine they needed, or their family was dying of thirst.

Mike had made a commitment to protect the people of Charlotte, but he had also made a commitment to his family.

The city was falling apart, facing an unprecedented threat. He was just a detective with a gun and a badge. The masses had already worked themselves into a frenzy. It would take an army to restore order, and if normal communications were down, then it stood to reason that the military was in the same boat. Unless they had planned for this sort of thing, but Mike didn't remember it coming up on any of the news reports over the past year.

Heading downhill, Mike switched gears on his bike, coasting down the sidewalk, which was clear for the moment.

The hill leveled out and Mike flipped to a lower gear again as he began another ascent. It was the last hill before the Charlotte city limits. From that point, it was another five miles before he would reach his mother's apartment building.

Mike stood up on the bike, pedaling harder, his legs burning as he reached the top of the hill. But as he neared the crest, he paused when he heard the growing roar of people.

Throughout his career as an officer, Mike had encountered several violent scenarios. One of them had been riots during one of the presidential elections. With people heated on both sides of the aisles, the angry rhetoric being displayed by the candidates only fueled the individuals at their base.

Charlotte had been under siege one night by the maddening crowd. Cars were overturned, storefronts were smashed and looted. People toppled light posts, streetlights, and stop signs. Anything that could be destroyed or demolished was done so in less than an hour.

All officers had been called up to assist, including Mike, who had trained with SWAT for crowd control tactics. He remembered heading downtown, standing at the front of the line as they administered gas cans to the crowd to get them to disperse.

The crowd fought back against the police, throwing bottles and trash, sticks and rocks, anything that was light enough to pick up, but heavy enough to cause damage.

Mike was used to being viewed in a certain way as a police officer. He knew that their image with the general population wasn't ideal, but that was the first time as a cop when he really believed it was him against the world.

Mike hated the "us versus them" mentality, but when dozens of glass bottles were smashed over his head as he struggled to subdue the crowd before they caused serious harm to themselves or the people around them, it was hard not to think it.

When it was all said and done, the damage that was caused by the rioting cost the city and its residents millions of dollars. But that day paled in comparison to what he found when he reached the top of that hill.

The sound of the city had changed from the noises of cars and busy movements to the screams and howls of despair from a city that had come to a complete standstill.

The highway that led out of the city was nothing but a gridlock of cars. People had abandoned their vehicles and were now either heading into the city or away from it and back into the suburbs and mountains to go home.

Mike lingered at the top of the hill, looking down on the city slowly tearing itself apart, and he knew that this would be infinitely worse than the riots he had experienced. What he was witnessing now was a complete societal breakdown.

But despite the danger and knowing what he was about to walk into, Mike didn't hesitate as he pedaled into the city. He needed to get his mother out of there, and he needed to do it before the city completely imploded.

Nearing the city's entrance, Mike was forced to ditch the

bike as the sidewalks and streets became too crowded for him to navigate. And because he knew that he wouldn't be able to carry his mother on the bike, he didn't make an effort to stash it so he could pick it up on the way back out. He would need to find a more suitable mode of transportation.

The outside of Charlotte was mostly surrounded by trees and smaller communities, homes, and businesses. But rising against the morning sky, Mike saw the skyrises of Charlotte's downtown.

Mike did his best to avoid the crowds, reverting to traveling between buildings and downside alleys so narrow only two people could squeeze through at one time. But even if he was just crawling at a snail's pace, Mike knew it was important to always be moving toward his goal. In times of crisis, every second counted.

Mike emerged from between two buildings, which dumped him back out onto the street and into another angry crowd. He avoided the crowd and crossed the street, weaving between the abandoned vehicles on the road. But ahead, at the intersection, he heard the familiar pop of gunfire.

The first shots came in a quick burst, and the chatter along the road suddenly ended. Everyone turned toward the source of the noise, which was coming from somewhere beyond the intersection ahead. The silence quickly ended when the gunfire started up again, and Mike watched as the horde shifted away from the intersection and toward him.

The gunfire was rapid, a constant barrage of bullets pushing the crowd toward Mike, who drew his weapon on instinct, and moved against the rush of people.

Mike wasn't sure what his plan was, but if he could bring down the shooter before he took down anyone else, then he might be able to save some lives. But when Mike neared the intersection, he saw multiple shooters.

Five men, all of them in masks, and all of them wearing bulletproof vests, armed with assault rifles, marched in a straight line, firing at anything that moved within their path, leaving a wake of bodies behind them.

The sight of the carnage brought Mike to heel. He quickly fired and off a round before the marching line of gunmen opened fire and forced him to find cover behind an old work van.

Mike leaned his back against the van, the vibrations from the bullets hitting the opposite side rattling his spine. He was crouched in a squat, the pistol gripped in both hands. His heart was pounding, and sweat rolled from his forehead and into his eyes. He quickly wiped the sweat from his forehead and then inched toward the front of the van, the gunmen still opening fire.

Once Mike reached the van's hood, he peered around the side and saw three of the five men turning down the street.

One of the gunmen spied Mike and fired in his direction. Mike retreated back behind the safety of his cover, and while he waited for an opportunity to return fire, he saw a group of people pinned down a few cars over.

Six people, all of them huddled behind the back of a truck, frozen with fear.

Mike glanced between the trapped citizens and the approaching terrorists. If they didn't move they'd be slaughtered like cattle. He had a choice to make. He could leave the people behind to die and move on to save his mother, or he could stay, which would put his life in danger, and ultimately the rest of his family.

Mike stole one last glance at the shooters on their

approach and saw that the cars in the street had forced them to break apart a little bit. Only one of the fighters had a good angle on both him and the people behind the truck. If he could pin that shooter down, there was a chance for escape.

Mike adjusted the grip on his pistol, and then he took a breath before he stood and found his target. He fired three rounds, missing his target, but distracted the terrorist long enough to provide the group of people time to escape.

Mike watched as the people fled to safety, but now pinned down behind the van, Mike needed his own escape plan.

The vibrations from the bullets grew more violent and numerous. Mike needed to move, and he needed to do it before the bullets tore a hole in the siding of the van so big that it turned into a window.

Mike opened the driver side door, keeping low as the windows blew out and bits of glass rained over the top of his head. He pressed down on the brake and shifted the vehicle into neutral. If Mike could push the van close enough to the next vehicle, then he would have enough cover to disappear into the one of the buildings across the street.

Keeping the door open, Mike leaned into the frame, planting his feet into the asphalt, and then pushed. His cheeks turned purple from the effort, and when the van didn't move after the first few seconds, he didn't think that his plan was going to work. But he didn't give up.

Mike pushed harder and he gained momentum. The gunfire was growing louder and more intense, and Mike looked up to find one of the terrorists nearing the front of the van.

Mike ducked down, driving his legs, the van rolling faster now. Finally, a gunshot blew one of the tires out, and the momentum ended. Out of time, Mike sprinted for the next car.

When Mike emerged from the van's cover, he fired blindly in the terrorist's direction, and the enemy reciprocated the gesture as he slammed into the next car, ducking low.

Adrenaline blurred Mike's vision. His heart pounded in his chest. He quickly checked his persons to make sure that he hadn't been hit, and when he was sure he was fine, he continued his retreat through the street, using different cars for cover until he reached the nearest building and ducked inside.

The windows of the storefront shattered when Mike entered, the terrorists continuing to chase him with gunfire, but he didn't stop moving.

Mike wandered through the small clothing boutique, groping at the walls to guide him as the light radiating from the front of the store was finally smothered by darkness.

The gunfire grew softer when he reached the back, and eventually faded. Surrounded by darkness, and catching his breath, Mike believed he was no longer in danger; until he heard something nearby.

Mike froze, aiming the weapon in the direction of the noise. He couldn't be sure that one of the men hadn't followed him into the building and was quietly stalking him in the darkness, but fear could be playing tricks on him.

Mike struggled to control his breathing, and he had to readjust his grip on the pistol. He was alone. He had to be. But when an alarm of metal crashed to his right, Mike turned on a dime, aiming his weapon into the darkness.

"Don't move!" Mike barked the order with an authority that he normally reserved for the most hardened criminals.

"Please, don't!" The voice in the darkness was panicked and worried. "I have my children with me. Just let us go. We don't want any trouble."

Mike's grip on the weapon loosened, and he lowered the pistol. He still couldn't see who was inside, but judging by their tone, he doubted they were a threat. "What's your names?"

"N-Nick." The voice cleared his throat. It was a man. "My daughters are with me. And my wife."

Mike relaxed, but kept his weapon at the ready. "Do you know if this store has a back exit?"

"Yes," Nick said. "This is the storage room. But there is a back door that leads to the alley between the buildings."

An alley wasn't ideal, but Mike didn't want to risk going out onto the main street in case any of the terrorists decided to linger behind.

"My name is Mike Thorton. I'm a detective with Charlotte PD. I need you to lead me out of here."

"Oh, of course." The relief in Nick's voice was evident. "It's just out this way."

Mike jumped when he felt a hand on his arm but quickly relaxed. He followed Nick and his family out of the storage area and back through the darkness. It was slow, and Mike tripped twice, but he finally managed to make it outside. Once his eyes adjusted, Mike caught a better look at the family.

Nick was short, shorter than his wife, who wasn't tall. The man had a full head of jet black hair and a matching beard which had been groomed to the shape of his face. His daughters flanked him on either side, both of them around Casey's age, and they couldn't have been more than a year apart. The wife was blonde and in much better shape than her husband. The woman looked like she could have been a bodybuilder.

"Thank you so much." Nick glanced down at his girls, and then his wife joined him. "I heard the shooting and just grabbed my family and ran."

"Do you know what's happening?" the wife asked. "Why all of the power is off? And our phones and computers aren't working?"

Mike wasn't sure how much he would be able to explain, but he tried to tell them what he knew. "It's called an EMP." He went through the scenario, and he watched the expressions on Nick and his wife's face shift between shocked and terrified. "The power isn't coming back on. Things aren't going back to the way they were before. And help isn't coming."

Mike watched as the hope on Nick's face faded.

But the father forced a smile before he looked down to his daughters. "Hey, that's all right. We're going to be fine as long as we have each other. Right, girls?"

Nick's daughters buried their faces into his sides, and then his wife kissed him before looking at Mike.

"Is there anything we can do?" she asked. "I mean, someplace we can go?"

"You need to grab as much food and water as you can carry, along with any medication that you need, and get out of the city," Mike said. "Any highly populated areas are going to be hotbeds of crime and possible locations for terrorist attacks. If you know of a place that's isolated and close to a freshwater source, then that's your best bet. Once you're in a secure location, you'll want to gather as many resources as you can. If you know people that you can trust, then building a survival group will be important. But only bring people on board if you're absolutely sure that you can trust them. Nothing kills a bond between friends and family faster than desperation. And people are going to become very, very desperate."

Mike noted that while it was his voice that spoke, it was his sister's words. Words that Mike never believe would come to fruition.

"Good luck," Mike said.

"You too," Nick said.

Mike returned to the street, which had been emptied from the terrorist's assault, leaving behind their messy carnage. The sun had arched higher in the sky, and the heat had intensified.

Mike moved quickly, mindful of his surroundings and the bodies that littered the ground. With the heat of the day growing stronger, Mike knew that the stink of death and blood would only worsen.

5

Every time Lisa Thorton grabbed an item of clothing out of her dresser drawers to pack, she paused to look at photographs of her family sitting on top. And with each pause, she grew more terrified that she would never come back to this home again.

On an impulse when she first started to pack, Lisa took all the photographs off the walls and stuffed them into her bag. She couldn't stand leaving behind so many memories of her family. But with the entire suitcase filled with albums, she knew it wasn't practical to take them. She would have to leave most of it behind.

Lisa settled for the wedding album, and both Casey and Kelly's baby pictures. Space be damned.

Nearly finished with her own packing, Lisa poked her head out of the bedroom and yelled upstairs to her children. "Are you guys almost done?"

"No," Casey answered.

Kelly stormed out of her room and appeared at the top of the stairs, hands clenched into fists at her sides. "Mom, this is ridiculous. I don't have enough space in my bag to fit everything!"

Lisa sighed. "Honey, you just need to bring your camping clothes, and some underwear and extra shirts and socks. That's it."

Kelly twisted her face with indignation. "That's it? Are you insane? Do you know how much money I spent on most of my clothes?"

"Kelly, enough!" Lisa marched to the bottom of the staircase, going toe to toe with her daughter. "Hiking gear and cold weather clothes. Underwear and socks. That's it. That's all we have room for. Now go!"

Kelly huffed and puffed, but she eventually stomped back to her room.

"Mom?" Casey emerged from his room. "I think I'm done."

Lisa walked to the top of the stairs and then kissed the top of her son's head. "Let's have a look." She entered the room and was surprised to find that her son had followed most of the instructions. "Looks like you have everything but your coat." She turned back to Casey, who had his head down. "Sweetheart, why didn't you put your coat in the bag?"

Keeping his head down, Casey gently swung his arms back and forth in a lazy cadence. "If we take our coats, that means that we'll be gone until it gets cold again." He looked up at her. "We're not coming back to the house, are we?"

"Sweetheart, I don't know how long we're going to be gone. But it could be for a long time, and your father and I just want to make sure that you have what you need to—" Lisa was about to say survive, but stopped herself. "We just want to be prepared. That's all."

"But everything I need is right here!" Casey spread his

arms and gestured to his room. "I don't understand why we have to leave. I want to stay." He sat on the bed and crossed his arms, but the defiant gesture was lessened by the pouty lower lip.

Lisa joined her son on the bed and placed her arm around his shoulders. "I know that this is scary. And I know that you don't want to leave. I don't either. But sometimes we have to do things that we don't want to do, even if they are scary. We have to be brave."

Casey uncrossed his arms and looked up to his mother. "What if I can't be brave?"

Lisa smiled and then kissed the top of her son's head. "Oh, I think you can do it. You're one of the bravest people that I know."

"Like Dad?" Casey asked, a smile stretching across his face.

Lisa laughed. "Exactly like Dad."

Casey hopped off the bed and nodded firmly. "Right." He walked to the closet and removed his big winter coat, and then placed it into the bag. "Done."

Lisa kissed Casey's cheek and then stood. "Good job. Now, see if you can go and help your sister finish her packing."

Casey's eyes widened. "She has so many clothes."

Lisa returned downstairs to assess their food and water situation. Because they would be limited to perishable foods on the road, she gathered up all of the fruits and vegetables and set them aside. She figured they would eat those first, and then rely on the non-perishable items later.

After Lisa had gathered and organized their supplies, she walked to the garage where they kept their cases of bottled water. Mike always had some spare ones on hand for Casey during baseball season, or for any sudden trips that they needed to take that required hydration.

Once in the garage, Lisa heard someone shouting. It was muffled from the closed door, and at first she thought it might be Casey and Kelly going at it upstairs. But the booming voice she heard was a man's voice, and the conversation had the cadence of anger.

Lisa stepped out of the garage and walked back through the house until she reached the front living room. She peered out of the window and saw the altercation across the street in her neighbor's yard.

Three men were standing on Nasir Ashkani's lawn, each of them armed with some kind of blunt instrument. One of them had an ax.

Lisa hurried back to her room and opened the closet where Mike kept the gun vault. She quickly entered the combination, then reached for the .36 revolver along with the holster, and tucked it behind her back. She wasn't sure what kind of situation she was walking into, but if the people she was about to confront were armed, then she wanted to be too.

Lisa walked out of the room and then shouted up the staircase. "I need you two to stay upstairs and keep the doors locked."

Kelly was the first to the staircase, followed closely by Casey. "Mom, what's going on?"

"Did something happen?" Casey asked.

"Not yet, but something might." Lisa knew that her children were frightened. They had already been through so much that what they needed now was reassurance. But she didn't have the time to give it to them. "If something happens to me, then I want you to hide, and you don't come out until your father comes back, do you understand me?"

Both of them nodded, and neither said another word.

The pistol was heavy on her backside. She had gotten her concealed to carry permit a few years ago after Mike had finally talked her into it. She went to the gun range a few times a month to stay sharp, but as she stepped outside and started her walk across the street where the confrontation had grown even more intense, she wished that she had practiced more.

The last thing Lisa wanted was to put herself in the middle of a fight, but she knew once the first spots of violence spilled over into the neighborhood, it wouldn't be long before everyone lost their minds. Keeping her family safe meant keeping the neighborhood safe.

"It's your people that are behind this!" Jerry Mathis had a bat in his hands, and he pointed it directly at Nasir, who stood on his porch.

"I had nothing to do with this," Nasir said, standing his ground, but not daring to go any closer than his porch. "I want you to leave my property now!"

The two men Jerry had brought with him were other neighbors in the cul-de-sac. Don Bartz and Ken White. Both of them were armed. Don with the ax, and Ken with a crowbar. Lisa was thankful that neither of them had a gun on them, so she counted herself lucky.

"Jerry!" Lisa announced herself before she got too close and found herself on the receiving end of a reactionary swing.

The three men turned at the sound of Lisa's voice, and while Ken and Don both looked embarrassed, Jerry maintained his angered expression.

"Go home, Lisa," Jerry said. "This doesn't concern you."

Lisa slowly worked her way up to the front of the pack, making sure that she kept her back toward Nasir so the other men didn't see the pistol tucked into her waistband and concealed by her shirt. "Whatever this is about, I can promise you it will only end badly if you don't leave now."

Jerry refused to back down. "You see what's happening, Lisa. Hell, I heard you and Mike talking about it. We've been attacked." He turned away and looked at Nasir. "And this guy looks an awful lot like the people who've been wanting to tear this country down for a long time."

"I had nothing to do with this!" Nasir barked.

Nasir was a single father of two daughters who Lisa was sure was inside. "Jerry, Don, Ken, you are letting your fears get the better of you! We all know Nasir. He's lived here for years. He's our neighbor. Our friend." She looked at Don. "He was at your house just last weekend helping you with your roof, Don." She turned to Ken. "And your son and Nasir's youngest are in the same classes at school, Ken." She shook her head. "This isn't the way that we should be handling things right now."

Both Ken and Don slumped their shoulders, but Jerry refused to back down. Lisa didn't think there was any reasoning with him now. The only thing that was going to stop them was a show of force.

"Jerry, you need to go home," Lisa said, her tone dropping an octave. Her adrenaline spiked, and she was already coated with sweat from both the heat and the situation. "Don't do this."

Jerry wouldn't take his eyes off of Nasir. He had the look of a mad dog that was off the leash. The man was practically foaming at the mouth. He was out for blood. "The only way

I'm going home is after I put this son of a bitch out of his misery!" Jerry charged forward.

Nasir stood his ground, probably thinking he was the only line of defense between the madman and his daughters.

While Jerry charged up the steps, Lisa reached around for the revolver in her waistband. She had practiced the motion during her training with Mike. She had a decent pull time from her revolver in a controlled setting, but this was real life.

Lisa's heart hammered in her chest, and her muscles thrummed like a plucked guitar string. It took three tries before she finally managed to get her hand on the revolver's grip, and by that time Jerry was already on the porch, swinging the bat down as hard as he could against Nasir's body.

But the porch was crowded and narrow, preventing Jerry from gaining any momentum with his swings.

Lisa finally removed the revolver from its holster and placed herself in a strong shooter's stance, feet planted wide, both hands on the gun, arms forward and straight, but she struggled to keep soft hands on the grip. She brought Jerry into her sights. It was less than a twelve-yard shot. She had hit bullseyes farther than that at the range.

But when she had Jerry in her sights, the magnitude of shooting another person with the prospect of actually killing him sunk in, and she couldn't bring herself to do it. Instead, she aimed the weapon at the sky and squeezed the trigger.

The gunshot thundered and silenced the grunting noises of the two men grappling on the porch, everyone turning to Lisa, who now had the gun aimed back at Jerry.

"That's enough, Jerry!" Lisa struggled to catch her breath,

and she was white-knuckling the grip on the gun, but that was only because she was afraid she might drop it.

"Are you going to shoot me, Lisa?" Jerry asked a hint of fear in his voice.

Lisa kept Jerry in her sights. "I don't want to, but I will." She looked to Ken and Don. "You two take him home and make sure he cools off."

Don and Ken exchanged a quick glance, but then slowly walked to the porch steps. Don extended his hand. "Jerry, let's go. C'mon man."

Jerry looked from Lisa to his companions, and then to Nasir who was on the ground, bloodied and struggling to breathe. He snarled. "This isn't over." But despite the threat, he backed off, following Don and Ken off of Nasir's property.

Lisa kept her gun trained on Jerry as he left, and he locked eyes with her with the same dead-eye glare that she had seen him give Nasir.

"You picked the wrong side, Lisa," Jerry said.

Lisa kept quiet, and she didn't lower the weapon until she saw Jerry disappear back into his house with Don and Ken. When they were finally out of sight, she gasped for breath, her body turning to jelly as she checked on Nasir.

Nasir had managed to prop himself up on his elbow, but he couldn't sit up all the way. Blood poured from a nasty gash on top of his head, lines of crimson dripping down over his forehead.

Lisa tucked the revolver back in its holster as she crouched by Nasir's side. "Are you all right?" It was a stupid question. The man had just been beaten with a baseball bat. Of course he wasn't all right.

"I don't think anything is broken," Nasir grunted as he straightened himself up and leaned back against his house.

He shut his eyes, pressing his lids down hard, his face wrinkled up in an expression of pain. "My head won't stop pounding."

Lisa nodded. "Yeah, you'll have a lump. Do you think you can stand?"

Nasir reached for Lisa's hand to help him up. Once he was on his feet, he took a moment to stabilize his legs. Lisa let go of him, and when he started to fall, she caught his full weight in her arms.

"Whoa," Lisa said, struggling to keep them both upright. She transferred him to one of the porch chairs. "Just sit for a minute." She took a closer look at his head and saw that he'd need stitches. "Do you have a first-aid kit in the house?"

"Yes," Nasir said. "It's in the kitchen. Cabinet's above the refrigerator." He winced again and then cleared his throat. "My girls—"

"They're safe inside," Lisa said, but she was unsure of how long that was going to last. "Listen, I want you and your daughters to stay at my house. It'll be safer there."

Nasir looked at her with wide eyes. "Safer for us, maybe, but not for you."

"We'll cross that bridge when we get there," Lisa said. "Let's get you and your girls out of here, and get you fixed up."

Nasir, knowing his options were limited, reluctantly agreed, and Lisa helped him inside to gather his family. But she looked back one last time at Jerry's house, wondering when the man was going to come after her again. She had been to enough dive bars during her earlier years with Mike to know the look of a man who didn't know when to quit, and Lisa imagined that going back to his house to lick his wounds was only going to intensify the desire for revenge.

Lisa didn't think that he would just come back for her, but for her kids as well, and it was in that moment that Lisa wondered if she should have just stayed out of this disagreement. And she wondered if these were the kind of choices she would be forced to make in this new world. Choices of life and death.

6

The interior of Charlotte was already being torn apart. Buildings were looted. Cars were vandalized. Street signs had been toppled. Anything that could be broken had been smashed. The streets were littered by destruction.

Over the dense murmur of the crowded streets was the sporadic noise of gunfire. The noise reverberated off the building walls. But the gunfire had become nothing more than background noise, and every time it thundered overhead, no one bothered to flinch.

Mike moved quickly through the streets, doing his best to avoid staring down at the bodies of the dead. He wasn't sure how many terrorists were in the city, but he knew it was a lot. He just prayed that his mother wasn't among the casualties.

Mike took a right onto the street of his mother's apartment building, and he sprinted the last stretch, muscles fatigued from the long journey he'd already traveled. He had sweated through most of his clothes, and he kicked himself for not bringing water with him. He had been in such a hurry to leave that it didn't even cross his mind.

Mike entered the building's lobby, boots crunching over the broken glass along the marble floor. But he only made it a few steps before he stopped.

The light from the street only reached so far into the lobby, but managed to reach the bodies littering the floor.

Mike drew his weapon. He bypassed the elevators, knowing that they wouldn't work, but he stopped when he heard the soft muddle of voices coming from somewhere inside the lobby.

Mike searched for the source of the noise, and his inquiry brought him closer to the elevators. People were trapped inside.

With no power, the inside of those elevators was pitch black. Trapped inside with no food, no water, no way to properly dispose of their waste, combined with the rising heat, their fate looked grim.

Mike examined the closed elevator doors. He knew there was no way to open them without the elevator key. As he walked to the stairwell, their voices growing softer and weaker, Mike was flooded with guilt and shame, but there was nothing he could do.

Mike quickly bounded up the steps, two at a time for the first three floors, but then stopped to pace himself. His mother lived on the thirty-fourth floor, just two levels below the penthouse.

It was to his father's disdain that he hadn't been able to afford the top suite, but they had bought the condo for a good price, and the HOA fees were reasonable as compared to other skyrises in the city. Plus, they still had a mountain view. And Mike suspected that it was just as good a view that they would find on the penthouse floor.

Mike stopped to rest three times on the walk up the stairs, and halfway up he vomited in the corner of the stairwell. It wasn't anything except bile since he had barely eaten any breakfast, but the hot taste that lingered on his tongue was terrible.

The inside of the stairwell was like an oven. With no A/C running for the past several hours and the hot summer sun beating down on it for the same amount of time, it had made the ascent to get his mother almost unbearable.

It was so bad that Mike wasn't sure his mother would be able to make the trip down. She was nearing seventy. But he would cross that road when he came to it. He needed to get to his mother first.

Panting and completely drenched in sweat, Mike reached the thirty-fourth floor and shouldered open the door to the hallway. Too tired to even push, Mike could only lean his body weight into the door to make it open.

Doorways lined the hallway like a hotel, and a few of the doors were open. Sunlight from the rooms spilled into the hallway and illuminated a path for Mike to follow. It wasn't much light, but after climbing thirty-four flights of stairs in complete darkness, it might as well have been high noon.

Chatter drifted from the open rooms, but Mike didn't stop to look inside and instead went all the way to his mother's door, which was closed. He tried the handle first and found it unlocked. He entered.

"Mom?" Mike squinted when he stepped inside. All of the curtains to the windows had been opened. "Mom, are you in here?"

Mike staggered from the foyer and into the living room

and kitchen area. The place was immaculately tidy. The building provided maid service, but his mother still insisted on cleaning the apartment herself every other day. She had always been a neat freak.

"Mom?" Mike walked into the bedroom, finding it empty. He then checked the bathroom, also empty. He looked in the spare bedroom, and the second bathroom, both empty like the others. His mother wasn't here.

Mike turned once in a circle, but his mind continued to spin even after he was still. He returned into the hallway. "Mom? Mom!" He shouted, no longer trying to stay quiet, and the few muffled voices that he heard from inside the rooms grew silent.

"Michael?" The voice preceded a well-dressed woman stepping from one of the condos and into the hallway. Martha Thorton barely cleared five feet, but she carried herself as a much-taller woman. And that's what Mike saw now as the pair made eye contact. "Michael, how on earth did you get here?"

Mike walked only three steps before he broke out into a jog and scooped up his mother into his arms, thankful that she was alive.

"Michael, my goodness, you are all wet!" Martha leaned back from her son's embrace and frowned, getting a closer look at him. "What happened to you?"

Mike grabbed his mother's arm. "Mom, we need to get out of the city." He pulled her back to her room, her friends poking their heads out to see what was happening.

"Martha, are you all right?"

"I don't know," she answered. "My son seems to have lost his mind."

But Mike was thinking clearly now, probably more

clearly than he ever had. He pulled his mother into the apartment and didn't stop until he reached her room. "You need to pack a bag." He opened her closet and grabbed all of her clothes off the rack and threw them on the bed. "You can't take all of those, but pick out the stuff that would be good for walking outdoors. You'll also need to bring a winter coat. I don't know how long we'll be gone."

"Michael, this is insane." Martha walked over to the clothes piled on her bed and struggled to keep up with her son, who was speeding around the room.

"Where did you and Dad keep your luggage?" Mike stopped to look at his mother when he exhausted all of the locations in the room.

"Michael, enough." Martha planted her foot down. "What is going on?"

Mike paused and got a good look at his mother. The light from the window in the room highlighted her attire. She was dressed in an elegant black gown, complete with matching black high heels, and a dark shade of lipstick around her mouth. She had done her makeup to perfection, she had always been good at that sort of thing, and she wore a black beret perched perfectly on the top of her quaffed hair. Looking at her, Mike remembered his father's funeral was scheduled to happen at this very moment.

"Mom." Mike took her hand and did his best to speak as slowly and plainly as possible. "Something happened. There was an attack on the country. No power. No water. No phones. No cars. The city is in chaos right now, and I need to get you out of here before that chaos decides to make its way up to the thirty-fourth floor."

Martha was quiet for a moment, studying her son. He was sure that she would make a fuss about it. But it must have been the way that Mike looked that convinced her that her son was telling the truth. "And where are we going?"

Mike drew in a breath, gathering the courage to tell her. "We're going to Katy's cabin."

Martha laughed and then dropped her son's hands. "You might as well go without me."

"Mom, this isn't the time to hold a grudge," Mike said.

"Hold a grudge?" Martha arched one perfectly-groomed eyebrow. "The girl didn't even have the decency to call her father after he got sick. I can understand not wanting to come to visit. But not to call? Or even write?"

Mike rubbed his forehead, which was so slick with grime and sweat that his fingers slipped right off. "Mom, we don't have time for this. There are people hunting civilians in the streets. If we don't get out of the city soon, then we'll die. Do you understand?" Mike hardened his tone, and he hoped she would let go of her stubbornness and listen to her son for once.

Martha's expression softened. "I don't think she's going to want me there, Michael."

"Of course she will." Mike walked to his mother and held her hand. "You're her mother."

Martha winced. "I don't know how much of a mother I was to her." She bit her lower lip and then lowered her gaze to stare at the tips of her shoes. "She argued with her father so much, and the two butted heads so often I just decided to stay completely out of it. But maybe I should have done more, maybe I should have tried harder—"

"Mom." Mike gently grabbed hold of his mother's shoulders. "Whatever happened in the past won't matter. We're her family. She'll let us stay. I know it." And he truly believed that, because as much as Katy could be a pain, he knew that beneath all of those layers of loneliness and solitary confinement, there was a woman who still cared, despite the apathy that she wore like a second skin. "But we need to hurry up and leave if we're going to have a chance to make it out of here." He let go of his mother and moved toward the window.

It was difficult to see how bad things had gotten from this high, but if he were to close his eyes, he knew that he could still see the blood on the streets and the lifeless bodies the terrorists had left behind. He turned back to his mother. "Figure out what you're going to bring."

Martha straightened a little bit and then cleared her throat. "I don't think I should go."

Mike couldn't believe what he was hearing. "Mom, this isn't the time to—"

"Your father is gone," Martha said, raising her voice. "You have your family outside of the city. Katy lives off on her own." She fiddled with her hands, her fingers knobby and swollen from arthritis. "And if it's as bad as you say it is outside, then I don't think I'll make it very far."

Mike stood slack-jawed, and when he couldn't find the right words, he simply moved closer to her again and touched her hands. "I am not letting you die here. Do you understand me? I am not losing both of my parents in the same week. I don't care if I have to carry you out of here on my back, I am getting you out of this city, and I am taking you to Katy's cabin."

It was strange standing up to his mother. As the oldest, he had always done exactly what his parents had told him to do. It was Katy who had been rebellious. He never understood why she felt the need to act out so much, but they were questions to be answered for another time.

"So are you going to pack, or am I going to have to do it for you?" Mike asked.

Martha repressed a smile, but Mike was glad to see that she hadn't completely given up hope. "Fine. But I'll be taking you up on that offer to carry me if I get too tired." She grabbed Mike's face and pulled it down to her and kissed his cheek. "You're a good son." She let him go and walked over to the mountain of clothes on the bed, and then turned back to Mike. "The luggage is the spare closet in the second bedroom."

Mike nodded and then retrieved the luggage. But while his mother packed, he needed to come up with a solution that would get them out of the city in a hurry. He paced back and forth, his brainstorming broken up from interruptions by his mother's friends who came down to check on her in the hall.

Mike wasn't sure how they would react to the news of what was happening, but his mother assured him that they would be fine to handle the information. And so he told them the truth.

Despite Mike's suggestion that they leave, all of them had decided to hunker down and wait it out, and when Mike objected to the strategy, it was his mother's friend Doris who spoke for the group.

"Son, I have been on this planet for eighty-two years," Doris said. "If this is how I go, then so be it. But I'm not going to leave my home just because things have gotten hard."

The sentiment echoed through the rest of the group. It was an admirable quality to wait out the storm, but Mike knew that all of them underestimated just how violent this storm would become.

None of them would survive the week.

Once Martha was packed, Mike led her down the hallway, carrying his mother's luggage, which was going to make the trip more difficult since her mother didn't own a backpack. And while Mike had spent the past several hours traveling through death and the heat of the summer, fighting against terrorists and the elements, reaching his mother had reinvigorated him.

But Martha forced Mike to slow his pace, and they made frequent stops for her to rest. Mike's incessant coddling was starting to wear his mother's patience thin.

"For Pete's sake, Michael, I'm fine." Martha huffed. "If I need a break, or if I get tired, then I will tell you. I'm old, but I'm not dead."

The trip down was easier than the long trudge up. When they finally reached the bottom of the stairwell, Mike paused to glance back at his mother.

"No matter what, you need to stay close to me," Mike said. "It's going to be bad out there, Mom, and the most important thing to do is to keep moving." He suddenly remembered the people in the elevator, how they would stay trapped inside until their bodies slowly shut down from starvation and hunger. Or their organs failed because they didn't have the medication they needed to survive. "No matter what we see, or hear, we don't stop. Okay?"

Martha nodded. "I'll be right behind you."

"All right," Mike said, one hand on the luggage, the other holding his pistol. He shouldered open the door, and their senses were bombarded by the elements.

The sun blinded them, and they both cringed from the shrill screams of the dying. The gunshots which had been distant pops before he entered the building were much louder now. The terrorists had moved closer.

Mike slowed when they reached the intersection, looking in every direction to determine the safest route while everyone else darted past him in directionless jerks.

The loudest gunshots were coming from the north side of the city. Staying west would be their best shot at staying out of harm's way.

"C'mon, Mom." Mike waited until his mother was right on his heels. She kept hold of his shirt as they crossed the street, and Mike made sure that he could always feel that pressure from his mother's hand. When the gunfire faded farther to the north, Mike believed that he had made the right decision.

Mike looked back at his mother, smiling. "I think we're going to be all right. We just need to keep heading west, and we'll be out of the city in no time."

Martha only nodded, and Mike saw the strain on her face. She was already exhausted, but she didn't complain.

The pair neared the next intersection, and just before they got close, the streets were flooded with people running south, climbing over the cars, trampling those that fell, and the sight of the stampede forced Mike to stop.

"We need to get out of the street now!" Mike directed his mother toward the nearest storefront as the tidal wave of people headed straight for them. And just before they reached the door, something near the intersection erupted, the explosion knocking both Mike and his mother to the sidewalk.

7

*T*he ringing in Mike's ears was dull at first, but it grew louder as he slowly regained consciousness. Face down on the concrete, his entire body ached.

Mike moved his arms and legs in slow, uncoordinated movements until he gained enough momentum to sit on his knees.

The ground was covered in grey soot, and as he examined himself, he slowly realized he was too. He coughed and blinked away the grey granules of dust around his eyes.

A massive grey fog had descended over the city. And through the ringing in his ears, he heard muffled screams and the dull percussive blasts of guns. With his hearing impaired, Mike wasn't sure how close the danger was, but he couldn't stay here. He needed to get him and his mother—

Mike's heart skipped a beat. He had lost her. He quickly turned left and right, scanning his surroundings, but the debris of smoke and dust had limited visibility to less than a few feet.

"Mom!" Mike's voice was nothing but a throaty croak. He stood, his legs wobbling, but he didn't collapse. He took one step into the growing cloud of dust, his panic turning to dread. "Mom!" He barked the words more harshly, hoping that wherever his mother was that she would be able to hear him. "Mom!" He hunched forward as he screamed into the abyss, but his only answer was muted gunfire.

Mike stopped. He was letting his panic control the situation. He needed to think. He took stock of his person. He had lost the luggage and his service pistol, but he still had the revolver that he placed on his ankle.

Mike removed the revolver and then wiped away more of the grey dust, but only succeeded in smearing it around his face. He was covered in it from head to toe. He retraced his steps, able to do so by the prints that he left behind on the sidewalk. He paused, knowing that he had held his mother's hand right before the bomb had gone off and that the pair were close.

Mike circled the area in small grids, making sure that he moved in straight lines so he wouldn't backtrack, and as tedious and trying as it was, it worked. "Mom!"

Martha lay on her back, arms lifted over her head. Mike dropped to her side, checking for a pulse, and then made sure she was still breathing. Once the vitals were confirmed, he tried to gently shake her awake.

"Mom?" Mike struggled to keep his voice steady. "Mom, I need you to wake up." But Martha wouldn't respond.

More gunfire echoed in the cloud of fog, followed by screams and the quick patter of feet.

No longer able to wait for his mother to wake up, Mike scooped Martha up. She looked so frail in his arms.

Mike continued forward on the sidewalk, using the building to guide him and continue his journey west. The clouds of dust thickened the farther west he moved, and Mike wondered what kind of bomb would have caused that explosion. But when he finally reached the intersection, he had his answer.

A crater at least seven feet deep and fifteen feet wide currently occupied the space where the asphalt had been just moments ago. The blast had disintegrated everything that was nearby. Mike looked up at the nearby building and saw that the first five floors were completely exposed, the side of the building having been blown away.

The blast had incinerated anything that was nearby, but Mike saw the remains of a few people who were unable to completely escape the bomb's blast radius. Seeing the after-math of the explosion, Mike knew that he and his mom had survived by blind luck.

Another gunshot pulled Mike's attention away from the blast radius to the north, but this one was much closer than before.

Mike retreated to the cover of the building behind him to hide. The dust was starting to clear, and visibility improved. From his position near the mangled concrete and metal, he watched the street.

Random people sprinted down what remained of the road. All of them were covered in the same grey dust, and they looked nowhere but straight ahead with a dead-eyed glare.

And then a gunshot would echo, and one of the runners would drop. The momentum from their run would cause them to fly forward, and they would skid over the pavement before their body came to rest.

It was hard watching the people fall. And with everyone that died, Mike felt something inside of him shift. Something primal and angry. But because he still had his mother with him, Mike knew that he needed to stay out of it. He couldn't save everyone.

8

*N*asir sat in one of the kitchen chairs while Lisa did her best to sew up the stitches on his head. Nasir had been a doctor in his home country of Pakistan, and he was able to walk her through the necessary steps.

But while Nasir handled the stitches well enough, Lisa struggled to keep her composure. Each time that she was forced to thread the needle through a piece of Nasir's scalp, pushing through the blood and hair, she had to swallow the vomit that crawled up her throat.

Finished, Lisa set aside the needle and thread, and then removed the bloodied gloves she wore per Nasir's instructions and tossed them into the trash. She then watched as Nasir picked up a mirror and checked her work.

"I don't see my brain, so it looks like you did a fine job, Mrs. Thorton." Nasir smiled and then set the mirror down as he picked up the gauze he'd use to wrap his head.

"I just touched your bloodied scalp, Nasir," Lisa said. "I think we can go by a first-name basis now."

"You're probably right." Nasir finished with the gauze and

then set it aside. He turned around to find his girls in the living room with Casey. One of them was a year younger, and the other was two years older.

Lisa noticed Nasir's lingering gaze on his children, Khatera and Maisara. "They'll be safe here."

Nasir turned, his expression grave. He had suddenly aged ten years in that one turn. "I can't believe this is happening."

Lisa wasn't sure if he was referring to the EMP or the fact that his neighbors had turned on him at the drop of a hat. "Mike will be back soon." At least she hoped. "And once he returns, he'll sort everyone out." Though Lisa wasn't sure how he'd do it. She hoped Mike's status as a detective would help convince people not to panic, but with society crumbling around them, she doubted people would recognize the law anymore.

"Thank you again," Nasir said. "If you hadn't shown up when you did. If you hadn't had the gun... I don't know what they would have done to me. Or my girls." His eyes reddened at the mention of his daughters, but he held back the tears. He cleared his throat and then changed the subject. "Do you know what's happening out there? Anything specific about the attack?"

Lisa told him what Mike had told her.

"So things are only going to get worse." Nasir rubbed his eyes. "This all seems so impossible."

"I know," Lisa answered. "Even now I think that I'm going to wake up from this nightmare and I'll be back in bed. But things just keep going from bad to worse to the unimaginable." She leaned back in her chair and then looked past Nasir to her son and Nasir's daughters.

Watching the three of them play together, laughing, Lisa

couldn't understand why everyone couldn't play nice with one another.

But she knew how deep prejudices could run. Not everyone was afflicted with it, but there were too many whose bigoted and racist views hindered progress.

"Has it always been this bad for you?" Lisa asked, looking back to Nasir.

"What do you mean?" Nasir asked.

"I mean with…" Lisa gestured outside toward Jerry's house. "These kinds of situations."

Nasir nodded and then shifted in his chair. "It was bad when I first moved here and my English was not good. People assumed that just because I couldn't speak the language that I didn't belong. And the fact that I'm Middle Eastern…" He lowered his gaze to the table, saddened. "I knew coming to this country would be difficult, but despite what people say, there are still opportunities here. If you work hard, you can pave your own way. It really is one of the greatest things about this country that I have come to love. And I knew that my hard work would pay off for my daughters." His sadness lifted at the mention of his girls. "They are very bright and they have wonderful spirit. But they had little prospects in my home country. I wanted to give them a better life after their mother passed."

Lisa had never heard Nasir mention his wife. "When did she die?"

"It was five years ago," Nasir answered. "It was a car accident. Freak thing. She had gone to the market to pick up some food. The girls were at daycare, and someone ran a light, and she died on impact. I was devastated when I heard the news. It affected my work, our home life. I needed to leave the city, that place, our home, because everything only reminded me of my wife."

Lisa reached for Nasir's hand. "I'm so sorry. For everything."

Nasir smiled and composed himself. "We've fought our way through it, and we'll fight our way through this."

Lisa let go of Nasir's hand. She admired his spirit, his courage, and his love for his daughters. She couldn't imagine going through what he did after losing his wife. But now she supposed they were all in the same boat together, forced to leave their homes. She only prayed that Mike would make it back to her alive and she wouldn't join Nasir as a grieving widow.

"What will you do now?" Lisa asked, curious to see if Nasir had any kind of plan. She didn't want to assume about any preparations that he might have.

"I don't know," Nasir said. "As intimidating as you were, I don't think it's going to stop Jerry and others from coming after me. I suppose I'll have to take my girls somewhere."

"But where?" Lisa asked. "Do you have any family?"

"The only family I have left is back in Pakistan," Nasir said. "Maybe the government will open up some shelters to help deal with the disaster. It would probably be safer to take my girls there than to stay here. Plus, I don't know how long our food stores are going to last without any power to run refrigeration. I have a generator with some gas, but not enough to last more than a few days."

Lisa knew that she had a choice to make because when Mike returned, they would leave immediately. And the moment Lisa turned her back on Nasir and his daughters, they would fall prey to the wolves that were sniffing around the neighborhood.

She considered giving him a weapon. They had another pistol in the safe that she could give him and show him how to use. But how long would he be able to hold all of those people off? How many bullets would he fire without any formal training before he actually hit something?

The more that Lisa thought about it, the more she was convinced that if they left Nasir and his family behind, they would die.

But what would Mike say about bringing other people? Not to mention how Katy would react to bringing strangers to her front door.

Lisa weighed the options, and she knew that there was only one thing that she could do.

"Nasir," Lisa said, pulling the man out of the pit of despair that he had circled into. "How much luggage do you and your girls have?"

9

*M*elvin Harris shed his convict clothes as soon as he could, dropping them among the crowd of people along the highway. Fear and panic had triggered the stampede, and he stuck to the middle of the herd to keep himself hidden from the authorities. People were so preoccupied from fleeing danger that no one noticed the half-naked man next to them.

Melvin didn't stop moving until he reached the end of the highway and re-entered the city. The first order of business was finding clothes. He needed to blend back into society, and naked people drew too much attention.

With every storefront being looted, it was easy for Melvin to simply stroll into the nearest store, grab what he needed, and walk out. People should have started looting years ago.

While Melvin had no qualms about his freedom, he was suddenly curious as to what had happened. It had been a stroke of good luck that traffic had stopped and all forms of communication had shut down, but to who did he owe this miracle? He lifted his face toward the sky, basking in the warmth of the sun.

In the end, it didn't matter. He was free. The only thing he was concerned with now was making the most of his situation.

It had been exactly three months, two weeks, and three days since the last time he killed. And it was all he could think about as he sat in his tiny cell day and night. Thoughts of murder had floated through his mind, even at a young age. But there had always been an outlet for him. A way for him to express his inner fantasies. And those thoughts festered as he lay locked away in a cell.

Melvin emerged from the clothing store as a new man. But while he walked out of the place with a well-worn apathy, he noticed that everyone else was running around like a chicken with their heads cut off, and every time a gunshot thundered into the air, the frantic animals ducked and screamed and scurried even faster.

Melvin smiled at their helplessness. None of them were prepared for the world to come crashing down on their heads.

He slowly broke out into a jog, and while he pretended to keep his directions sporadic and panicked, he was always watching, always looking, always on the move for his next victim. He didn't think it would be difficult. There was a smorgasbord of delights for him to try, and when a half-dozen masked men with machine guns made their way down the street, Melvin found his next meal.

A cluster of people veered off into the nearest building to evade the terrorists mowing down anyone who crossed their path. Melvin understood the thrill of taking a life, but he believed that those men were doing it all wrong.

The killing was an event. It was a game of cat and mouse. And it was only when the mouse was nearing the edge of death that either animal felt alive. It was a rush more than anything he experienced in his entire life. Melvin was glad to be back in the game.

Once everyone was inside the building, people scattered, darting to different darkened corners of the restaurant. Melvin thought it was a stupid place to hide, but he wasn't in charge of the panicked herd.

All Melvin was concerned with was finding the right mark for his fun, and he spotted her in the very back of the store. Alone.

The gunmen continued their killing spree down the street, firing randomly into stores, and the glass of the front of the restaurant shattered, triggering more screams. It was pathetic how they cowered. They were nothing but emotional meat bags. Right now, he needed to pretend to be one of them.

Melvin whimpered to himself when he neared the back of the store where the woman had gone, but he purposely kept his distance.

Melvin cowered and scrunched up his face until it was red and wrinkly and snot was coming out of his nose and tears filled his eyes, a tactic he had used before.

After a few minutes, the terrorists passed the building, and the sounds of their gunfire faded, along with the sharpened screams of everyone huddled in the restaurant.

Slowly, people started to stand, and with the enemy gone, they left the restaurant to go wandering out into the street, continuing their never-ending search for safety. But Melvin knew that there were no safe places anymore.

Once the restaurant had nearly emptied, Melvin poked

his head up from the hunched position. He saw the woman was still near him, huddled in the corner. She hadn't moved a muscle even though the danger had passed. At least the danger of the terrorists.

"Hey," Melvin said, putting on his weak and eager voice. "Are you all right?"

The woman only trembled, keeping silent. Melvin took the opportunity to get closer to her, but when he made his move, she retreated farther into the darkness.

"Whoa," Melvin said, holding up his hands. "I just wanted to make sure that you weren't hurt." He waited until she actually looked up at him before he took another step. "Are you okay?"

The woman nodded. "I think so. I mean… I'm not sure." She sniffled and then wiped her eyes. She had been crying.

"Do you know what's going on?" Melvin asked, keeping up his act. "I was out getting groceries and then all of a sudden everything just… stopped."

The woman came out of the corner a little bit, but she still kept her distance. She wasn't about to get close enough so Melvin could grab her, but that was all part of the game.

"I don't know either," she said. "I was driving, and my car just shut off. I hit the truck in front of me, and then everyone got out and just looked around. Then there was gunfire and people started running. So I ran."

The woman was growing more emotional the longer she spoke, and before long, she had her face buried in her forearms. Melvin knew that this was his opportunity. He moved closer, starting out by placing his hand on her shoulder, waiting to see how she would react. When she didn't recoil from his touch, her fate was sealed.

"What's your name?" Melvin asked, trying hard not to salivate.

The woman wiped her eyes and took a whimpering breath. "Peggy."

"Peggy, you need to listen to me," Melvin said. "We need to get out of here before those people come back and try to hurt us, okay?"

Peggy nodded and then took Melvin's offered hand as he helped her stand. "Where are we supposed to go? Those people are everywhere."

Melvin nodded, but then leaned closer and kept his voice to a whisper. "I have a brother in the army. He called me right before all of this went down. He said they knew about the attacks and that they're going to try and stop them, but until they do, they have relief centers set up around the city. They're safe zones, Peggy. We need to get there before more of those people come back."

Peggy's eyes lit up with that sweet familiar look of hope. "O-okay. Where is it?"

Melvin grabbed her hand as he led her out of the back of the restaurant. "It's not far."

And while Peggy was no doubt thinking of what she was going to do when she was finally safe, the only thing that Melvin thought about was how he was going to kill his twenty-ninth victim.

he fog and the shooting were behind them, and Mike still carried his mother in his arms. Sweat dripped from his chin and nose. Even though his mother was small and light, carrying her under the conditions of the blazing heat after the distance that they had just traveled had nearly made him pass out twice. He needed to stop to check on her vitals, but he was afraid to stop because he didn't want to discover that he was carrying around his mother's corpse instead of her unconscious body. But he knew it couldn't be avoided.

Mike found a quiet, isolated spot between two buildings. The area he had wandered into wasn't as crowded as downtown, but they were still in the city, and they were still being hunted. He gently set his mother on the ground and then placed two fingers against her neck.

Time slowed as Mike waited for a sign of life, and he exhaled in relief when he felt a pulse. She was alive.

Martha stirred, groaning, and shifted uncomfortably on the concrete.

Mike placed both hands on her. "Mom? Oh my god. Mom, how are you feeling?"

"Sore." Martha opened her eyes. "What happened?"

"There was an explosion," Mike said.

Martha winced, and Mike helped her sit up. "Where are we?"

Mike looked around for a landmark to get a better bearing on their location. "We're closer to the burbs now, somewhere on the west side of the city."

Martha frowned. "But we were downtown the last time that I remember." She studied her son carefully and then widened her eyes with awe. "You carried me all that way?"

It was the sound of surprise in his mother's voice that made Mike blush. "It's not like you're that heavy, Mom."

But Martha didn't mean it as a slight, and she gently grabbed her son's hand. She squeezed it and smiled. "Thank you."

Mike helped his mother to her feet and then offered her his arm as they walked back out onto the street.

"How much farther?" Martha asked.

Mike knew the answer, but he didn't want to speak it aloud. It would be another few hours before they escaped the shadow of the city. But after the trek he'd just made, Mike wasn't sure if either of them had the strength to make it.

The heat, the exertion, and the stress of the situation had all compiled and sucked the life out of him. He was exhausted.

Martha reached for her son's face, gently cupping her weathered and dusty palm against Mike's cheek, and smiled. "It's all right, son."

Mike knew she had read the doubt on his face, and she was trying to let him know that it was okay for him to go. It was the simple reassurance from a mother who no longer wanted to be a burden on her son.

"No," Mike said, shaking his head. "I'm not going to leave you."

"Michael—"

"Mom." Mike placed his own hand over her mother's. "I will find a way."

Mike examined the cars in the street, noticing a few older models that might still work. But the problem wasn't finding transportation, it was the clogged city streets. Even if Mike were able to find a car or truck that would start, he wouldn't be able to maneuver around the thousands of stalled vehicles. Maybe he shouldn't have ditched the bicycle.

A thought pricked in the back of Mike's head, and he arched his eyebrows. He just needed a bigger bike. "Mom, I know how we can get out of here."

His mother looked up at him, skeptical. "I don't think I can walk anymore, son. My legs are toast. I can barely breathe from the dust in my lungs." She shut her eyes and twisted up her face from the pain, then gently shook her head. "I don't have anything left."

"You don't have to walk," Mike said.

He scooped his mother up in his arms and carried her into a nearby building tucked down a side street.

Inside it was dark, but not pitch black. A high window provided enough sunlight for Mike to see the building was a storage facility. The place was crammed with pallets of boxes stacked from the front of the building all the way to the back. Plenty of places for his mother to hide in case danger came lurking, but Mike didn't plan to be gone for that long.

Mike found a spot deeper in the building to place his mother and gently set her down. The floor was concrete, but he found some package stuffing for her to sit on that would make it easier on her joints.

"I want you to stay right here," Mike said. "If someone comes, just do your best to hide and stay quiet." He glanced around the facility. "I can't imagine anyone would come back here, but just to be on the safe side—" He reached around for his belt and placed a knife in her hand.

The blade had a dark handle, and the steel looked dull in the darkness, but Mike knew it was sharp.

"I don't think I'll be able to do much good with this," Martha said, handling the weapon awkwardly. "I barely have enough strength to lift it on my own hand."

Mike firmly grabbed the wrist that held the blade, and his mother looked up at him. "I'm not going to be gone for very long. I'm just going to get the bike and then come right back. I'll be back before you know it." He kissed the top of his mother's head and then stood to leave.

Mike wanted to look back as he left, but he didn't. Because if he died, he didn't want the last image for his mother to see of him as the little boy who turned back to see his mother one last time. Instead, he wanted it to be of the man who charged ahead to take action in a world that was falling apart.

When Mike noticed the street sign nearby, he realized he was close to McClellan's Motorcycle Shop. And if older model cars worked, Mike believed the same would be true for older motorcycles, like a 1960 Harley Panhead, which his partner had obsessed over.

Energy renewed by his mission, Mike moved quickly down the street, keeping off the road and on the side-walk. The buildings to his right provided a natural source of cover and allowed the bulk of his attention to be focused on any potential threats that were ahead or to his right.

The terrorists that attacked the city had done a good job of flushing the majority of the people out of the street and searching for cover. All that was left behind now were the broken-down vehicles that had been abandoned and the bodies rotting in the streets.

The heat of summer was compounding the decomposition, and the stink of death had intensified. It wouldn't be long before the entire city smelled of decay, but Mike hoped to be long gone before then.

Only two streets away from the repair shop, Mike transitioned from a jog to a run. But when he crossed the next street, Mike skidded to a stop and ducked behind a car. He watched three masked men corralling a group of women from the street and into a nearby building.

Each man had a woman, and they handled their lady roughly as they entered a small building.

Mike lowered his forehead onto the hood of the Buick and shut his eyes, wishing he could unsee what he had seen, but it was too late for that now.

Time wasn't on his side, and he needed to get his mother out of the city.

But the girls those men had shoved into that building were young. One of them too young, and Mike couldn't help but think of his daughter at home. If someone had seen Kelly or Lisa being pushed into an abandoned building with dark intentions, he hoped the person who saw wouldn't sit idle. And neither would he.

Mike reached for his revolver and then moved quickly toward the building where the terrorists had taken their victims.

The building was a standalone and only one story, which meant there was limited space for the bad guys to perform their heinous acts. But that also meant once Mike entered the building, he would be forced to react quickly.

His exhaustion from the day had stolen some of his confidence that he would be able to kill all three men before one of them reached for their weapon, but as he neared the building, he heard crying from inside.

Mike was already out of time.

He opened the door, sunlight flooding into the darkened front room. The light revealed the men with their pants down and the girls struggling to fight back against their rapists.

All three men turned at the intrusion, all of them unarmed.

The first bullet Mike fired struck the man nearest to him in the chest. With the door closing behind him and the sunlight disappearing, Mike pivoted his aim to the next man, squeezing off one round that winged his target in the shoulder. He quickly lined up his shot again and fired a third round, which pierced the man's throat.

The door was completely closed by the time Mike positioned his aim toward the third and final assailant, but the third man had enough time to charge Mike and slammed his body into the door before he could line up a shot.

The force from the collision caused Mike to accidentally squeeze the trigger, the shot ringing out in the darkness, followed by the sharp, piercing screams of the women.

Both men spilled from the building and onto the sidewalk. When Mike smacked against the concrete, he lost his grip on the revolver. Stunned from the collision, Mike was open to attack, and the terrorist took advantage by climbing on top of him and choking him.

Mike reached for the man's wrists, bucking his hips and kicking his legs all at the same time in hopes of causing the man to fly off of him, but the man was bigger than Mike and too heavy, and the exertion from the day had drained the last of his strength.

Mike stared into the terrorist's angry eyes. The man bared his teeth, squeezing Mike's neck as hard as he could with as much pressure and as much force as he could muster. Mike's vision slowly started to fade, and he lost his grip on his attacker.

The pressure in Mike's head was so intense he thought his brain would explode out of top of his head, and his vision was starting to go black.

A dull thud broke through Mike's daze, and nearly instantly, the darkness lifted, and the pressure around his neck was relieved.

Mike jolted upright, coughing and hacking, and glanced down at the man who had nearly killed him. He was dead.

The back half of the terrorist's skull was missing, and blood and brains were dripping out of the back. Mike quickly shoved the rest of the dead man off of him and retreated from the corpse. He stared at the dead man in shock, unsure of what happened until he looked to his left and saw a woman with one of the gunmen's rifles in her hands.

The woman had a wild look in her eyes, and her grip over the weapon was so tight that her arms were shaking. She stared at the man she had killed, makeup smeared over her face, and her hair and clothes disheveled.

Mike slowly stood, arms out by his sides, not wanting to spook her.

The woman turned to Mike, aiming the weapon at him in the same motion.

"It's okay," Mike said. "You can put that down now. I'm not here to hurt you."

The woman looked down at the rifle in her hands, and she stared at it like she was seeing it for the first time. She frowned, then slowly bent over and placed the weapon on the concrete. When she straightened up again, she hugged herself and then retreated to the open door where the other two girls slowly emerged, each of them wearing the same look of shock and disgust.

The four of them were quiet for a moment, the silence lingering until the girl that had killed the terrorist and saved Mike's life cleared her throat and spoke up.

"Thank you." Her voice was quiet and small.

Mike nodded. "Are you all right? Did they—" He cut himself off as his own cheeks flushed with embarrassment, and he averted his eyes. "I'm sorry."

"No, it's okay." The girl in the back stepped forward. "They didn't." She shuddered. "You got here just in time."

Mike nodded, and while he should have felt good about the encounter, he found himself replaying the moment in his mind. He had been on the police force for over twenty years, and in that time frame, Mike had fired his weapon only twice. And in both instances, Mike had never killed anyone.

And he just killed two men in less than thirty seconds.

Mike turned around and away from the bloodied man on the street. His mind was swimming in a heap of confusion.

But when Mike looked across the street, he saw people had emerged from the buildings. Dozens of people, all of them slowly crossing the street and gathering around the fallen terrorist who had been tearing down the only world that they had ever known.

Everyone circled around the dead man, staring at him as if he were some kind of indestructible demon, killed. And when they were done looking at the dead man, they looked at Mike.

"You saved them," a man said.

Mike looked to the three girls. "They were in trouble. It's what needed to be done."

But judging by the shamed look on everyone else's faces, Mike realized that everyone standing around had watched the terrorists take those women into the building. None of them had done anything to help.

"I haven't seen any of them dead before," a woman said, staring down at the gunmen, but keeping her distance.

One of the men moved from the crowd and walked over to the rifle that the woman had dropped on the concrete. He picked it up, keeping it at arm's length from him as he looked the weapon over. And just when Mike was about to ask the guy if he needed a hand with it, the man flipped the weapon around and handled it like he'd owned one for years.

Mike wasn't sure what the man was going to do, but when the pair locked eyes, he saw the hardened glare of determination.

The man turned toward the others. "We can't run anymore. If we want to take our city back, then we'll have to fight."

A wave of agreement rippled through the crowd, and Mike watched as the expressions of shame and regret hardened into the stares of men and women who now had a purpose.

"We need to give them everything we have!" The man raised the weapon into the air, and the gesture triggered a roaring, rallying cry from the group.

Led by the man who had picked up the weapon, the forty or so people marched down the street, joined by two of the women who had been attacked. Mike watched them leave. He wasn't sure what would happen to them after they were gone, but he was glad to see that people were fighting back.

Mike turned around to collect his revolver off the floor and saw that one of the women that had been attacked stayed behind. It had been the woman who had shot the man that was about to kill Mike.

"Do you have anywhere to go?" Mike asked.

It was the only question that he could think of at the time, and he wished that he would have chosen something more sensitive.

But the woman nodded, then stared down at the man she had killed. "I've never killed anyone before." She looked at Mike. "Does it go away?"

Mike frowned. "Does what go away?"

The woman shrank into herself and then stared at her feet. "Their face."

Since Mike had just killed his first, he wasn't sure. He cleared his throat, ridding himself of any uncertainty. "They didn't leave us any other choice. If I hadn't killed them, then they would have raped you and your friends. And if you hadn't killed him, then I would be the one dead on the ground." He spied his revolver and then walked over and picked it up.

Mike checked the ammunition in the chamber, and then snapped the barrel shut. "I need to be getting back."

The girl was pretty. Young, but pretty. And when she

walked over and gently kissed Mike on the lips, he didn't pull away.

The gesture wasn't meant to be romantic. It was only a peck. A moment of acknowledgment of their connection. She said nothing else as she stepped away and walked in the opposite direction of the mob that was determined to quench their thirst for blood.

Mike stood in the middle of two paths, one of them running away from the fight, and the other heading directly for it. Mike looked down at his gun, then to the dead man on the ground. He wondered how many more men he would have to kill before this was all over. And then he wondered how many of those men would haunt his dreams like they would haunt that girl's dreams.

All he knew for sure was that he would continue to fight for a very long time.

11

*M*ike arrived at the motorcycle repair shop without further incident, and he was glad to find the place hadn't been looted. He figured most people thought since all the cars stopped running that stealing a motorcycle would be pointless. But that wasn't true. You just had to know what to look for.

Mike prayed that the bike was still in the shop. His partner, Kevin, was a motorhead. He loved everything about bikes. The man couldn't get enough of them, and Kevin never stopped talking about the vintage Harley that he couldn't afford that was in this shop. And when Mike neared the back, he saw it was still here.

The 1960 Harley Panhead had been placed onto a stand, but it was connected to a ramp that could bring the bike down. Mike wasn't sure if there was gas in the tank, but he figured he could siphon some out of the abandoned cars on the road.

Mike was careful to bring the old bike down. It was

heavier than it looked, and the cycle nearly got away from him on the way down the ramp before he hit the brakes.

Because the vehicle was locked in the showroom at all times, the key was already in the ignition. Mike had gone riding with his partner a few times, but it had been a while since the last trip. Still, he hoped the old adage of riding a bicycle applied to a motorbike too.

Mike found two helmets and put one on his head and strapped the other to the passenger seat in the back. He turned the ignition and then kicked down hard on the starter, and Mike didn't even have enough time to hold his breath before the engine sputtered to life.

Mike laughed and throttled the engine, letting it warm up. He checked the tank and saw that it was half full. It was plenty of fuel to get him and his mother the rest of the way home. And from there, they would have his father's truck, and that would be more than enough to get them to Katy's cabin.

Mike cut the engine and then walked the bike through the store. It was too messy for him to drive through, though he considered giving it a try since he would be driving through cluttered streets anyway.

Once Mike had the motorcycle outside, he looked behind him and picked up two pairs of sunglasses.

Eyes protected from the sun, Mike mapped out a path on the road. There were a lot of wrecks, but there was plenty of space for him to weave around. He just needed to take it slow.

Mike donned his helmet, started the bike, and then eased off the clutch and twisted the throttle. The bike crawled forward slowly, and then he hit the throttle too hard, and he lurched forward. Mike wiggled the handlebars, sliding from side to side, and he managed to course correct, but he nearly went headfirst into the back of a pickup truck.

Once Mike was moving, he managed to keep a steady pace, but in addition to the blocked roads, he was also worried about attracting terrorists.

The motorcycle might have worked, but it was incredibly loud. With the quiet of the city, he was betting the engine echoed for a few miles.

Mike returned to the alley without incident, and before he could park the bike, he saw his mother step out of the building and walk down the alley. He was about to get off to come and help her, but she gestured for him to stop.

Martha arrived at the bike, and Mike handed her the helmet.

"Thank you," Martha said, shouting above the engine.

"I would have come to get you," Mike said.

Martha waved her hand dismissively. "I heard you coming from a mile away. And I needed to walk on my own to make sure I still could."

Mike waited for his mother to finish with her helmet and then leaned the bike to the side, so it was easier for her to mount.

"Just wrap your arms around me and squeeze as tight as you can," Mike said.

Martha nodded as she hopped up onto the bike. Her arms were bone-thin, and the grip was so loose when she interlocked her hands together that he was having second thoughts about his plan.

"Are you sure you can hold on?" Mike shouted.

"I'm fine! Just hurry!"

Mike nodded and then eased forward. He started slow,

not even moving out of first gear, but after a few streets the city traffic cleared some, and he was able to speed up.

With the traffic clearing and Mike picking up speed, he thought that things were finally turning around. But he let those hopes rise a few seconds too soon.

The last pair of high-rise buildings were up ahead before they escaped the city limits and entered the surrounding suburbs. From there, Mike could follow the back roads all the way to his house.

But through the seventh-floor windows of that last pair of high-rises, Mike saw a pair of rifles protrude into the open, and gunfire rained from above.

The bullets struck the vehicles around the motorcycle, shattering glass and tearing apart metal. The bullets which struck the pavement ricocheted off and veered in random directions.

Because the roads were still crowded, Mike had limited space to maneuver, but he saw an opening to his left and he throttled the gas, rocketing them out of the street and down the nearest side alley.

The sound of gunfire chased them, but they were well out of range before any of the bullets touched them.

The narrow walls of the alley amplified the noise of the bike's engine, and Mike stopped halfway through the alley to make sure his mother was all right. He cut the bike's engine and then turned around. "Mom?"

Martha Thorton had her face pressed against her son's back, and when she didn't respond, Mike's thoughts went down every darkened alley in his imagination. "Mom, are you all right?"

Martha stirred. "I'm okay."

Mike relaxed, but then realized they might not have a way

out of the city. "I think those terrorists might have shooters stationed at every outbound road around Charlotte." He glanced behind him one last time and then looked forward to the street where the alley spilled out into.

"Michael?" Martha asked.

"Hang on tight, Mom." Mike started the engine again and then felt his mother's arms squeeze around him as he released the clutch and twisted the throttle, rocketing them down the alley. An urgency had gripped Mike, one that he couldn't quite place. He needed to get home.

Mike bounced out of the alley and into the next street. He took a sharp right, continuing his journey west. He stayed on the sidewalk, which was clear of any obstructions, and he made sure to keep his peripheral vision on alert as he waited for any sign that the enemy had more shooters in the buildings above.

They did.

Once again gunfire thundered from above, and Mike was forced back down another alley, and he barely made it out of the range of the shooter. Mike and his mother were trapped.

Mike killed the engine and looked back to his mother. "I don't have enough open space on the road to go fast enough to evade them, and there isn't enough cover on the streets for me to hide from them. We're stuck, Mom."

Martha nodded as if the news he'd just told her had to do with the grocery store running out of milk. She looked back to the original road, and then to her son. "Is it me that's slowing you down?"

"What? Mom, no," Mike said. "They just have too many shooters, and I can't go fast enough on this thing to get out."

"And why can't you go faster?" Martha asked.

Mike opened his mouth to answer, but then stopped

himself when he realized he was going to say that he was afraid that she'd fall off, or she'd get hit, or something would happen to her.

Martha reached for her son's chin and gave it a hardy shake. "You listen to me, Michael. I will not be the reason you don't go home to your family today. I will not be that burden. But if either of us is going to survive what the world is now, then we're going to have to take risks. And those risks might involve putting your old mother in harm's way. Do you hear me?"

Mike knew she was right. Now wasn't the time to hesitate. When he was in the police academy, he was told that the most important aspect of the job was to be decisive. If you ever found yourself in a life-or-death situation and you hesitated, it could cost you your life, the lives of other officers, and the lives of other civilians. "The moment I turn the corner out of this alley, I'm going to speed up and I'm not slowing down until we're past the threat."

"You just worry about getting us out," Martha replied. "Let me worry about me."

Mike nodded. "Hang on."

Mike started the bike again and drove toward the alley. He glanced at the speedometer of the old bike and knew that he would be topping out the speed.

He had never gone faster than sixty on a motorcycle, but if he were going to make it difficult for the shooter and minimize their chances of being hit, then he'd need to top the bike out at one hundred miles per hour.

Mike slowed just before he neared the end of the alley so he wouldn't wipe out when he turned the corner. The moment he was out of the alley and exposed himself, the gunmen opened fire. So Mike opened the throttle.

The old bike jolted forward from the sudden acceleration, and while Mike was worried about his mother holding on, he nearly lost his grip on the bike too. But he managed to hold fast and shifted gears, watching the speedometer quickly tick past forty, fifty, sixty, and seventy miles per hour.

The gunfire grew louder, the shooters in the windows unloading everything they had at them as Mike rocketed down the sidewalk.

The storefronts passed in a blur. The vibrations from the engine as it peaked at the top speed made his bones rattle.

But Mike was moving so fast that he didn't dare look down. One wrong move and he would find himself on the pavement, and both of them would be dead.

The gunfire continued all the way until after they passed the building, but Mike slowed gradually, only easing off the gas until he was completely sure that they were well out of the gunman's range.

Mike glanced down and saw that his mother was still holding onto him, and he smiled. "Mom, are you all right?"

She slowly loosened her grip and then looked at her son. "I'm fine."

Mike glanced back behind him. He couldn't believe they survived. He remembered all of the bodies he saw on the streets, all the people who didn't make it, and all of the people who would continue to die as they tried to flee a city they had once called home. He thought of the people that had rallied around him after they saw him kill an enemy they thought to be too strong to bring down.

But most of all, Mike thought of his family. He turned away from the city and looked ahead. He knew the journey would still be dangerous, but he wasn't as afraid as he had been before.

"Mom, are you ready?" Mike asked.

Martha wrapped her arms around her son one more time. "How fast are you going to go now?"

"As fast as I need to get us home." Mike cranked the engine to life and then took off, the tires skidding out on the pavement as Mike and his mother left the city behind them.

12

*M*elvin wiped the blood from the knife with a rag he had found somewhere in the abandoned apartment where he had led his prey. It had been easy to get the girl up here, almost too easy. And as he stared at her lifeless corpse which was still tied to the bedposts where he had put her, he felt... empty.

The thrill Melvin had experienced before he was imprisoned had diminished. He had still enjoyed himself, but it wasn't how he remembered.

The woman had already been so terrified of the other monsters lurking in the city that she was blind to see who he really was. A lesson she learned too late in the end.

"Never trust a strange man." Melvin wagged the still-bloody knife at her like a scolding finger, then turned away from the girl and walked to the window which provided a view of the streets below.

With all of the chaos and violence in the streets, Melvin thought this would have been his paradise. He was in the eye of the storm, a place he had always believed he would thrive.

JAMES HUNT

But part of his fun was the challenge of tricking people. The game of leading them into a trap that he had designed. And now everyone was running around like cockroaches after the lights turn on. It was like shooting fish in a barrel.

The pickings were too easy. He needed to find himself a challenge.

Melvin turned away from the window and examined the apartment he had used to kill the woman. The fact that there were no police meant he didn't even have to worry about fixing up the crime scene. It would be days, weeks, maybe even months before anyone came looking for that woman, and when they did eventually stumble upon her rotten corpse, people would assume she had been killed by the masked men who were shooting up the city like a bunch of Neanderthals.

Melvin clenched his fists in anger. It drove him mad that people wouldn't know it was him. He needed to find someone in this city that could challenge him. He needed to feel the thrill of living on the edge, of not only outsmarting his victims but the authorities as well.

And then an interesting thought formed in Melvin's mind, something he would have never considered before the world had turned upside down. But now it made sense.

Melvin had killed twenty-eight people (twenty-nine if he counted the wandering doe behind him, but Melvin wasn't sure she was worthy enough to earn a spot on his list of victims), and he was convinced the authorities weren't anywhere close to capturing him. But he was wrong, and his fun came to an end. That was when he met Detective Michael Thorton.

The detective was a good-looking man, someone Melvin would have put as a mark for himself. It wasn't a sexual attraction, merely a connection. He had no preference between men and women. Everyone bled the same color. And that was all that mattered to him.

If Melvin wanted to recapture the excitement which had been lost due to the collapse of society and the rule of law, then he was going to have to find a lawman that wanted to put him back behind bars. And he couldn't think of a better candidate than the man who had caught him: Detective Thorton.

But while Melvin had gotten to know the detective well during their interrogation time, he had no idea where the detective lived. To find that information, then he would need to return to the one place he had always tried to avoid: the police station.

Melvin had been taken to Detective Thorton's precinct after he had been arrested. He was certain that the detective's station would have the necessary files on all of their police officers and detectives. Personal information like their home address.

Melvin's pupils dilated, the excitement and adrenaline returning in the way he had originally remembered it. This was the rush that he was looking for. This was the feeling that he wanted to recapture.

Melvin smiled and headed for the door, leaving the blade behind along with the corpse. "Well, my love, this is goodbye. I wish I could say that this was one of the better experiences that I've had, but I'm afraid to tell you that it was rather boring."

The woman remained motionless, her head tilted to the left, her hair covering her face. But her mouth was open, and her tongue had fallen out.

"But it's not your fault, really," Melvin said. "Don't beat

yourself up about it. I'm sure you would have been great for someone else, but alas. You were not mine to take."

Melvin smiled again and then walked out the door.

The streets were a little quieter than before, but there were still random gunshots followed by piercing screams. It was rare Melvin found himself in a position to be hunted, but with the number of those masked gunmen, he couldn't count himself out as a piece of meat to be slaughtered.

All it would take was one stray bullet, some crazy person to sneak up behind him, and then it would be all over. This was the kind of wild that he knew normal people felt on a day-to-day basis. But it had taken the end of the world for Melvin to feel that way.

The idea of dying out in the streets like some common idiot only fueled Melvin to stay ready and alert. He needed to be constantly aware of his surroundings. He still had the gun he stole from the officers after he escaped, which he kept tucked into his waistband and concealed beneath his shirt.

Melvin was light on his feet as he moved throughout the city, which he was incredibly familiar with. He knew the detective's precinct was on the south side of the city, which appeared to be clear of most of the terrorists that had descended upon Charlotte.

Melvin wondered what the terrorists' endgame was. Did they want to take over the city? The country? Or was their primary objective sweeping over the land like a shadow of death, killing as many people and destroying as many things as they could?

Melvin hoped it was the latter. The world was always so much more interesting when people decided to turn the status quo over on its head. Because just look at what it was doing to Melvin Harris, a serial killer, a man who had spent his life evading the police, now about to break into a precinct full of officers.

It truly was the end times.

Melvin arrived at the precinct, and he took his time on his approach. Since he had already shed his shackles and his prison clothes, he doubted anyone would recognize him.

A closer look at the precinct revealed the building in tatters. The windows were shot out, the bodies of cops lay strewn about the steps leading up to the front doors, which had been broken down. Several civilian bodies also lay mixed in with the sea of blue.

But as easy as it looked to just walk into the building, Melvin's instincts told him to stop. It was the perfect set-up for an ambush. He looked at the spray of bodies on the steps again. It was here he realized that the position of the civilian bodies was of people trying to enter the precinct.

And call Melvin crazy, but there was no reason for police to shoot civilians who were wandering into the building looking for help.

The masked terrorists had set a trap for anyone looking for the police. Instead of finding help, they'd only get a bullet to the head.

Melvin studied the front of the building and saw a window that had been smashed out. The glare from the sun prevented him from seeing inside, but Melvin knew that it was the perfect position for someone to set up a rifle.

"Clever," Melvin said, whispering to himself.

Melvin doubted there would be more than two men in the building. It was a scavenger assignment, picking off the weakest who were coming to the authorities for help. But Melvin still made sure to keep himself ready for any surprises. He was too close now to be killed by some amateur rebels.

Melvin entered through the back door, and like he thought, it was unguarded. He was quiet as a church mouse as he moved through the building.

It was nearly pitch black inside, and Melvin paused for a few seconds to let his eyes adjust. He had always seen well in the darkness. He didn't know exactly why, but he always assumed that it had to do with his desire to kill. He knew of many predators in the wilderness that hunted at night. Melvin always considered himself more of a predator than a man.

Melvin maneuvered through the halls of the precinct easily once his eyes adjusted to the darkness. He could never see as clearly as if there was light, but he managed to see enough to know that the lumps of shadows that he stepped around on the floor were bodies.

That and the smell.

Death had a certain scent, a sharp sour stench Melvin savored. He often spent time with his victims after he had killed them, waiting for them to rot and decay, so he could revel in their smell. It was a primal urge to be a part of death and destruction, and Melvin had dedicated his life in pursuit of that desire.

Voices drifted from the front of the building, and Melvin froze. He closed his eyes so he could concentrate harder. It just sounded like gibberish.

Melvin listened closer and he realized the two men, he was sure they were men, were speaking a completely different language.

Melvin couldn't decipher the language, but he was able to tell the kind of conversation that the men were having. It was a delicate balance, a light cadence that went back and forth that was only exchanged when someone let their guard down.

They must not have had a person wander into their trap for a long time. They had grown bored and sloppy. It was perfect for Melvin's plans.

Melvin emerged from the back hall and into the main bullpen. He saw the pair of men that had been whispering. Both of them had their backs to him. He took a moment to pause and make sure that there was no one else lurking in the darkness, but when he was certain that the coast was clear, he moved forward.

The slow walk gave Melvin time to consider his options. He had the pistol, and the gun would be the quickest way to get rid of them, but it was also loud. If those men had friends nearby, the gunfire might cause them to come and check on them. But Melvin also considered the fact their assignment was to shoot people. Two more gunshots wouldn't draw any more attention to them.

But would using the gun be more fun than snapping their necks? Or choking them to death? Or watching them bleed out?

Melvin's smile stretched wider as he moved closer. He removed the pistol from his waistband and aimed it at the back of the head of his first victim. Melvin had never liked to kill someone by surprise, so he made sure to click the hammer back so the pair of men would turn around.

Melvin squeezed the trigger, killing his first target, and the second man barely had enough time to scream before Melvin shot him in the face.

Two shots. Two deaths. Easy.

Melvin lowered the weapon and then searched the pair of

bodies for anything that might be useful. He figured the men who had come to upend the west had some tools that would come in handy.

Melvin pilfered a nice hunting blade, another pistol with extra magazines, the assault rifle with extra magazines, and a pack to store his new toys.

The terrorists also had several explosive devices: a dozen mines with tripwire detonators, and a handful of grenades.

Melvin gathered everything and donned the pack, then paid his respects to his fellow killers.

"Thank you, boys," Melvin said. "I'll leave you to the rest of your mission."

With the threat dealt with, Melvin turned his focus on finding the file that he came to collect. One of the men was a smoker, and while Melvin didn't partake (it was a nasty habit), he did take the lighter to guide him.

Melvin could only keep the flame moving for a few minutes at a time before the flame grew too hot on his thumb. And while the intermittent light was annoying, it served his purpose until he stumbled upon the filing cabinets in a random room next to some larger offices.

With the cabinets and drawers labeled and in alphabetical order, a quick scan of the drawers led Melvin to Detective Michael Thorton's personal file. He looked inside the jacket and saw Michael's picture.

"So serious," Melvin said, mocking the stoic expression.

He took a moment to look at the man's commendations, noting that he was a decorated officer within the community, but was upset that there was no mention of his capture of Melvin. "I mean, I did kill twenty-eight people."

Melvin moved onto what he was really looking for, the detective's current residence, which was with all of his other personal information. He was married, which Melvin already knew because of the wedding ring that he remembered seeing on Michael's hand. But he was glad to learn that Michael also had two children. A boy and a girl.

"One of each," Melvin said. "How fun."

Melvin tore out the address from the file, and then spit on Michael's picture before tossing the folder to the floor. He couldn't wait to play his games with the detective. He couldn't wait to see the surprise on the detective's face when he showed up at his front door. He would force the detective to watch him kill each member of his family slowly.

Distracted by his fantasy of Detective Thorton on his walk toward the front of the precinct, Melvin had let his guard down. He was no longer alone.

"Freeze, Melvin!"

Melvin stopped. He recognized the voice, and as he slowly lifted his gaze from the floor to the man standing in the doorway, he couldn't hide his surprise when he saw Detective Kevin, Michael's trusted partner, pointing a gun at him. "Detective. Good to see you."

Kevin was silhouetted in the light of the door, and it was difficult to see his expression. But the man's clothes were tattered, and he was dirtied and bloodied. The journey back to Melvin hadn't been easy.

"Put your hands on your head, turn around, and walk backward to me," Kevin said, barking the orders with authority.

Melvin didn't do as he was told, instead choosing to take a moment to assess his situation. The detective hadn't shot Melvin on sight, which was peculiar considering that the law had all but eroded into nothing. Which meant that Kevin was still holding onto the idea that things were going to get better, that there was some kind of civilized structure outside of the city. It was the naïve detective's first mistake.

"I said, put your hands on your head! Turn around and walk backward toward me! Now!" Kevin took two steps inside the precinct, and even with the distance between them, Melvin could see the fiery gaze in the detective's eye.

"What happened to your friends, Detective?" Melvin kept his tone innocent, still refusing to obey Kevin's orders. The detective would have to shoot him if he wanted to stop him from leaving this place because the only way out for Melvin was in a body bag. "Did he die?" Melvin faked a little gasp. "I'm so sorry. But..." He frowned, pretending to be confused. "I only attacked one of the officers. Where is the other one? Did he leave?" Melvin smiled. "He did, didn't he. He took off and ran because that's all that people do now. A little trouble comes their way, some adversity that they don't know how to handle, and then they take off running before that danger kills them. I hope you don't hold that against him."

Kevin had his arms straight out in front of him, squeezing the grip of the pistol as though he could crush it with his bare hands. "I'm not going to ask you again."

Melvin laughed. "See, I have to disagree with you on that, Detective. Because if you wanted to shoot me, then you would have put a bullet right through my forehead the moment you walked through that door and saw me." He pressed his index finger against the center of his forehead and smiled. "But you didn't. Because you want to take me in alive. Because you want me to pay for what I did. You want justice to prevail and for me to be carted away and for a needle to go into my arm."

Kevin nodded. "Yeah. That's the plan."

Melvin took a step forward and then stopped when Kevin jolted. "Easy. I'm just getting closer like you asked me to."

"That's not what I asked you to do." Kevin took two more steps to match the ones that Melvin had taken. "Hands on your head. Turn around. And walk backward toward me."

Melvin knew that he shouldn't test his luck too much with the man, so he complied. "You'll have to guide me if I stray off course."

"Just keep walking," Kevin said.

Melvin knew that Kevin was exhausted and nervous. Why wouldn't he be? He was currently alone in a room with one of the biggest mass murderers in the country. Any sane person would be worried about what Melvin might do.

Melvin saw the wide-eyed stare in Kevin's gaze. The man was barely holding it together. Who knows what kind of horrors that Kevin might have seen that would have caused him to question his own morality? Those types of situations always put stress on the mind and the body. And that stress had made Kevin slow to react.

The moment that Melvin was within arm's reach of Kevin, he knew that the detective would order him to stop and get on his knees. It would be easier to control Melvin from a higher position. He would then clamp a pair of hand-cuffs down around his wrists and remove any weapons that he had on him.

And as Melvin got to his knees per Kevin's orders, all he had to do was wait until the detective had one of the cuffs around his wrist, a position that would make it impossible for Kevin to keep the weapon trained on him, and he would make his move.

And it went off without a hitch.

Melvin pivoted on his knees, spinning around as he used

his one free hand to grab the blade that he took off of the terrorist's body and then plunge it deep into Kevin's abdomen.

The detective lurched forward from the blow and dropped the pistol. He collapsed to his knees and then turned to look up at Melvin. Blood pooled in his mouth, and he wore that familiar look of surprise, the kind all of Melvin's victims wore the moment he killed them.

Melvin lived for that expression. The fear, the uncertainty, and then finally the acceptance of their fate. A fate decided by him.

Melvin finished off the detective by pulling the knife up and across the side, opening up Kevin's torso like a can of tomatoes as he collapsed on the ground.

It was a big mess, and Melvin grimaced when he saw the blood on his shoes. But then he remembered the situation that he was in. He didn't have to hide what he had done. He looked like everyone else out in the streets now. A man just trying to survive.

Before Melvin left, he collected Kevin's badge. It was smeared with blood, but Melvin took that as just one more token to remember the detective by. "I'll give Michael your regards."

Melvin walked out of the precinct and clipped the detective's badge to his belt, then mapped his route to Michael Thorton's house.

$\mathcal{L}$isa kept the gun on her person at all times, and she had moved the children out of the living room. There were too many windows, and she didn't want to give Jerry or anyone else an easy opportunity to hurt her family.

Lisa also gave Nasir the spare pistol. She had been hesitant to give him the weapon since he wasn't familiar with guns, but Lisa knew that having him armed might give them an edge if something were to happen. And he caught on quickly with the proper gun safety protocols.

It had been hours since the altercation with Jerry and the others, and while Lisa hadn't spotted any movement from the house across the street, she couldn't shake the feeling that they were still planning something, still watching. Waiting for the right time to enact their revenge.

"Mom?" Casey reached the bottom of the stairs. "Can we get some water? It's really hot."

The summer temperatures were already in full swing, and everyone had a nice ring of sweat around their collars. It was only going to get worse, and Lisa wished the kids could go outside to try and catch a breeze, but it was too risky.

"Of course," Lisa answered. "Take some up for the girls too, okay?"

Casey nodded and then headed into the garage where they had already packed all of their water in the back of the truck. Lisa almost walked out to the garage with him to make sure that he was safe, but she didn't want to make him more frightened than he already was.

"Lisa?" Nasir walked up behind her. He had been watching the back door. "Should I go back to the house? Grab some additional supplies for the trip?"

After Lisa had told Nasir the plan for taking the truck to Mike's sister's place in the mountains, he had been grateful, but he too was worried that he might not be accepted with the rest of the family.

"I have some canned food and bottled water," Nasir said. "I'm sure it would come in handy."

Lisa knew it would, but she wasn't sure what would happen to Nasir if he walked out of the house and exposed himself in the street. She had already risked so much to save him, and she didn't want to see him get hurt over a few cans of food.

"I don't think it's safe," Lisa answered. "And Mike should be home soon."

At least that's what she kept telling herself so she wouldn't go crazy. But the more time passed without seeing any sign of her husband, the harder it was to keep all of those horrible thoughts from taking control.

"You're sure that this is okay?" Nasir walked forward with the timid posture of a child. It had been the fifth time he'd asked that, and Lisa was growing tired of reassuring him.

"Nasir, I'm not leaving you and your daughters here," Lisa answered. "It's not safe for you or for them. Now, head back to the door. Keep a watch on things, all right?"

Nasir nodded. "Thank you, Lisa."

Lisa turned back toward the window and stiffened when she saw Jerry leading a group of five men across the street toward their house. Jerry was armed with a rifle, the others carried bats and other blunt instruments.

"Nasir! They're coming! Stay on the back door in case they come around!" Lisa shouted, keeping her eyes locked onto the group of gunmen heading toward her. She retreated toward the stairs. "Kids! Stay up there and lock the doors!"

Kelly appeared at the top of the stairs. "Mom, what's going on—"

"Do it now, Kelly! Keep your brother and Nasir's daughters safe! Go!" Lisa waited until she heard her daughter's bedroom door shut before she returned to the living room.

Without thinking of the consequences, Lisa charged toward the front door and then ripped it open, taking aim at Jerry's head.

"Not another step!" Lisa used the door to help act as cover, but she was exposed enough that Jerry could take a shot if he wanted to. "Turn around and go home!"

Jerry did stop, and he held up his hand, signaling for his men to follow suit. "We don't have to do this the hard way, Lisa. I know you, and I know your family. All we want is the terrorist that you have hiding inside, nothing more. You let us have him, and we'll leave you alone."

And while Lisa wasn't going to hand anyone over, she was ashamed to admit that, at least for a split second, she considered giving in to Jerry's request.

After all, this wasn't her fight. Her priority was to protect her family. But deep down, she knew it wasn't right to let an innocent person be lost to the whims of prejudice.

"This is your last warning to head back," Lisa said.

Lisa prayed that she wouldn't have to resort to violence. She didn't want this any more than she thought that Jerry did. But she was surprised to see him raise his rifle in response and shoot her living room window.

The glass shattered, and the kids screamed upstairs. Lisa fired one retaliatory shot, but she missed, and then retreated back into the house, shutting and locking the door. She hurried back into the living room and then flipped over the couch to provide another barrier for protection. She peered over the top and saw two men heading around the back.

"Nasir, they're coming to you!" Lisa shouted, then focused her aim on the three men that were coming up her front driveway.

Lisa had always struggled to hit moving targets, and she wasn't able to line up a shot fast enough before Jerry and the rest of his goons managed to slide up against the garage door and out of her field of vision. "Shit."

The front door would provide a better angle on the garage door, and Lisa returned to it, keeping below the line of sight on the window.

Two gunshots thundered from the rear of the house, pulling Lisa's attention toward Nasir, and she prayed that he was able to hold them off.

Lisa returned her focus to the door and then crouched low as she unlocked it. She opened it, peering through the crack, and before she could aim her pistol, Jerry was already poised to shoot.

Jerry fired, missing the door and striking the side of the house, but it was enough to send Lisa back behind cover, and enough time for one of Jerry's goons to rush toward the living room window that had been shattered and jump inside.

Lisa screamed when the man rolled forward, and she aimed the weapon at him, and fired. The revolver bucked in her hand, and the bullet strayed left. A few seconds later, Nasir appeared from the kitchen, his gunfire forcing Jerry back.

"Lisa! C'mon!" Nasir moved toward the stairs, and Lisa followed.

Nasir was the first at the top of the stairs, and he stopped to let Lisa pass. When they were at the top, they paused, each of them on either side of the stairs behind the cover of the wall.

"We can hold them here," Nasir said. "It's too narrow for more than one of them to come up."

Lisa nodded. It was a good plan in theory, but what Nasir had failed to grasp was that they were now trapped upstairs. No way out. No way down. Unless they wanted to jump twelve feet out a window.

Below them, voices were hushed and hurried, and Lisa waited for someone to appear at the bottom of the stairs. She looked at Nasir, catching his attention, and spoke quietly.

"Conserve your ammunition," Lisa said. "Only shoot at what you know you can hit."

Nasir nodded, and then they waited.

A few minutes passed, and just when Lisa was hoping that the group had given up and decided to go home, Jerry spoke.

"C'mon down, Lisa," Jerry said. "It's all over now."

"We have the high ground," Lisa said.

Lisa waited, hoping that her confidence would send him packing, but a few seconds later, she saw Barry poke his head around the corner. She fired quickly, missing Barry and sending him running.

"That's enough, Lisa!" Jerry said. "You and I both know that you can't stay up there forever."

"And you and I both know that my husband will be coming back soon," Lisa said. "And he'll be returning with the full force of the Charlotte PD!" She added the lie in hopes the idiots would buy it, and for a moment, she heard the doubt creep into Jerry's voice.

"He ain't bringing the police with him," Jerry said.

"Yes, he is," Lisa replied. "Now is your last chance, Jerry. Throw the rifle at the bottom of the stairs and walk away."

It was quiet for a long time, and Lisa thought that he might actually listen. But then Jerry peered around the corner and fired a shot up the stairs.

14

*O*n the drive home, Mike fought the urge to ask his mother if she needed a break, remembering what she had told him about making sure that she was strong enough to survive the journey. She was right about needing to stand on her own two feet. And while Mike loved his mother, his main priority was his wife and children. They needed him more than his mother did.

Society was crumbling all around him, and Mike prayed he never had to choose between saving his mother and saving his wife and children. He couldn't imagine being placed in such a dire situation, but he knew that they were in a world where 'dire' was the new normal. It was sad but true. He saw it everywhere on his ride back.

Crime ran rampant in the streets. People looted and stole, fought and bickered, all of them propelled by the fear of the unknown and the uncertainty of tomorrow.

Never before had the country experienced such catastrophic failure. All of the pressure points had been exposed. With no power, no communication, and no transportation, people were in the dark.

And while it pained Mike to see so many people hurting one another instead of helping, not to mention the amount of crime, he knew that stopping would only cause more trouble for himself.

Mike saw the stares of people as he passed on the motorcycle. The rumble of the bike's engine announced their arrival long before they were seen, some of them waving their hands, running after him, wanting to know how he was able to move, thinking that because he was mobile, he knew what was happening.

But despite the stares and the cries for help and the unsettling sights that Mike passed, the journey was uneventful. The motorcycle was nimble enough to handle all of the tight spots that Mike encountered, and by the time that he neared the neighborhood, he managed to get the hang of it pretty well. And he had a better understanding of the appeal of riding a motorcycle.

Mike turned back, unsure if his mother could hear him. "We're almost home! How are you doing?"

"Fine!" Martha's voice practically vanished into thin air the moment the words left her mouth.

Mike nodded and offered a thumbs-up, which his mother reciprocated. He knew she was tired.

The roads started to curve more once they reached the neighborhood. The panic and chaos of the inner city hadn't reached the suburbs yet, which boded well for their escape. For a moment, he thought things were turning around. But that ended when he veered onto his street.

A crowd had gathered outside of his house. Heads turned at the sound of the motorcycle, and Mike was unsure of what happened. But when he saw Jerry step from his house with a rifle in his hand, firing a shot into the air and dispersing the crowd, Mike veered the motorcycle up the nearest driveway for cover.

Adrenaline funneled through his veins, and Mike was in such a rush that he forgot that his mother was on the backside of the bike and she was knocked to the grass. He parked the bike, then helped her to her feet.

"I'm fine," Martha said. Her cheeks were a bright red, and she was drenched in sweat. A few bugs clung to the skin and sweat of her neck. "What is going on at the house?"

"I don't know," Mike answered. "But I need you to stay here and don't move until I come back. Okay? No matter what happens, I need you to stay here."

Martha nodded, and Mike crept toward the front of the house he had ducked behind. It was Kerry Mueller's house. And if they were home, they were keeping it to themselves.

Mike stopped just before he reached the front of the Muellers' house and peered around the side. Jerry was still in the front yard, and he had sent two goons ahead to fetch Mike. It was Ken and Barry from across the street. Ken held a baseball bat, and Barry had a crowbar. It looked like Jerry was the only one with a gun.

Mike emerged from the cover of the house, revolver aimed past Ken and Barry toward Jerry, who raised his rifle in retaliation.

"Drop the gun, Jerry!" Mike took three steps forward, and Ken and Barry stopped. He knew that Jerry didn't hunt or visit the range often enough to be accurate from his current distance.

"You first!" Jerry said. "I haven't done anything to your

family, Mike, and my quarrel isn't with them! I've tried to tell your wife that, but she won't listen!"

Mike couldn't imagine what could have happened, but whatever it was, Mike's first priority was disarming the enemy. An enemy who Mike had over for dinner more than once.

"I'm not going to ask you to drop the weapon again," Mike said.

Barry and Ken, both of them with a deer in headlights expression, turned back to Jerry, hoping that he would listen. But he didn't.

Jerry squeezed the trigger, and just as Mike anticipated, he missed. Mike returned fire, and while the accuracy on his revolver wasn't as good as the rifle, he managed to get close enough to push Jerry back for cover.

Barry and Ken took off running the moment bullets started flying, and Mike advanced to the next house up, darting around the back.

Mike was only two houses away from his own, crossing through Buddy Dyer's backyard, when Jerry finally reared his ugly head from around the corner of the next house. But the long barrel of the hunting rifle cost Jerry some time as he had to swing it all the way around and plant his foot before he could take aim, and Mike disappeared to the front of the house as Jerry pulled the trigger.

Mike paused at the front of the house, catching his breath as he waited to see where Jerry would go. Between the motorcycle's engine and the sound of gunfire, Mike's ears were ringing. It made it difficult to tell if someone was sneaking up on him, so he was forced to keep his head on a swivel.

After a minute of no sign of Jerry, Mike sprinted forward,

moving across the front of Buddy's house and heading into his own front yard, when a gunshot thundered behind him.

Mike ducked. Another bullet fired, closer than the first as Mike passed through the front door and landed hard on his stomach. He glanced behind him and kicked the door shut with his foot.

But when he saw the front window had been smashed. Mike got to his feet, revolver gripped tightly in both hands, and retreated to the stairs as Jerry appeared in the window. He looked up to the second floor, shouting. "Lisa!"

"We're up here—"

A bullet zipped past the left of Mike's head, and he leaned away as another bullet almost hit him. The relentless gunfire pushed Mike from the base of the stairs and toward the kitchen, putting a wall between him and Jerry.

Jerry unleashed more gunfire, redecorating the inside of Mike's house with lead. But the display of force dispensed all of his ammunition, and when he paused to reload, Mike took his shot. He planted his feet and raised his revolver, aiming for Jerry's arm, and squeezed the trigger.

The bullet connected with Jerry's left arm. Blood soaked the sleeve of his shirt, and he dropped the rifle, using his opposite hand to cover the wound, screaming.

But Mike didn't break stride as he moved toward Jerry, now aiming the revolver at the man's head, kicking the rifle out of reach as Jerry fell to his knees.

"Enough!" Mike said. "Lie on your stomach! Now!"

The color had drained from Jerry's cheeks, and despite the bullet wound, he complied, slowly lowering himself to the floor, letting go of his arm.

Mike didn't have his cuffs, but he had some zip ties in the garage. He got a closer look at the wound on Jerry's arm and saw that he only grazed the man. It was nothing more than a flesh wound.

"Lisa!" Mike yelled, his voice cracking from fatigue. "Lisa!"

"We're coming down!" Footsteps followed, and then Lisa appeared in his peripheral, holding the spare weapon from the gun safe. When the pair finally locked eyes, Lisa sprinted to her husband, flinging her arms around his neck. "Thank God you're all right."

Mike kept his weapon trained on Jerry even though the man was unarmed, wounded, and on his stomach. "Are the kids okay?"

Lisa let go of Mike and nodded. "They're upstairs. Nasir and his girls are with them too."

Mike frowned. "Nasir?" He looked to his wife. "Why is he here?"

Lisa looked down to Jerry, and suddenly it all clicked in Mike's head without her saying another word. Mike sighed, shaking his head.

"Jerry..." Mike wanted to press his heel against the bullet hole in the man's arm and press down. "What were you thinking?"

"He's one of them, Mike," Jerry said, his left cheek still flat on the carpet, spots of blood darkening the floor. "He's part of the attack!"

Mike ignored the ravings of the mad man and turned to Lisa. "I have zip ties in the garage. I need you to get them for me."

Lisa hurried into the garage and returned with the requested items. With the fight run out of Jerry, Mike holstered his weapon and placed the zip ties around the man's wrists and ankles, and then told Lisa to grab a bandage to put over the wound.

"Where's your mother?" Lisa asked.

Mike suddenly realized that he had left his mother out in the sun. "She's alive, but I kept her back when I saw what was happening at the house. Is everyone ready to go?"

Lisa hesitated.

"What?" Mike asked.

Lisa struggled to find the words and then moved herself and Mike away from Jerry. She lowered her voice. "I told Nasir that he and his girls could come with us to the cabin."

"Lisa, you know that we can't—"

"They don't have anywhere else to go," Lisa said. "And if we leave them here, then more people are just going to come after them. Nasir is a good man. He helped me defend the house."

"And you only had to defend the house because you brought him over here in the first place." Mike placed his hands on his wife's shoulders. "I know that your heart is in the right place. But if we take them with us, we'll be painting a target on our backs."

"Because of where they come from?" Lisa asked, a bite in her tone.

"Yes," Mike answered. "As messed up as that is, yes, because of where they come from and who they look like." He frowned and gestured to Jerry. "He has known Nasir for the past five years, and look how quickly he turned on a neighbor. Imagine what someone would do who didn't even know them... Lisa. They can't come."

"It's okay."

Both Mike and Lisa turned at the sound of the voice and

were surprised to find Nasir standing at the bottom of the stairs.

"I don't want to put your family in any more danger than I already have," Nasir said. "I will find a way to protect my family on my own." He walked over and handed the pistol to Lisa. "Thank you for what you did. You saved mine and my girls' lives."

Lisa looked down at the weapon and shook her head. "Keep it. You might need it."

Nasir stared at the gun and then nodded. "I'll grab my girls and leave you be." He offered his hand to Mike, and the pair shook. "Good luck to you, Mike."

"You too, Nasir." Mike let Nasir go, but just before the man turned, Mike saw the sadness in his eyes. It was the same look that Mike had seen on every person that he passed in the city.

Mike watched Nasir head upstairs, and once he was gone, he caught the stare from his wife. "Don't look at me like that. You know as well as I do that taking him would be a bad idea."

"He's a doctor," Lisa said. "And he and his girls are already packed. We have room in the truck—"

"Lisa, enough." Mike rubbed his temples, his mind aching from the stress of the day. He moved toward the front of the house. "I'll get my mother. Bring the kids downstairs." He stepped on the glass from his front living room window, which was nothing more than an open space now. "I want to get out of here before things get worse."

Mike didn't holster his weapon, keeping the revolver in his hand as he eyed the rest of the neighborhood. There were no signs of Barry or Ken, and the crowd that had gathered in his yard had decided to remain hidden behind closed doors. He just hoped that everyone chose to stay there.

Mike jogged back to the Dyer house where he left his mom and found her sitting on the grass with her back against a wall. She was hunched forward, and Mike assumed that she was only catching her breath. "Mom, we need to go—"

It was the sight of blood on his mother's hand that caused Mike to stop, and then he noticed the dark blotch from the wound on her stomach where the blood had soaked through the shirt.

Martha slowly lifted her gaze to look Mike in the eye. Her face had gone pale and grown sweaty, and her voice was frail and quiet. "Michael…"

"Mom!" Mike rushed to his mother's side and put pressure on the wound. He was speechless, unsure of how this could have happened. "Mom, what—"

"I followed you," Martha said, locking eyes with her son. "I heard your voice, and the gunshots, and when I turned the corner…" She lowered her gaze to the wound on her stomach.

A bullet to the gut was bad news, especially in their current situation. They needed to leave, but he knew they wouldn't find help on the road.

Nasir.

"Jerry!" A woman's voice echoed from down the street. "Jerry!"

Mike reached for his mother's other hand and firmly placed both of them over the wound. "Keep pressure on it." He was afraid to move her. "I'll be back." He kissed her forehead and then hurried to the front of the house.

The woman screaming was Pam, Jerry's wife. And she

was holding another rifle as she approached Mike's house, flanked by three more men, another of whom was armed with a gun.

"Jerry!" Pam screamed again.

"I'm in here!" Jerry's muffled voice answered, and at the sound of her husband's voice, Pam and the others broke into a jog.

Mike knew the moment they were inside the house, they would be overrun. And the close-quarters combat with the firearms would create a bloodbath. Mike jogged across the lawns to make sure that the others were aware of his presence, but before he could make it to the next house, gunfire erupted from inside his own home.

Pam and the others ducked, then scattered in different directions, but none of them turned tail to run. Instead, they broke off into two groups. One heading right, the other heading left.

Mike engaged the group that headed to the left. He didn't want to kill his neighbors. He didn't want to draw more blood, but if they didn't stop, then he would pull the trigger. Life wasn't without its consequences.

Thankfully, all it took was one gunshot in their direction to send them away.

With Pam and the other group pinned down by the garage, Mike snuck around the back and then announced himself before he entered through the back in case Lisa or Nasir were stationed nearby. "It's Mike! I'm coming in!" He shouldered open the door and saw Nasir lower the weapon.

"More people are out front," Nasir said.

"By the garage, I know." Mike placed his hand on Nasir's shoulder. "My mother is hurt. I need your help. Get your girls and get into the truck."

Nasir frowned. "What happened—"

"Go, we don't have a lot of time." Mike pushed Nasir toward the stairs. "Hurry!"

Gunshots were exchanged from the front of the house, and Mike entered the living room to find his wife near the window, going tit for tat with Pam and the others. Jerry was still on his stomach and on the floor, blood seeping through the bandage, feeding his wife information.

"Mike's in here, Pam!" Jerry's face was bright red from the strained effort to try and keep his head up. "He's armed! He's—"

Mike kicked Jerry across the jaw, and Jerry went silent. Mike joined his wife's side. "Go upstairs and get the kids, then head for the truck. I'll meet you out there soon."

Lisa nodded, and Mike took her place, providing cover fire. Once Mike saw Lisa and Nasir bring the kids down and disappear into the garage, he caught sight of Ken trying to sneak through the back. "Nasir, run!"

Nasir sprinted forward on command with just enough time to evade Ken's gunshots and Mike's retaliatory gunfire.

With Ken in the rear and Pam in the front, Mike didn't have the firepower to hold off both of them on his own. He retreated from the window, making sure the shooters saw him move toward the garage, and then followed him into the house.

It was pitch black inside the garage, and Mike smacked his knee on his workbench as he moved toward the front of the garage. "Lisa, start the truck!"

When Mike reached the garage door, he fumbled for the manual release handle and heard the truck's engine turn over, then sputter to life.

The inside of the garage was flooded with sunlight, and

Mike sprinted back to the truck and jumped into the driver's seat. "Everyone, hang on!" Mike pressed the clutch and then hit the gas, the truck lurching forward. He sped down the driveway.

Mike floored the gas pedal as he veered left, heading back to pick up his mother as Pam and Ken finally entered the garage.

Bullets chased them, but none of them hit their intended targets. Mike slammed on the brakes when he reached the Dyer's house and then sprinted out of the truck. He saw his mother in the same place where he left her, and he prayed that she was still alive.

Mike scooped Martha up and into his arms, her body limp.

"Drop the tailgate!" Mike yelled, seeing Nasir in the back, and the man did as he was told. Mike transferred his mother into the back of the truck as smoothly and gently as he could, and then slammed it shut. He pointed to Nasir on his way back to the driver seat. "Keep her alive!"

Pam and the others still hadn't given up their pursuit, Pam firing another shot from three houses down. This one struck the back left taillight, but Mike was back behind the wheel, and he sped away, leaving the home that he had built with his family in the rearview mirror.

15

The front of the cab was crowded. Mike and Lisa bookended their children, Casey and Kelly squished in the middle. Both of the kids had remained quiet since they left the house, and he noticed that his son was shaking.

Mike's mouth was dry, his tongue sticking to the roof of his mouth. One hand on the wheel, he knocked on the window behind him and then opened the sliding panel. "How is she doing?"

The wind whipped through the cab, and Mike caught Nasir's eyes in the rearview mirror.

"She's still breathing, but she's lost a lot of blood," Nasir said. "We need to get her a transfusion quick, or she's not going to make it."

Mike wracked his brain to think of where they could go. He figured that his sister would have some medical supplies, but she was too far away to help them at the moment. And any hospital that they tried would either be overrun or abandoned.

"The clinic off Highway 21," Lisa said. "It's where we take the kids whenever they're sick and we don't want to go into the city."

Mike nodded. It was close enough to arrive there in time, and Mike hoped that it was far enough away from the city to avoid the crowds and chaos.

"Is Grandma going to be okay?" Casey asked.

Mike patted his son's knee. "We're trying to make that happen, buddy."

"I can donate blood," Kelly said. "I'm O negative. That's the universal donor, so mine should work for her."

Mike smiled. "That'd be helpful, sweetheart. Thank you."

But despite the plan and well wishes, Mike wasn't sure if it would be enough. It would depend on how skilled Nasir was on the operating table, and if the clinic hadn't already been looted and destroyed.

Mike stuck to the back roads, which gave him enough room to navigate with the truck, and it also kept them out of the watchful eye of the general public. But it did lengthen the time of their trip, costing them precious time.

When the clinic came into view up ahead, Mike saw a crowd outside the building. He pulled into one of the vacant parking spots and shut off the engine, keeping the keys with him. He turned to his wife and saw that she still had the gun in her hands. He locked eyes with her. "No one gets near the truck."

Lisa flexed her grip over the pistol as she nodded.

Mike then turned to his son. "Help your mother, and be nice to your sister." He looked to Kelly and squeezed her hand. "I'll come and get you when it's time for the blood."

"Okay," Kelly said.

Nasir had the tailgate open and was talking to his girls in

their native language, and while he spoke it quietly, he caught some unwanted attention. Mike helped Nasir carry Martha from the truck and through the clinic's front door.

The only light in the clinic was the sunlight through the windows, Mike was surprised to discover the inside mostly empty. A few people sat in the chairs in the waiting area, but there was no one at the nurse's desk.

"The supplies must be through there," Nasir said, pointing to a closed door.

Mike followed him, and when they passed through the door, he saw candles had been lit inside the rooms, most of which were open. Mike found the nearest one and brought his mother inside, laying her down on the table.

Mike placed his hands over hers and the wound, and he took stock of her condition. Blood had soaked her shirt so much that he couldn't tell if she was still bleeding.

"Michael," Martha said, her voice nothing but a whisper within a breath. "Thank you for coming back to me."

Mike gently squeezed his mother's hand, tears forming. "We don't leave family behind. Ever."

Martha's breathing was shallow and quick. The flickering candlelight of the room made her look more skeleton than human.

Nasir entered, carrying a box of supplies that he dropped on the counter next to the bed. "There's only one doctor that stayed behind. He has his hands full with another patient." He quickly rifled through the supplies and finally ended on a syringe that he used to pull some liquid from a bottle. "This will help with the pain and regulate her pulse." A few squirts erupted through the tip of the needle and then he jammed it into Martha's arm.

A few seconds later and his mother lost consciousness.

"Get your daughter," Nasir said. "We need to start pulling her blood."

Mike released his mother's hand and let Nasir do his work. He stepped out of the building and saw that no one had come over to the truck. He also saw that Lisa had brought Nasir's daughters into the cab, all five of them crammed across the long bench seat.

"Kelly, we need you," Mike said.

The others made way for her, and Mike glanced around while she stepped out. The clinic was on the outskirts of an old neighborhood. It was scarcely populated, well beyond the city limits. It was mostly county and state land out here. The people who lived here kept to themselves. Much like the folks that were staring at Mike and his family outside the convenience store from across the street.

It was a group of men. Mixed ages. But none of them averted their gaze when Mike looked at them. He was about to reach for his revolver when Kelly finally joined his side.

Mike brought his daughter into the clinic, holding her hand until they reached Martha's room. Nasir had cut through the fabric of her shirt and was washing away the blood, dabbing at the fresh streams that sprouted up from the wound, which was surprisingly small considering the amount of blood that was generated.

"There was no exit wound," Nasir said. When he noticed Kelly, he pointed toward the box. "Grab the tubing and needle, and sterilize the crook of her elbow with some peroxide. Use a cotton swab to clean the area."

Mike retrieved the necessary tools and then had Kelly sit down in a chair. She kept her eyes on her grandmother while Mike cleaned the skin where Mike thought that Nasir could draw blood.

"Hey," Mike said, pulling his daughter's attention to him. "She's going to be all right."

Kelly pulled her lips into her mouth, just like her mother whenever she was nervous. "Yeah."

Once Mike finished cleaning the skin, he looked to Nasir. "She's ready."

"Good," Nasir said. "Now, attach the tubing to the bag, and set it on the ground next to the chair. Then grab one of the needles and find a vein."

Mike shook his head. "I've never done this before."

"I can't take my hands off of your mother right now," Nasir said. "You'll have to do it."

Mike took a breath and attached the tubing and then found a needle from the box. He screwed the end into the other end of the tubing and searched for a vein that he could use.

Kelly pointed to one. "That's where they drew blood last year for my physical. The nurse said it was the biggest one."

"Right." Mike carefully pinched the needle between his fingers and then hovered it just above the vein that Kelly had identified. He wasn't sure how hard to push, so he gently pressed the needle into the vein, but he missed. "Sorry."

Kelly looked away, biting her lower lip and shutting her eyes. "It's okay."

Mike tried again, this time piercing the vein. A little bit of blood oozed from around the needle, and Mike examined the tubing to see if blood was going through. It wasn't.

"Nothing's happening," Mike said.

"Pump your hand into a fist, Kelly," Nasir said, still focused on Martha's wound.

Kelly pumped her hand into a fist, squeezing tight, but still looking away from the needle in her arm. Mike watched the tubing hoping to see some red blood flowing, and after a few more seconds, they were both rewarded.

"It's working," Mike said, relieved. He looked up to his daughter, who slowly glanced down at her arm. "Good job, Kelly."

"Mike, I need your help," Nasir said, his tone urgent. "Sanitize your hands all the way up to your elbows, and then put on a pair of gloves."

Mike's knees cracked when he stood, and he sterilized himself quickly. He then donned the gloves and walked to the other side of the table. "What do I need to do?"

Nasir reached over with his bloody hand, grabbed Mike's right hand, and placed it over the wound. "I need you to help me control the bleeding until we can get her a transfusion. Keep a firm pressure, and do not move until I tell you, okay?"

Mike nodded and then glanced to his mother's expressionless face. He hated seeing his mother so weak. Growing up, she had always been such a strong woman, but time caught up to everyone. Mike only hoped that Nasir could buy her more time.

Nasir worked deftly with the instruments, searching for the bullet. After a few minutes, his eyes lit up. "I have it." Sweat had beaded thickly on his face as he looked to Mike. "Try not to move. I don't know how good of a grip these tweezers have."

Mike nodded and, without realizing, held his breath. Nasir slowly removed the instrument from the hole in his mother's stomach and then removed the .22 caliber bullet fired from Jerry's rifle. He then set the bullet in a bowl and reached for the needle and thread.

"The bullet was small, so that's good," Nasir said. "Should be minimal scarring on her lower intestines, which is where it was lodged." He threaded string through the needle. "It's not a good place to be shot, though. And because we don't have an MRI machine or X-Ray…"

Mike frowned, waiting for Nasir to finish. "What?"

"The likelihood of her surviving something like this at her age is… unlikely," Nasir answered.

Mike had been so worried about getting her fixed that he didn't consider what kind of recovery she might have. And for a brief moment, he considered just letting her go. But then he remembered what his mother had told him on the motorcycle before they left the city. He couldn't keep moving forward while being afraid that his elderly mother couldn't handle what was coming down the road. It would be a difficult fight for her, but it wasn't his place to think she couldn't survive. "We'll worry about what comes next when it happens."

Nasir nodded and stitched Martha's wound. Once Mike was released from his duties, he walked over to Kelly and saw that the blood bag was full. He slowly and carefully removed the needle from the vein and then handed the bag of blood over to Nasir, allowing him to handle the transfusion. He then walked Kelly back outside to the truck, and when he looked across the street, he was glad to find the clustered group of men that had been staring at him gone.

"How is she?" Lisa asked.

Kelly hung by the door next to Mike, leaning against her father as she kept a cotton ball pressed down over the point where Mike had drawn blood. "Nasir got the bullet out and is stitching her up." He shrugged. "Only time will tell after that."

Lisa nodded and then hugged Casey. Nasir's two daughters sat in the middle and kept their heads down. Mike reached for the closest one and gently touched her shoulder.

"Your father did a very good thing," Mike said. "You should be very proud of him."

The little girl nodded, but she didn't smile, and then looked back down. She was the younger of the two, and then her older sister looked over to Mike.

"Will we have to leave now?" She asked.

Mike frowned. "Leave? What are you talking about?"

"We heard you talking to our father about how it was bad for us to be around you," she said. "Do we have to go back to our house now?"

Mike's mouth hung open, and shame flooded through him as he realized that the girls had overheard his conversation with Nasir. He looked to Lisa, who wore the same saddened expression as the girls. "No. Both of you and your father are coming with us. We're friends. And friends help each other. I should have remembered that sooner."

The girls brightened at the news, and while Mike knew he had made the right choice by moral standards, he wasn't sure if it was the right choice in this new world order.

With the heat and stench of the clinic unbearable, Mike and everyone waited outside until Nasir walked out. Blood covered his hands and traveled up to his elbows. His shirt was stained with matching splatters of red, and his shoulders slumped. The man was exhausted.

"She's stable," Nasir said.

Lisa leaned forward. "Is she going to make it?"

Nasir shook his head. "I don't know. It's going to take time to see how well she responds to the surgery. And I still don't know what kind of internal injuries she might have sustained from the impact of the bullet. I'll monitor her vitals closely while she recovers."

Mike shook the doctor's hand, thanking him again for his

help. "We couldn't have done it without you. And I'm sorry for what I said at the house. I was wrong."

"I understand," Nasir said. "It was a difficult situation. You just wanted to protect your family. That's all anyone wants to do in times of crisis. But I appreciate your change of heart. Do you want to see her?"

Mike nodded, then followed Nasir back into the clinic. When they reached her room and he saw Martha on the table, she was so still he thought she might be dead. But Mike relaxed when Nasir walked to the bedside and smiled.

"Her pulse is still strong," Nasir said. "It's a good sign."

Mike joined Nasir on the opposite side of his mother and held her hand. It was small and frail, a far cry from the strong and comforting touch that Mike remembered from his childhood.

"I need to check on a few other patients to help the other doctor that stayed," Nasir said. "But I'll come back to help you move her when it's time for us to leave."

Nasir headed for the door, but Mike stopped him before left.

"How well-stocked is this place with their medical supplies?" Mike asked.

Nasir frowned. "I'm not sure."

"Find out," Mike said. "Discreetly."

Mike wasn't sure how Nasir would feel about it, but the man nodded, and he left. Mike didn't like the idea of having to steal equipment from the medical facility, but he knew how important certain medications would be moving forward.

It wouldn't take much for something as simple as the flu to kill someone, and Mike didn't want that to happen to anyone in his family. Plus, he thought that showing up with some medicine would help smooth things over with Katy over the fact that he had the beginnings of a caravan heading her way. Plus, if Mike was going to make the commitment to take care of people, then he needed to make sure that he had the resources to do so.

And in a world where the law had crumbled, Mike knew that he would be forced to break it. He just hoped that he would be able to make those hard choices when it was time.

16

---

*I*t was a long walk from the city to the suburbs, but after being locked up in a cell for the past several months, Melvin didn't mind the stroll. He closed his eyes, basking in the sunshine. The police badge clipped to his belt was a nifty accessory in this new world.

People were very trusting to authority figures in times of crisis because deep down, they hoped that they would hold all of the solutions to their problems. But that was just a lie the authorities used to manipulate the masses into remaining calm when shit hit the fan. However, Melvin was able to use it for a different manner of control.

Two more kills had been added to his count, post-prison life, and he was falling into a nice groove. It had been easy to get them to do what he wanted. All he had to do was flash the badge and lead them into a darkened alley. The blade took care of the rest.

Both of them had begged for mercy, and it was the panicked cries for help that he lived for. Nothing made him feel more powerful than holding the life of someone in the palm of his hand.

Of all the people that Melvin had killed, he had never had one that faced their pending doom with any dignity. All of that flew out the window the moment they were trapped and knew what Melvin planned to do to them.

Despite the myth of machismo, Melvin had learned that men and women groveled in the same way. No one wanted to die.

But now, Melvin needed to ascend to the next level. In a world where the average person could be so easily killed, he needed to challenge himself and find an individual who would resist the urge to beg. He believed Detective Michael Thorton was that kind of man. At least he hoped he was. If not, then at least he got his exercise for the day.

The sun was at its highest point in the sky and starting to work its way in the downward arc of sunset when Melvin reached the small suburban neighborhood the detective called home.

It was a typical middle-class area, but now it looked more like a war zone.

Cars were broken down in the streets. Looting had already occurred in some of the homes that he had passed, and people had the same general sense of panic as those in the city. It was only on a smaller scale.

Melvin counted the house numbers on his right until he neared the detective's house, and when he finally stood before the correct house, Melvin frowned.

The garage door was open. Shell casings littered the driveway. The front living room window had been shattered, exposing the center of the house to the elements, and the front door was wide open.

Had someone else beat him to killing the detective already?

Despite the appearance of the house, Melvin remained cautious on his approach. He entered through the garage, hoping to keep himself concealed for as long as possible. It smelled of gas and exhaust, which was surprising considering that he hadn't seen any vehicles working since he left the city.

Perhaps the detective was more resourceful than Melvin previously believed.

The door to enter the house through the garage was cracked open, and Melvin drew his weapon. He carefully nudged the door open with the barrel of his gun, giving him a better line of sight inside.

Melvin paused there for a moment, waiting, watching, listening. But the longer he waited, the more certain he was that there was no one waiting to ambush him, and he entered.

The interior of the house was in bad shape, and from the looks of things, it was quite the fight.

Furniture had been toppled. Windows smashed. Glass covered the floor. Bullet holes had torn through walls. Blood stained the carpet.

Melvin paused in the space between the living room and the kitchen, glancing around. No one was home. If the detective and his family were still alive, then they were far away from this place.

"Damn," Melvin said.

But perhaps not all was lost. He might be able to determine where Michael Thorton had gone with his family. He was wearing a detective's badge after all.

Melvin walked to the staircase and ascended to the

second floor and found two bedrooms. The children's rooms. Judging from the way that both were decorated, he assumed that the boy was younger and the girl was a teenager, probably in high school.

Melvin studied each room, searching for anything that might lead him to understand what happened to the family, any clues to where they had gone, but he learned nothing useful.

Melvin returned downstairs and saw another door on the opposite side of the house from where he entered. He pushed the door in and smiled. This was the master bedroom. This was where the detective and his wife laid their weary heads at night to rest.

Goosebumps covered Melvin's flesh as he entered the room. Inside he felt that connection he'd been searching for, the one that made him feel like he did before he was caught.

Melvin crossed the room and sat on the edge of the bed, imagining the detective doing the same thing when he woke in the morning, contemplating the day.

Melvin turned his head to the left and saw a dresser with a few photographs stacked on top. He stood and walked over to investigate.

The pictures were of the detective's family, and Melvin saw that he had been right about the children. The wife was pretty. It was the perfect nuclear family.

One of the pictures on the dresser had all four of them on vacation standing in front of a big geyser. All of them were pointing and smiling in awe at the rise of the hot water behind them. It was a cheesy photo, and judging by the age of the children, it was a few years old.

Melvin flipped the picture over and removed it from the frame. He rarely kept any keepsakes from his victims, but this was a special occasion. Melvin was heading into a bigger world. He was hunting someone who was a hunter himself. And he knew that this was going to be a kill that he wanted to savor and remember.

Melvin neatly folded the picture into quarters and then placed it in his pocket. He glanced around the room one more time and then saw the closet in the back of the bedroom where a safe had been left open. Intrigued, Melvin walked over to investigate.

It was a small safe, no bigger than a few square feet. Melvin reached in and felt papers stacked inside. He removed the papers and returned to the bed.

Most of them were documents, wills, important tax information, all of the papers filed with the boring legalese. Melvin had killed a lawyer once, and in that instance he truly believed that he was doing the world a service.

But hidden amongst the documents and wills, Melvin found a particular piece of paper wedged between the boring items that didn't belong. It was an envelope with a letter inside. It had already been opened, and the return address on the envelope was a P.O. Box from somewhere outside of the Charlotte area, but still within North Carolina.

Melvin removed the paper from inside and flipped it open. It was a letter.

Mike,

I know you don't want to hear this, but I can't come to Dad's funeral. I thought I might change my mind, but I couldn't bring myself to do it. I know you'll be upset, but that's just the way it is.

Give the kids a hug and a kiss for me.

I hope you'll forgive me one day, and if you ever want to visit, my door is always open for you. You're the only family that I have left.

Love,

Katy

Melvin couldn't wipe the smile from his face even if he wanted to. Nothing was more important to most people than family, and Melvin had learned something important about his newest mark.

Melvin tucked the letter back into the envelope and then glanced at the PO Box number on the front. It wouldn't give him an exact address of where Katy lived, but he knew that it could get him close enough. He tucked the envelope into his pocket and then heard the unmistakable crunch of glass coming from the living room.

Melvin quickly stood up from the bed, wondering if the detective hadn't left after all, but then realized that was folly. There weren't enough places for them to hide here.

Melvin gripped the pistol tightly and then maneuvered toward the bedroom door and waited, listening for the intruder.

Another crunch of glass gave away the intruder's position, and Melvin knew exactly how he was going to play this scenario.

"Charlotte PD, freeze!" Melvin spun around from the bedroom, aiming his gun at a pair of men who were also armed in the living room. "Drop your weapons, now!"

"Who the hell are you?" The taller of the two spoke up, his rifle pressed up against his cheek as he brought Melvin into his sights. He had a lump on the side of his head, and his clothes and hair were disheveled.

"I'm Detective Harris," Melvin said, which brought both men's attention toward to the badge clipped on his belt. "Where's Michael Thorton?"

"He's gone." The second man was shorter and his voice less commanding. The sidekick.

Melvin arched his eyebrows. "Are you going to put that down? Or are we going to have a problem?"

"Depends," the tall man said. "What do you want with Michael Thorton?"

Melvin was able to understand the context of the question, and based off of the disarray of the house and the fact that the family had packed to leave in a hurry, Melvin deduced that the Thortons had some trouble with the neighbors. Melvin could use that to his advantage.

"Michael Thorton was being investigated by Internal Affairs," Melvin said. "We think he might have had something to do with everything that's happening across the country."

The taller man lowered the rifle, and his eyes widened with excitement. "I fucking knew it!" He turned to his friend. "Didn't I tell you, Barry? I bet they planned it with those fucking Middle Eastern bastards. Damn traitors."

Barry lowered his weapon as well, but he didn't share the same level of enthusiasm as his fearless leader. Instead, he squinted his eyes, studying Melvin. "You look familiar. Have we met before?"

"We might have," Melvin answered. "I used to work pretty closely with Michael. I even visited his house a few times with my wife for dinner."

Melvin was sure that Barry recognized him from the news coverage, but the authority of a badge was to never be underestimated by the common man. It acted like blinders for anyone that tried to get too close.

"Yeah," Barry said, nodding along, convincing himself the lie was true. "That must be it."

"I'm Jerry," the tall man said, walking across the living room and extending his hand. "I live across the street."

"Good to meet you, Jerry." Melvin reciprocated the shake and then nodded to Barry. "You too, Barry."

"I tried to stop Nasir, the guy Mike must have been working with, but they managed to get the jump on me," Jerry said. "I don't know where they went, but I know what they were driving."

Melvin smiled, wondering how long he should let the two idiots talk before he killed them. "Any information you could provide would be helpful."

17

*M*ike's anxiety calmed once they were on the road again, but the stress didn't completely disappear. He knew that in this new world order that there was no place that was truly safe. Not even his sister's cabin, which was out in the middle of nowhere.

The path to the cabin took Mike and his group off of the paved roads, and they traveled the hidden dirt paths that had been carved out on his sister's mountain. Once upon a time, they were logging roads. And while they hadn't been maintained, the paths were still clear enough to drive through. So long as you had four-wheel drive.

Because it was so remote, people hadn't branched out this far yet to build any new towns or cities. And that was the main reason why Katy had bought a chunk of land out here in the first place. She wanted to be as far away from civilization as she possibly could.

Mike had always thought she was crazy, but after surviving the initial effects of the EMP, he was glad that his sister had been so prepared.

It had been over three years since Mike had actually seen his sister, and he was afraid that neither would recognize one another. And he hoped that his sister didn't start shooting at them the moment she saw the truck. He didn't think that would be a good start to rebuilding their relationship. But it did give him an idea.

Mike eased on the brakes and stopped. Lisa looked over from the passenger seat and frowned.

"What's wrong?" Lisa asked.

"We're almost there," Mike answered. "This is the only back road into her place, and no one knows about it but me." He took a breath and then looked at his wife. "I should make the rest of the trip on foot alone. Talk to her."

Lisa tilted her head to the side. "Do you really think it'll make a difference how she finds out? She's not going to be happy about Nasir and his daughters no matter what."

Mike understood his wife's logic, but she didn't know his sister like him. "Maybe. But there are some things that I need to speak to her about before everyone comes up. Trust me?"

Lisa reached her hand across the seats and grabbed hold of Mike's hand tightly. "Always."

Mike kissed his kids and then checked on his mother, who was still asleep, but according to Nasir, her vitals were still strong. He kissed his mother's hand and then started his journey up the final leg of the hill alone.

He wasn't able to calm the butterflies in his stomach, and they only grew more frantic the longer he walked. He didn't know what he would say to his sister when they saw one another.

Katy had never been a forgiving person. The tension between Mike's sister and father had created a rift in their family as wide and vast as the Grand Canyon. But Mike had never learned what caused their falling out.

The dirt path narrowed to a walking trail that would be too small for the vehicles to pass through. It was overgrown with brush and dirt, but well shaded by the trees overhead. After a few minutes of walking alone, he grew lost in the quiet and the calm.

The mountain and the woods were a far cry from the chaos that he had seen in the city. There were no bodies in the street. No blood splashed along concrete. No roads clogged with broken vehicles. No death. Only life.

Mike stopped and then closed his eyes. He tilted his face toward the fading sun. It was warm. He listened to the breeze rustling leaves and branches. He heard the distinct chirp of birds and the buzz of insects. It was the sound of life. And he preferred these much more than the screams and gunfire that he had escaped from in the city.

Mike opened his eyes and then restarted his journey. He walked for a while, still finding no signs of his sister's cabin, and he began to wonder if he had taken a wrong turn somewhere.

Ten minutes later, Mike exhaled relief when the path opened up to a small clearing in the woods and he saw the backside of the cabin. But the next step forward, he heard the unmistakable pump of a twelve-gauge shotgun.

"Don't move."

Mike spread his hands out so Katy could see them. He turned, slowly.

"Hi, sis," Mike said.

Katy's hair was wild and untamed, but she attempted to keep the unruly curls out of her face with a ballcap and a ponytail. She was dressed in camouflage, everything long-sleeved and tactical. She had always been strong, but life outdoors had only sharpened her edges.

"You going to put that thing down?" Mike asked, hoping that she couldn't sense the worry in his voice. "Or are you going to pull the trigger before I even have a chance to explain why I'm here?"

"I know why you're here," Katy said, still not lowering the shotgun. "But you shouldn't have come."

Mike grimaced. "Katy, we're your family. And will you put the gun down?"

Katy hesitated for a moment, but then finally lowered the barrel of the weapon. She kept it at the ready though. She still didn't fully trust him. "I'm not running a shelter out here, Mike."

Mike crossed the rest of the path and got a better look at his little sister. "You never called. Why?"

"I don't want to do this now." Katy shouldered the shotgun and then walked past her brother, but Mike snatched her arm and spun her back around.

"No," Mike said. "You don't get to walk away from this. Not now."

Katy reclaimed her arm, and for a moment Mike thought she was going to aim the barrel of the gun at him and blow him away, but she didn't. "I get to walk away whenever I want, Mike. That's the deal that I made for myself when I decided to live out here. This is my life. My land. And you can get the hell off of it."

Katy started back up the path, and for a second Mike considered letting her go. He wasn't sure if she was worth trying to save, but then he remembered the people that were counting on him. Because while she might be able to walk away, he couldn't.

"Kat," Mike said.

Katy stopped, but she didn't turn around. He hadn't called her Kat since she was a teenager.

"I don't know what happened to you," Mike said. "I know you're mad, but my family needs a place to stay that is safe. And right now, your cabin fits that bill. If not for Mom or me, then for Kelly and Casey."

Mike waited, hoping that the thought of helping her niece and nephew would break through whatever hate that she felt towards the rest of them. Because deep down, he knew that Katy cared about his kids. They might be the only people she cared about at all anymore.

"Mom's hurt," Mike said, his voice catching unexpectedly. "It's pretty bad."

Katy finally turned around to face him, but she didn't take a step forward. "What happened?"

"She was shot when we were leaving the neighborhood," Mike answered. "One of the people we brought with us, Nasir, he was a doctor in Pakistan. He got the bullet out, sewed her up, but he's not sure if she'll survive or not."

Katy stared at the ground for a moment, and Mike waited anxiously to discover what she was going to decide. Mike didn't have a backup plan, so all of his chips were riding on his sister's decision.

"How many did you bring?" Katy asked, looking up from the ground.

It wasn't a yes, but Mike thought it was a step in the right direction since it wasn't a no. "Eight, including me."

Katy nodded and then chewed on her lower lip. She walked back over to her brother and stared up at him with conviction. "I've only got one extra bed, so I hope they don't mind sleeping on the floor."

"Thank you," Mike said.

Katy nodded and then took a deep breath. "Did you bring supplies?"

"Food, water, even some medicine and medical supplies that Nasir helped pick out," Mike answered. "Hopefully it will help."

Katy snickered and shook her head. "Brother, out here, hope will get you killed."

18

*M*ike returned with Katy to the group, and their family reunion was less than joyful. While Lisa was cold and stiff, the kids acted afraid of their aunt, something Katy, who had always been self-conscious, picked up on immediately.

But Mike should have seen that coming. He had lamented enough to Lisa about how mad he was about Katy not showing up for the funeral, and the last time that the kids had actually seen their aunt was at least five years ago. They had changed. So had Katy.

When Katy finally walked to the back of the truck and saw their mother lying on the blankets that they had brought from the clinic where Nasir had saved her life, Mike saw Katy's first expression of worry. He was glad to see that beneath that hard exterior, she still had a human side, even though she didn't let it come out very often.

Once the introductions were finished, Katy led the group up the path and through the woods until they arrived at the cabin.

A large patch of land had been cleared, the cabin built from the fallen timber. Aside from the cabin, Mike saw her old Jeep covered beneath a camouflage tarp out front. The left side of the cabin housed bees and a chicken coop. Pigs occupied the back of the cabin, and the right side housed a small garden.

"Do we have to poop outside?" Kelly asked, whispering to her mother.

"We'll have to do a lot of things differently now, so it's best if you just get used to it." Lisa placed her arm around her daughter, though Casey had a slightly different outlook than his sister.

"It'll be nice to be one with nature," Casey said.

"You're such a freak," Kelly replied, rolling her eyes.

"Takes one to know one."

Before the bickering transformed from childish to out of hand, Mike intervened. "I don't want either of you to get on one another's nerves right now. Understand?"

Both Kelly and Casey nodded, then sulked away, heads down. But at least they weren't arguing.

"You didn't have to snap at them like that," Lisa said.

Mike knew she was right, but he didn't have time to sugarcoat things anymore. "Just because we're here doesn't mean that we're safe from danger."

Lisa stepped closer. "I understand the threat we're facing, Mike. But that doesn't mean we have to lose everything about who we are." She walked around him and joined their children.

Mike helped Nasir carry his mother inside, and Katy led them to the spare bedrooms. "You keep an eye on her." Mike turned to his sister. "Where do you keep most of your supplies? We should start putting everything together."

Katy raised her eyebrows. "And you know this from your years of survival experience?"

"I'm just trying to help," Mike answered. "If you have a better solution, then—"

"My solution is that this is my house, and my property, and everything that happens here, everything that people touch or use, doesn't happen unless it's with my permission," Katy said. "If you or anyone else that you brought here has a problem with that, then they can leave now."

Mike wanted to argue, but he chose to heed his own advice that he gave his children. It was best not to cause a scene if there was nothing to argue about. "You're right. This is your place. And you're the expert in this scenario. We'll do whatever you think is best."

"Good," Katy said. "Now, the best thing we can do with supplies is to make sure that we split them up. It's important to have different stores in different areas, that way if one storage place is compromised, we don't lose all of our supplies."

Mike nodded. "That's smart."

"I know," Katy said, then glanced back to their mother who was on the bed before punching Mike in the arm and stepping out of the room. "C'mon. We need to talk."

Katy and Mike stepped out of the cabin. Katy shifted her weight from her left foot to her right, then hooked her thumb in her belt loop. It was a telltale sign that she was worried about something.

"What's wrong?" Mike asked.

"I was going to come and get you," Katy answered.

Mike was stunned. It wasn't something he had expected to hear.

"But there's a reason why I stayed." Katy leaned closer,

keeping her voice hushed. "We're not as safe as you think we are up here."

Mike frowned. "What are you talking about?"

"The town that's nearby?" Katy asked. "The one where I keep my P.O. box? I think it's some kind of central hub for the people that are responsible for all of this."

"How many people do they have?" Mike asked.

"A lot, and more are coming every hour," Katy answered. "They've started to send scouting parties out to comb the surrounding area, but so far none of them have made it this far north. I don't think they believe anyone would live so far out in the middle of nowhere."

Mike grew worried. "Do you think they'll make find us up here?"

Katy shrugged. "Hard to say. If the group stays small, we should be fine, but if it gets any bigger... then it's anybody's guess."

The prospect of having the same enemy that Mike had spent all day trying to evade just down the road was unsettling. But he wasn't going to make this a bigger deal than was necessary because he knew that he needed to keep a calm head before jumping to conclusions.

"So what do you think we should do?" Mike asked.

Katy chortled. "We're not in front of everyone else right now, so you don't have to pretend to value my opinion."

"That wasn't an act," Mike said.

"Whatever you say."

"Hey." Mike stepped in front of his sister. "I'm serious. I came here because I didn't know where else to go. I didn't know who else could help me protect my family. And I would like to hear your thoughts on the matter."

Katy didn't smile, but the scowl that seemed to have

become a permanent fixture on her face softened, and Mike counted the small victory.

"Well," Katy said, trying to reset her face so that Mike couldn't see how his words had affected her. "We'll need to keep an eye on their movements in town. I checked a few hours ago, but I wanted to get a better look as the sun was going down to see where they put everyone."

Mike frowned. "Put everyone?"

"They rounded up everyone from their homes and then put them to work," Katy said.

Mike glanced up at the sky. "How long will it take to get down there?"

"With you? About an hour."

"Then we better get moving," Mike said.

19

---

*K*aty allowed Mike to borrow a small pack and a rifle from her arsenal, which she made sure to keep under lock and key. She also made sure that the only people that were allowed to have guns was herself and Mike. No one else was to be armed unless required by an emergency situation, and only Katy could declare such an emergency.

While the pair were gone, Lisa was left in charge, though there wasn't much for them to do. Katy had already completed most of her chores for the day, but she made sure to let everyone know that they would be pitching in to help in the morning. Which started before dawn.

Alone on the trail with his sister, the pair fell into a comfortable silence. But while Mike didn't mind the silence, he was hoping to use the time as an opportunity to talk.

"You really like it out here," Mike said.

"Yup," Katy replied.

Mike walked behind her, trying to keep up with her quick

pace, and waited for the path to widen before he sidled up next to her. "You go into town a lot?"

"Only when I need to check the mail," Katy answered. "Or if I'm running low on certain luxury items that I can't make myself."

And judging from her attire and her lifestyle, Mike surmised that there wasn't much his sister couldn't make on her own.

"Are you close with any of the people down there?" Mike asked.

"I'm not close with anyone, Mike," Katy answered. "And I know what you're doing."

"What am I doing?"

"You're trying to break the ice. Loosen me up." Katy looked at him. "But I don't want to catch up. I don't want to know how you're doing, or what you've been up to. I don't care about that stuff anymore. I haven't cared about it for a long time." She faced forward again and gestured to the woods that surrounded them. "This is my world. Out here, it's quiet enough to hear my own thoughts, and those are the only ones that concern me."

Mike had worried a lot about his sister when she had first moved out here. He had worried that she would get sick and have no one to help her get better. He worried about someone coming after her in the middle of the night while she slept. He worried if she would starve or die of exposure. He had lost a lot of sleep because of her over the years. And now he wondered why he had wasted so much of that time on her now.

"I killed men in the city," Mike said, deciding to change the subject.

Katy turned toward her brother, surprised by the revelation. "How many?"

"Two," Mike answered. "I haven't really had any time to process it. I haven't even told Lisa about it yet, because the moment I got home—" He shook his head, stopping himself. "It doesn't matter. I think I just needed to say it out loud, so it didn't keep bouncing around in my head and driving me crazy."

Silence fell between them again for a little while longer, but finally, Katy spoke.

"I'm sorry you had to do that," Katy said. "Killing isn't easy."

"No," Mike said. "It's not. Not even when the person you killed deserved it. Not even when you were trying to protect yourself against all the odds. You versus them, and you know that if you die, then there won't be anyone to take care of your family." He stared down at his boots, the sweat stinging in his eyes, and he quickly wiped it away.

"The first time I killed anyone overseas was during a rescue operation in Afghanistan," Katy said. "A group of Marines had gotten pinned down and was surrounded by the enemy. Ground forces didn't have time to pick them up before they were dead, but flying in was risky too. Command decided to approve the mission, and my team went up."

Mike watched his sister as she told the story. He had never heard her talk about her time overseas in the military. When she came back from her tour, she didn't re-enlist, and that was when she started to isolate herself more.

"It was night time, so we thought that would help provide cover," Katy said. "Anyway, we landed, and the enemy was closer than we thought. Gunfire almost tore apart the chopper, and we had to carry the wounded on board. It was hard getting a grip on some of them because there was so much blood." She stared down at her hand, and Mike wondered if she could still see the blood. He knew he could if he closed his eyes. "I was on point for cover on the last run back, and one of the insurgents managed to sneak up from behind. He didn't have a gun on him, but he had both of his hands high above his head. He was screaming something in Farsi, and he was heading right for the chopper. He was a makeshift suicide bomber. I raised my rifle to shoot, but I froze before I pulled the trigger. I don't know why I did that, but something came over me. Maybe it was the blood I saw, or all the wounded that I helped carry onto the chopper for evac, but when I stared into the man's eyes through the scope of my rifle, I saw the enemy up close. We talk about the enemy all the time in briefings and around the camp, but it was always hypothetical. At least it felt that way to me. But when I finally saw the enemy up close, when he was running toward me with the full intention of killing me and everyone on my team, I still hesitated. I ended up getting the shot off in time, and the grenades exploded near his body. We joked that the family would have had to bury him in pieces. And while I laughed along with everyone else to pretend I was normal, when we got back to base, I locked myself in an outhouse that had been roasting shit all day and cried. I don't think I ever cried so hard as I did that night. And for what? Because I shot some terrorist that wanted to kill me? Because I ended someone's life before they could end mine? It didn't make any sense to me then, but after being out here alone with really nothing else to do but think, I managed to come to terms with the fact that killing, no matter who it is, or why, takes a toll on the soul of the person who performs the killing. It stains you. And while the stain does fade, it never really goes away. It's a part of you. Always."

Mike stopped, and he waited for Katy to turn around. "Thank you."

"I wasn't really trying to help," Katy said. "Just thought that you should know that what you're feeling isn't unnatural. People aren't meant to kill one another. We don't have claws or thick hides. We don't have fangs or powerful jaws. We're meant to work together, to be in groups and communities. We're made to solve problems with these." She pressed her finger into her temple, then lifted the rifle in her hands. "Not these."

Mike stepped closer to Katy. "If you think that we're supposed to be in groups, then why did you come out here to be all alone? Why didn't you come to stay with Lisa and me and the kids? I offered to put you up until you figured things out."

Katy nodded but looked away. "I know you did. But other things happened over there that I still hadn't figured out how to deal with. I'm not sure I've even done it now. I just knew that the only thing I wanted was to be alone." She shrugged. "And then I guess I just got used to it."

Seeing his sister like this, hearing her talk in length about her experiences, it made him want to hold her, to reach out and tell her that everything was going to be all right, and she didn't have to work through her pain alone.

But Mike knew that they hadn't repaired their relationship in that way yet. And he knew that this moment was a good milestone for them. He didn't want to ruin that by pushing it too far.

Katy finally broke the silence, since Mike didn't know what else to do. "Shouldn't be much farther. C'mon. I want to make sure we still have some light so we can see what they're doing."

With the conversation behind them, their pace quickened, and Mike found himself lighter on his feet. He wasn't sure if it was the admission of the killing or the fact that he was getting his second wind, but Mike was glad to have his mind cleared, and some of his energy returned.

With a faster pace, it didn't take long for them to reach the town, and Katy brought Mike over to a cluster of bushes that they used as cover. When they first sat down and Mike glanced at the town, he didn't see anything out of the ordinary.

But Katy only pressed her finger to her lips, then pointed back to the town. "Just watch."

And so Mike did. He watched the town for a long time and then noticed two men step out of a building. The distance made it difficult to see, but when he peered through the scope on his rifle, he saw the pistols strapped to their waist. But it was when he looked at their faces that he was surprised.

"They're Americans," Mike said, then peeled his eye off the scope and turned to his sister. "They're working with the people who set off the EMP?"

Katy nodded.

"Who else have you seen?" Mike asked.

Katy shrugged. "It's a mixed bag."

Mike returned his attention to the people down below. He couldn't believe people from his own country would want to harm it like they had done. It was unthinkable. Maddening.

"Mike," Katy said, gently placing her hand on his arm.

"Why don't you take your finger off the trigger and we take a moment to think about what we're going to do, all right?"

Mike glanced down and not realize that his finger was on the trigger. He quickly removed it. "We'll need to get a closer look if we want to really know what they're doing. Is there any other vantage point we can use?"

"Yes," Katy answered. "But you need to be dead quiet."

The pair remained low on their approach, and Mike mirrored Katy's movements.

"Ask, and you shall receive," Katy said as she lay on her stomach and peered over the side of a rock that acted as their cover.

From their current position, they had a clear view into the heart of the town, and it was a far better angle than their previous spot. Here, Mike could see the center of the enemy's operations.

"Looks like they're gathering supplies," Mike said.

"They've been raiding nearby houses all day," Katy said.

Mike frowned. It was a far different strategy than the one that he had seen used in Charlotte. In the city, the masked men fired at anything that moved. He couldn't think of a good reason why the terrorists here would be collecting the people from the town. It seemed like too much for them to take care of. Not that he thought the hostages were getting five-star accommodations.

"What else have you seen, or heard?" Mike asked. "Anything out of the ordinary?"

Katy shook her head. "Nothing really. I actually thought it was strange that I didn't hear more gunfire from everyone. It was like they took the town without any real violence."

"The only way to pull something like that off is with

people that are on the inside," Mike said. "Do you know anyone in the community that is strange? Loners?"

Katy's face slackened. "You're describing me."

"You know what I mean," Mike said.

Katy thought about it, and then she finally nodded. "Actually, yeah. I remember one guy, Tommy. He was always screaming at people. He was drunk most of the time, but he could get pretty violent and rough sometimes with the locals."

"Sounds like the perfect candidate for someone to radicalize," Mike said. "Do you know where he lives?"

"Other side of town," Katy answered. "But I don't know if we can get there before dark."

Mike didn't like the idea of being stuck out here for so long in the middle of nowhere, but he also wanted to figure out what was going on. He hadn't been able to find answers in the city, but he might be able to find some answers out here.

"Let's go," Mike said.

"You're sure?" Katy asked.

"Yes," Mike answered. "The more we can learn about what's happening, the better we can prepare for what they might do."

Mike again followed Katy down into the town, but they made a wide loop around the south side, so not to alert any of the guards stationed on the lookout. Katy did a good job of making sure that the enemy didn't know that they were coming.

Once the town was behind them, Mike saw a small cluster of mobile homes on the side of one of the hills in the area.

"Not much cover for us to approach," Mike said.

"It doesn't matter," Katy replied. "Tommy's place is right there."

The mobile home was on the edge of a community on one of the hillsides. It was clustered around several thick shrubs, and there were plenty of places where they could sneak around.

"I'll follow your lead on the way up," Mike said. "But when we get near the house, I'll take over."

Katy cast him a look. "You do remember I was in the military, right?"

"Seven years ago," Mike answered. "And I went through my SWAT recertification three months ago. I'm the one who has the fresher pair of eyes and hands."

Mike could tell that she wanted to protest, but she didn't. Instead, she nodded and then led the way up the mountain.

Mike didn't complain on the journey up, but his legs were starting to turn to jelly. The long day had taken its toll on him. "You do stuff like this every day?"

Katy glanced back at him. "You mean walking?"

"I mean hiking," Mike answered through labored breaths. "Smartass."

Katy stopped, and Mike nearly bumped into her.

"Come on, I didn't mean—"

Katy spun around and clamped her palm over Mike's mouth, pressing her finger to her lips to keep him hushed.

Mike nodded and then followed Katy's finger as she pointed between a cluster of trees northeast of their position. They were already next to Tommy's house.

Mike did his best to remain quiet as they moved closer to the house. He looked for any movement in the windows and listened for any voices coming through the walls of the home, but the closer they moved toward the structure, the more Mike was convinced that there was no one home. Still, he wanted to make sure that he did his due diligence before he chalked up the mission as a loss, and he was rewarded when he heard voices.

But they weren't coming from the house. They were heading toward the house.

Katy tapped on Mike's shoulder and then pointed them out. Two men were on the main dirt path that led up the hillside to the small community of mobile homes.

Katy leaned closer to Mike's ear and dropped her voice to a whisper. "The one on the left is Tommy. Never seen the one on the right before."

Mike watched the pair closely. Both of them were engaged in heavy conversation, but Mike wasn't close enough to hear any specifics.

They stopped when they neared the walkway path that veered toward from the dirt road to Tommy's home. They talked for a few more minutes, then shook hands and broke apart, Tommy heading toward his house. Alone.

Once Tommy entered the house, Mike took a moment to take stock of the rest of the area. The homes were spread out, but if any of them were still occupied, then it wouldn't take much to alert the man's comrades.

The house only had two points of entry from what Mike could see, a front door and a back door. If either of the entrances were locked, then they'd have to draw him out. Mike nodded, liking that plan the best.

Mike turned around. "You stay here, watch me, and when you see my signal, I want you to make noise."

"What kind of noise?"

"It doesn't matter."

"Okay."

"He'll come out to investigate, and I'll subdue him."

Katy arched one eyebrow up. "Are you sure you're up for this?"

"I'll be fine," Mike answered. "Just be ready."

Katy nodded, and Mike made his way up toward the house. He remained hunched low on his approach and did his best to keep quiet, though he didn't have as much experience traipsing through the woods as his sister did.

Mike arrived at the house unnoticed, and he positioned himself by the front door. The idea would be when Tommy rushed outside to check on the noise, Mike would knock him out with the butt of his gun, hitting the guy as hard as he could.

Once Mike was in position, he found Katy in the woods and then flashed a thumbs-up. A few seconds of silence passed and then she threw a rock at the side of the house. It cracked against the old wood, and the moment it made contact, Mike heard a commotion inside the trailer.

Less than three seconds later and Tommy burst out of the front door, gun in hand, and was completely blindsided by Mike, who clocked him in the forehead. The man's body went limp like a noodle, and he hit the ground.

Mike then quickly glanced around and made sure that they were alone and no one was alerted to their presence. When no one else reacted to the encounter, Mike pulled Tommy's body back inside and waited for Katy to join them.

20

$\mathcal{M}$ ike made sure that Tommy was tied up nice and tight and his mouth was taped shut before he dumped the bucket of water over the man's head and woke him up. Katy stood back and watched as Mike handled the interrogation. She didn't like being on the sideline, but since they were both sticking to what they knew best, Mike retained the lead on this one.

Tommy blinked his eyes open, water dripping off of him and onto the dirty floor. The inside of the trailer was just as disgusting and gross as the man who occupied it. But once Tommy realized he was bound, he thrashed about, screaming into the gag.

Mike let the man go on about this for a little while longer, hoping Tommy would tire himself out once he realized that no amount of screaming or shouting was going to get him loose.

But that took a while.

"How much longer do you want to do this?" Katy asked.

"How well do you know this guy?" Mike asked.

"Well enough to know that he's got a pair of lungs on him," Katy answered. "We can't question him without taking the gag out, and we can't take the gag out because he'll start screaming and giving away his position the moment we do." She leaned closer to him. "We need to get him out of here and take him to the cabin."

"And give away our position?" Mike asked.

Katy tilted her head to the side. "Well, we wouldn't be letting him go, Mike."

Mike never considered the option of killing the man. Not after they had captured him. But he knew that it was something that they would have to consider. If this man had been so willing to turn against the people in his community for a group of murderous psychopaths that wanted to watch this country burn, then Tommy would have to face the consequences.

Mike walked over to Tommy, the man still thrashing against his restraints and screaming into his gag, and hunched forward so he could look the man in the eyes. Tommy calmed down for a minute, but then started screaming again.

"Tommy," Mike said. "You need to tell us what you're doing if you want to make sure that all parts of your body remain in working condition. Do you understand me?"

Tommy quieted for a minute, but then Mike heard a very muffled 'fuck you' through the gag.

Mike nodded. "Okay." He bent down and started to untie Tommy's boots.

"What are you doing?" Katy asked.

"Hand me my rifle." Mike tugged at the boot and peeled it off Tommy's foot. The man's foot smelled musty and sour, and the sock that Mike removed was dirtied and soaked with sweat. He grabbed his rifle from Katy and then stood.

Both Katy and Tommy were baffled, but Mike offered Tommy one last chance to talk. "What are you and your comrades doing in town?"

When Tommy responded with another gagged 'fuck you', Mike slammed the stock of his rifle down on Tommy's foot as hard as he could. Tommy screamed through the gag, his entire body seizing up from the pain.

Mike had never been someone who had enjoyed torturing. And despite the movies, cops were never rough in the interrogation room. Everything was always done by the book. But the world had changed, and it wasn't like the guy didn't have it coming.

Mike waited until Tommy calmed down and then leaned forward to get into his face once more. "All I want is answers to my questions. They're all going to be yes or no, so it'll be easy for you to answer. I ask you a question, and you either nod your head yes, or you shake your head no. If you don't answer, then I'm going to hit you again. And I'm going to keep hitting you until you do, understand?"

Tommy took a few deep breaths, and just when Mike thought that he was going to have to hit the man's foot again, two of his toes already turning black and blue, Tommy nodded.

"Good," Mike said. "Do you have more than twenty men working in the town?"

Tommy shook his head.

"More than ten?" Mike asked.

Tommy nodded.

Mike counted up from ten until he landed on fourteen. "And the total number of fourteen includes you?"

Tommy nodded.

"Are you expecting more people to show up?" Mike asked.

Tommy nodded.

"Today?" Nothing. "Tomorrow?" Nope. "Two days from now?" Tommy nodded. "Two days from now. Okay, good. Now, I've reached the point where I need to undo your gag, Tommy. But our agreement is still in place. You scream, you act out, and I break the rest of your toes and crunch your foot until the bones have turned to dust. Got it?"

Tommy nodded.

Mike was careful when he removed the gag and kept the rifle poised to strike should Tommy not hold up his end of the deal. But Mike was relieved to find Tommy didn't act out.

"What the fuck is wrong with you, man?" Tommy asked, his face dripping with sweat, and then he turned his attention to Katy. "I know you. Shit, you're that crazy woman that lives up in the trees. People have been looking for you."

"Glad to know that you can't find me," Katy said.

"What are those people doing in the town?" Mike asked.

"We're using the town as a supply route," Tommy answered, spitting out his words between those labored breaths.

"Supply route for what?" Katy asked.

"What do you think?" Tommy spat the question back with petulance. "For killing! For punishing everyone who did us wrong!"

"Who's us?" Mike asked. "Why would Americans do this to their own people?"

Tommy laughed, shaking his head. "We ain't people like you. Or you." He looked at both Katy and Mike with accusing eyes. "Some of us are white, some of us are black, some of us are brown, but none of us are like *you*."

"And what are you?" Mike asked.

"We're anyone that's fed up," Tommy answered, and then he smiled, a hint of joy breaking through the pain. "And we finally got the upper hand." He laughed. "Oh boy, did we ever." He laughed harder. "Look at all of you now, running around with your heads cut off."

"How did you do it?" Katy asked.

"I don't know the specifics," Tommy answered. "I'm just a foot soldier. A man who saw an opportunity and took it. And I'd do it again in a heartbeat."

"What kind of supplies are your people bringing through here?" Mike asked.

"Food, water, guns, medicine," Tommy answered. "Anything that we can take away from people like you and keep for ourselves. We've got little stations like this all over the country. There are thousands of us living in communities. We're your friends, your family, your neighbors, and coworkers. We're everywhere. And we're going to win."

"Win what?" Mike asked, unable to grasp the desires of a mad man.

"The war," Tommy answered.

"You're a fool if you think that a few thousand people can overthrow this country," Katy said. "Once we get communications back up—"

"And how long will that take?" Tommy asked, growing aggressive. "It hasn't even been a day, and look at what people have done to one another." He turned to Mike. "You've seen it, haven't you? Death, chaos, people are out to save themselves. It's hard to defeat a country, easier to beat smaller groups. And by the time the military can communicate with one another about what's going on, the people in this country will have done most of the hard work for us, tearing each other apart. And sure, you might kill some of us every day, but so long as one of us is still alive, then the war will never be over. And that's how we win. We win by never losing."

Mike stepped away from Tommy, his mind reeling. The country had already suffered a terrible blow. He had seen it firsthand in the city. People had lost their minds, and the death toll was probably already somewhere in the millions, and that number would climb rapidly over the next several days and weeks.

No one had been ready. And they knew that.

The sound of choking pulled Mike out of his own terrible thoughts, and he looked over to find Tommy with his throat slit, Katy wiping the blade on the man's shirt to clean it of blood before she placed the blade back in its sheath.

"What are you doing?" Mike asked.

"We got what we needed from him," Katy answered. "We couldn't let him live. You knew that."

"He might have told us more," Mike said. "We could have—"

"We learned what we needed to learn," Katy said, her eyes grew cold and hard. "He told us what he knew, and we've stayed here longer than I wanted to. People might be expecting him back, and I don't want us to be here when they come looking for him."

Katy shouldered Mike on her way to the door. Mike turned back to Tommy, his head slumped forward and the front of his shirt covered in blood. It took a moment for him to come to terms with what his sister had just done. She had murdered someone. But so had he. Apparently, this was the way of the world now.

21

*I*t had been an interesting journey for Melvin once he left the detective's house, where he had his share of fun with some of the neighbors that had rallied against Michael Thorton. And while Melvin might have shared Michael as a common enemy with those bottom feeders that the detective called his neighbors, he needed to focus on his larger mission.

But that didn't mean he couldn't have more fun along the way.

It had been a bloody journey from Charlotte as he made his way west toward the P.O. box number that he had traced to the small town where the detective's sister lived. Or at least lived nearby. He had borrowed a map from one of Michael's neighbors, but he had the unfortunate audacity to bleed all over it after Melvin jammed a pen into the side of the man's neck.

Melvin rolled his eyes. "People."

But despite the flecks of blood that hindered his path on the map, Melvin made good time. He had picked up a bicycle, which he used to move faster down roads that had been clogged with traffic and broken-down vehicles.

But the farther west that he rode, the less traffic that he encountered, and he knew that he was getting close to finding his prey. He had also learned that he wasn't the only predator lurking about in the world.

The men that Melvin had seen in the city seemed to be sprinkled throughout the countryside. He hadn't bother engaging with these people because he had no desire to press his luck. From what he had seen in the city, they held the mentality of shoot first and ask questions later. With Melvin's MO of talking to his victims before killing him, he knew that they would have conflicting ideologies.

A sign for the town was up ahead, and Melvin decided to ditch the bike and go the rest of the trip on foot. If the detective was nearby, he didn't want to draw attention to himself by sticking to the main roads. He wanted to make sure that his arrival in town was a surprise.

Sticking to the trees off the road, Melvin saw the town up ahead. From what he could see from his current position, the place looked deserted. But the closer he moved toward the town, he saw that it was guarded.

At first glance, Melvin believed that this little community had banded together, fighting against the enemy that had descended upon the country, slaughtering innocents.

But upon closer inspection, Melvin saw only a few people in the town, the rest being pushed into one building. He realized that the men herding the masses were the same kind of men that Melvin had encountered in Charlotte.

Had the detective fled trouble, only to be captured by the people when he arrived? Melvin hoped not. If so, his new game would be over before it began.

Melvin was about to descend back onto the road and cross down below to the other side to get a better look and sneak his way up into the town when he saw a pair of bodies dart across the road and disappear into the woods near him.

Melvin ducked and flattened himself against the earth. He had become a natural at blending in, becoming a ghost when he needed to. It was how he had evaded capture for so long. But as he watched the pair move closer to him, Melvin almost blew his own cover when he saw who it was.

The detective.

He was with another woman, and judging by their resemblance, Melvin would have bet his last dollar that the woman was the sister that had sent the letter. They were moving quickly through the woods, and it took all of Melvin's willpower not to get up and immediately follow him. But he had picked up a few skills in tracking people through the woods. Sometimes it was fun to let his victims run and think that they could escape.

Melvin waited until the pair had gained a bit of a head start, and then he sprinted after them. He wandered through the woods for a while, but he finally saw the backs of their heads as they trudged up the mountain.

Melvin was downwind, so he doubted there was any chance that he could give away his position unless they had a dog's hearing. But he was able to hear snippets of their conversation. They were talking about the men in town. Something about their supplies and the captured townspeople, which made Melvin smile.

Even in the grips of chaos, the detective still couldn't deny his true nature to help people. It was what made them such a perfect match. Two forces on opposite sides of the law, and they were about to crash into one another for an epic battle.

Melvin maintained his safe distance for the next hour, climbing the mountain, unsure of where they were heading. They had traveled far away from the town, and Melvin wasn't sure where they would be going that was so far away from the rest of civilization.

Along the way, Melvin noticed the sister taking the lead and how she weaved around certain areas, careful to step over some invisible line. For a long time, this confused Melvin until he stumbled upon one of her traps.

Melvin caught sight of the tripwire only seconds before he was about to step down on it. He slowly, carefully, removed his foot and bent down to examine the wire, which ran five yards east to west. He followed the wire to the mine hidden beneath leaves and dirt.

"Clever," Melvin said, a smile on his face.

These were the same kinds of weapons Melvin had found on the terrorists. It seemed the detective's sister was better prepared than most.

Melvin continued following the detective but was much more conscious about his steps. Even with the slower pace, he managed to keep up with his prey. And when he saw the small cabin in the clearing ahead, Melvin brightened with pleasure. It wasn't just the detective that was at the cabin, but his entire family. Wife, kids, even a few friends.

Melvin was going to have fun. A lot of fun.

*I*t was Mike, Lisa, Katy, and Nasir in a circle, everyone huddled close while Mike explained what they found in town. Adults only. For now, he wanted to keep the kids out of any plans they came up with. He wasn't sure that would last forever, but he wanted to protect them from what the world had become for as long as he could.

And once Mike had said his piece, the response he received from his wife was one that surprised him.

"You can't help those people," Lisa said.

"What are you talking about?" Mike asked. "Those are the same terrorists that I saw in Charlotte, the same people that are attacking—*slaughtering*—innocent civilians. We have to help them."

"How?" Lisa asked. "You said there were fourteen people guarding the town?"

"Thirteen," Katy said.

"Thirteen," Lisa said. "Thirteen people against you two? How would that even work?"

"They're comfortable," Mike said. "This is the first time

that I have seen any of them in one place, and they haven't killed anyone. Which means that they might be waiting to use those people as leverage or torture them, or use them as some kind of cheap labor." He shut his eyes, knowing that he was getting worked up, and took a breath to calm down. "And the bigger problem is that they have people trying to find Katy. They know that she lives somewhere up on the mountain, but they just don't know where yet. And they want to completely secure the area before they expand. So if we can stop them before more of them show up, we increase our chances of survival."

"How much longer is this going to last?" Lisa asked. "Can't we just wait them out?"

"It could take over a year," Katy answered. "With the sheer amount of infrastructure that has been destroyed because of the EMP, it has crippled everything. It took our country over two hundred years to get to this point. It's going to take some time before we see any semblance of normal."

Lisa deflated. It was difficult news to hear. But they all needed to hear it. The future had transformed into a place of hard truths. And if they couldn't face those truths without conviction, then they weren't going to make it very far in the long run. All that mattered now was making sure that they survived. That was key.

"We would be safer in the long run if we eliminated any nearby threats now," Nasir said.

The answer surprised Mike. Since the man was a doctor, he thought that the idea of killing went against his moral code.

"I agree with Mike," Nasir said. "If I even get a vote."

Lisa sighed, shaking her head. "I don't know about this."

"Lisa," Katy said. "I understand that you're concerned. I

am too. This isn't a plan that I want to pursue, but the fact of the matter is people are looking for me. And the moment they find out where I am, they find out where you and the kids are. And I don't want anything to happen to them. At the very least, if we go after them now, we have the element of surprise. But if we wait until they stumble upon the cabin, then we'll be pushed up against the wall. And I don't think that's a fight we'll be able to win."

Mike braced himself for the torrent of vehement language that he knew his wife would unleash on a woman whom she didn't care for very much, but he was surprised to see Lisa only nod in agreement. But she still wasn't happy about it.

"Fine," Lisa said. "I need to get dinner ready."

"Use whatever you need to in the pantry," Katy said. "I can help if—"

"No, I'll take care of it," Lisa said. "You two have work to do."

Lisa departed for the kitchen, Mike turned his focus on him.

"I want you to stay behind," Mike said.

"I can fight," Nasir said. "And it's the least that I can do after what you've done for my daughters and me. I owe you."

Mike placed his hand on Nasir's shoulder. "It's not that I don't want you to fight. Lord knows that we could use the extra manpower. But you're a doctor, and your mind is far more valuable to us than your trigger finger right now. If one of us gets hurt, then you could fix it. If you get hurt, we're all screwed."

Mike hoped that the logic would sneak its way into Nasir's mind, and the man finally acquiesced to the plan. Nasir returned to his girls, and Mike turned to his sister.

"So how do you think we should play this?" Mike asked.

"Asking for my advice now, are you?" Katy asked.

"I told you that we need to stick with the experts and what we do best," Mike said. "And this is a war. I've never been in one, but you have. So how do we fight them?"

Katy nodded and then gestured toward the front porch. "Let's talk outside. I need a smoke."

Mike followed his sister outside and leaned up against the railing as Katy pulled a smoke from her pocket and lit up.

"When did you start smoking?" Mike asked.

"I've always smoked," Katy answered, taking a puff. "I was just really good at hiding it."

Mike nodded. "You've gotten good at hiding lots of things over these past few years."

Smoke from the tip of the cigarette drifted lazily up over Katy's face, making her expression hazy and nuanced. She didn't look like the young sister that he remembered growing up with. She had truly become a stranger to him. A woman whom he didn't know.

"I know it bothered you," Katy said. "Me leaving."

"It bothered more than just me," Mike replied. "It bothered the whole family."

Katy took another drag, nodding along. "Yeah. Maybe."

"No, maybe about it," Mike said. "My kids loved you. You had a great relationship with Lisa. Hell, I thought we had a good relationship. And then you just leave, abandoning us out of nowhere. And I still don't understand why."

Katy lowered her gaze to the wood floors, still puffing on her smoke. She was quiet for a long time. But when she finally spoke, her voice was quiet and small like he remembered when she was little and really scared.

"Dad disowned me," Katy said. "After I came back from

Afghanistan. That's why I took off." She took another smoke, still staring at the floor.

Mike winced. "What? Why would he disown you?"

"I told him about what happened," Katy said. "Over there." She finally looked up at him.

"Are you talking about the stuff that happened when you hesitated with the chopper team?" Mike asked. "Katy, that's nothing to be ashamed about—"

"It wasn't about that." Katy shook her head, and she scuffed her heel against the floor, growing agitated. "It was about something else. Something worse. Much worse."

Mike's stomach started to hollow out the way it did when he got nervous, and his mouth dried up. "Katy, what happened? What aren't you telling me?"

Katy took one last puff on the cigarette and then flicked the butt out into the dirt. "Nothing. Forget it." She made a beeline for the door, head down, but Mike grabbed her arm and pulled her back before she could escape. "Get off me!"

"No!" Mike shouted, his tone harsher than he intended, and when he saw her wince, he softened. "There isn't anything that you can't tell me, you know that. We've always been that way ever since we were little, remember? No secrets."

Katy crossed her arms, hugging herself, and her eyes reddened. She sniffled and then quickly wiped her nose.

"Katy," Mike said. "Please. Talk to me."

And then the dam finally broke loose. Katy scrunched her face as she cried, and she instinctively leaned into her brother, who placed gentle hands around her back. They stayed like that for a long time, and it was only after the tears had run their course that she finally broke free. It took a

187

moment for her to calm down, and Mike said nothing as he waited. Finally, she spoke.

"I was raped," Katy said. "When I was on my tour."

The words lingered in the air for a moment, Mike hearing them, but his mind refusing to accept their truth.

"What?" Mike asked. "How did… How did that happen?"

Katy kept her arms around herself, keeping her eyes on the ground. "It was on base one night. I had a few drinks with some of the guys from my platoon. I guess I had one too many because I stumbled back to my barracks and passed out." She took a breath and then exhaled. "But I woke up in the middle of the night, and my pants were down, and there was—" She shut her eyes. "There was a man on top of me."

Mike clenched his fists, squeezing his hands so tight that his knuckles popped.

"I tried to fight him off, but I was too tired," Katy said. "I tried to yell for help, but no one came. And then he finished, and left." Her eyes widened, and she stared ahead, her expression stoic. "I lay there for a long time, crying. It wasn't until morning when I was supposed to report for duty that anyone came looking for me. I had cleaned myself up by then, which I later realized was a mistake." She frowned. "I just wanted to get his stink off me, so I took a shower."

Mike remained silent. He had questions, but he wouldn't ask anything until he was sure that she had said her piece. But in the gaps of silence, dark thoughts filled his mind, all of them about what he would do to the man who did that to his sister.

"I reported what happened," Katy said. "Did the rape kit, but some of the evidence wasn't conclusive since I took a shower. I tried pushing it up the chain of command, but no one wanted to hear about it. The military doesn't like to ruffle feathers, and the last thing they wanted to do was start an expensive hearing. With so much pushback I dropped it, but I was able to get a psychological discharge. And that's when I came home and spoke to Dad." She cleared her throat. "I told him what happened, and he didn't believe me. He said that I was just looking for attention. 'Like I always do.'"

Mike's mouth hung open for a long time. He struggled to find the words. He didn't know what to say. "Why didn't you tell me?"

"Because I was so angry," Katy answered. "I couldn't believe he thought that I would lie about something like that. I mean, I know I got into some trouble in high school, but I wasn't that person anymore, you know?"

Mike reached for his sister's hand and squeezed. "I'm so sorry."

"I just know how close you were with him," Katy said. "And I thought that it would be better if I just left without causing more trouble than I already caused."

"Hey," Mike said. "That wouldn't have been trouble. You did nothing wrong."

"Yeah," Katy said. "I know that now. But it took a long time for me to get there." She glanced out to the woods, the last bits of the day fading away. "It was nice being out here. It gave me time to reflect, think about what happened." She turned back to Mike. "I wanted to come back for the funeral. For you. But I just couldn't. And now you know why."

Mike nodded. "Thank you for telling me. And I'm sorry for being so hard on you. If I had known—"

"It's okay, Mikey," Katy said. "I know you're not the bad guy. Neither was Dad, really. He was just… afraid to rock the boat. Even if it meant covering up something bad."

Mike wanted to talk to her more about it, but she looked

so tired and exhausted that he didn't press the issue. She eventually got up and headed for the door.

"We still need to plan for the morning," Katy said. "I think we should try and hit them at first light."

Mike nodded. "That's a good idea. They'll be the most vulnerable then."

But Mike had no idea how he was supposed to plan an attack tomorrow after what he just learned.

23

---

*I*t didn't take long for Katy to map out their strategy. She had been to the town enough times that she had a good idea of where everything was located. Their plan was simple. Katy would plant explosives around the town, causing a distraction, and when the bad guys rushed out of the building and sprinted toward the trouble, she would take them out with her rifle.

While Katy was shooting the bad guys, Mike would sneak into the library where they were holding everyone hostage, and arm as many of them with guns to fight back.

But Katy made sure to hammer home one very important detail: None of the enemies escaped.

If any of the terrorists in the town managed to flee, then they would be able to alert any nearby cells about what happened, drawing more attention to their area.

"Are you going to be okay with that?" Katy asked.

Mike wasn't sure how he felt about executing people. But there were no jails to house any prisoners, and no court system to prosecute them. Killing the enemy was the cleanest approach. "I'll do what needs to be done."

"Good," Katy said. "And listen, when you go to grab the people in the library, you want to find Mark Thompson. He's the closest thing to a mayor the town has, and if people are reluctant to help, then he'll help talk them into it." Katy yawned when they finished and wiped her eyes. "I'm going to sleep. I'll be up early to get everything ready."

"Okay," Mike said. "Just wake me up when you're up."

Katy flashed a thumbs-up and then disappeared to her bedroom. They had planned everything in the kitchen, and Mike sat there alone for a little while, still trying to wrap his head around what happened to his sister.

How could his father have said something like that? He knew that Katy wasn't lying about what happened. Was his father really that scared? Was he really that frightened that they would get so much bad press that it would ruin their family name?

Mike rubbed his eyes. The day had caught up with him, but his mind was still spinning with questions that needed answers.

Mike got up and stepped quietly through the living room where his family and Nasir's family occupied sleeping bags on the floor. Everyone had passed out an hour ago, exhausted from the day's events. Mike walked into his mother's room and gently sat on the edge of her mattress.

She was asleep, so still and quiet. And small. He reached for her hand and held it in his own. She had always been a small woman, very petite. But seeing her current state on the bed, she didn't look like she would make it through the night.

But then, between two sharp, shallow breaths, Mike watched as his mother cracked her eyelids open. They fluttered for a moment, and at first glance, Mike thought she was having a seizure, but she was only shaking off the heavy sleep that she had fallen into.

After Martha was able to hold her eyes open for longer than a few seconds, she finally set her gaze on her son, and she winced as she struggled to open her mouth. "Wa—" She shut her mouth and swallowed, unable to finish the word.

Mike grabbed the water glass from the nightstand and then brought it to his mother's lips, and she drank greedily from the cup. The water spilled over the sides of her mouth, and she coughed after a few gulps, spraying more water over the front of her.

Mike set the glass aside and then used the edge of the bedsheet to wipe the water up. When he was finished, he reached for her hand again and felt her reciprocate the squeeze. But it was weak. Very, very weak.

"What happened?" Martha asked, struggling to stay awake.

"You were shot," Mike answered. "But we got you all fixed up. All you have to worry about is resting now."

Martha stared at Mike for a moment, then glanced to the rest of her surroundings. She looked confused, then worried. "Where am I?"

Mike had come in here to find comfort, but the last thing that he wanted to do was make his own mother uncomfortable about their situation. But he also wanted answers to what happened. And despite his positive outlook for his mother's recovery, if she died, then everything that she knew went with her, and Mike needed to know. He needed to understand.

"We're at Katy's cabin," Mike said.

He waited for how she would react, and he suspected that

if she hadn't been so injured, he would have seen a more exaggerated expression from her. But she was hurt, and weak, and tired.

Martha nodded and then exhaled a sigh.

"Mom," Mike said, still holding her hand. "Katy told me what happened. Between her and Dad." He studied her carefully, looking for any tells or micro-expressions, but she remained stoic. "Did you know? Did you know about what happened to her and how Dad reacted?"

Martha was quiet for a long time. She simply stared up at the ceiling, not looking at Mike, and just when he thought she was going to fall back asleep, she closed her eyes and spoke. "Your father was a complicated man. A man that came from a different time."

Mike let go of his mother's hand. "Oh my god. So you did know? You knew what he said after Katy told him what happened overseas?"

Martha licked her lips, most of her concentration on her breathing and staying awake. "I wasn't in the room with them when they discussed it, and when I tried talking to Katy about it, she shut me out. I didn't learn about what really happened until after she left. I had to pull it out of your father. And you know how difficult something like that was with him."

Mike did know. Getting his father to open up and talk about anything that didn't involve work or cars was like trying to crack the safe at Fort Knox. "Did you try and convince him to call her? To try and make it right?"

"Of course I did," Martha said. "But where do you think Katy got her stubborn side? The man was a mountain when he didn't want to do something. He couldn't be moved. I would have had better luck negotiating peace in the Middle

East."

Mike shook his head, dumbfounded. He lowered his head and rubbed his eyes, a sour pit forming in his stomach. "God, how could dad do something like that?" He popped his head up. "I mean I know that he could be strong-willed, but over something like this?" He stood, his voice growing louder without his intention.

Martha tried to reach for Mike's hand, but he was too far out of reach, and she didn't have the strength to try and reach him. "Michael, sit down. Please."

Mike didn't want to sit down. He wanted to drive his fist through the wall. He wanted to scream. He wanted to be able to speak to his father one last time so that he could give the old man a piece of his mind. He was angry, and he needed to direct that anger somewhere before he exploded.

But it was the sound of his mother's voice that pulled him back from the edge, the way that it always did whenever he felt that uncontrollable anger course through him. The real bad stuff that he could normally keep at bay. There were only two people that could talk him down when he got like that. The first person was his mother. The second was his wife.

"I need to talk to you, Michael," Martha said. "Sit down. Please."

Mike finally rejoined his mother on the bed, and then allowed her to place her hand on his own hand. Sitting there as a grown man, he suddenly felt like he was eight years old again, waiting for his mother to tell him that everything was going to be okay. It was funny how that need never disappeared, no matter how old you grew.

"What your father said, and did, was terrible," Martha said. "And no one let him know that more than I did when I finally learned the truth. I don't know why he couldn't just admit he made a mistake. Maybe because he was too old or too embarrassed or too scared. I think he was afraid that if he had done something about it, then that meant the horrible thing that happened to his daughter was real. That Katy was raped, and that the men who did that to her were still walking free. And he just couldn't accept that fact. He wasn't strong enough to bear that burden."

"That's not an excuse," Mike said, his eyes reddening and growing wet. "He should have done something. I would have done something if that happened to Kelly. I wouldn't have even hesitated."

"I know, sweetheart," Martha said. "I know. But you are a stronger man than your father was. You're a better man. And he helped raise you to be that way. Don't forget that."

Mike knew that she was right, but at that moment, it didn't matter. He was still mad and was going to allow himself to stay mad.

"When he was sick," Martha said. "He told me that he was glad that he was suffering. He said that it was his penance for not doing anything when Katy came to him for help." A tear fell from the corner of her eye and rolled over the wrinkles of her cheek. "He might have done something bad, Michael, but he regretted it in the end. He really did. And by the time he wanted to make it right, Katy didn't want to hear any part of it."

"And how was she supposed to handle it, Mom?" Mike asked.

"I don't blame her for not wanting to listen," Martha answered. "I just wanted my family to be together again. I just wanted us all to heal from those old wounds."

Martha shut her eyes, and one more tear fell. But a few

seconds after that and she was back asleep. What little bit of strength that she managed to conjure was gone.

Mike gently removed his hand and then stood. He watched her for a little while longer before he left the room and joined his wife on the floor in their sleeping bag.

Mike lay awake for a while, his mind reeling from the events of the day and everything that he had learned. Even though he knew that he needed to rest, he wasn't sure if he was going to be able to fall asleep the way his mind and body were still wired.

But when Lisa rolled against him and placed her arm over his stomach, it was the warmth of her body that overpowered the thoughts racing through his mind, and he drifted off into a deep, soundless sleep.

SLEEP ELUDED Melvin most of the night. His mind just wouldn't stop racing. And he couldn't get comfortable sleeping on the hard, cold ground. He managed to pilfer some camping supplies on his journey, but the sleeping bag and extra blanket did little to protect him from the elements.

But it wasn't the first night that Melvin had to spend outdoors. When he was younger, he hid from his stepfather's violent temper, and the safest place he could find was the woods behind his house.

Melvin's stepfather would come home in a drunken rage, looking for a fight, but Melvin learned quickly to already be long gone by the time that mean bastard came home. It was his mother who never learned the lesson. She took the abuse, and then the next morning made his breakfast with a side of fresh bruises for her trouble.

But those days were long gone. He no longer hid from the hunter. He was the hunter.

Melvin had kept a close eye on the cabin, but he also maintained a safe distance. It was difficult for him to stay back and not swoop into the cabin in the middle of the night and slaughter everyone while they slept. But after the trap that he found in the surrounding woods, he wasn't sure what else the detective's sister had up her sleeve.

She was smart to have booby-trapped the area, creating her own security system. Melvin had only missed the trap by blind luck, and so he stayed put. And it had proven helpful.

Melvin studied the family. He watched them move, listened to their conversations. He wasn't able to hear all of what they said, but he caught enough to piece together what he had missed.

The detective and his sister were going to attempt to go down into the town and set the people free. It was a noble act, but then again, the detective was a noble man. And the detective's crusade ended up providing the perfect cover for Melvin's plans.

Because he couldn't sleep, Melvin spent most of the night preparing for his fun with the detective. He had a few ideas of what he wanted to do, but not all of the supplies to make his vision come alive.

But a quick trip into town under the cover of darkness easily fixed those problems as he slipped past the guards on duty, neither of them alert or wakeful.

Once Melvin rounded out his supplies, adding what he gathered from the town to the weapons in his pack he pilfered from the terrorists in Charlotte, he turned his attention to the woods. He wanted to become as familiar with the area as possible.

Melvin's eyes adjusted quickly to the darkness, and it didn't take long for him to understand the appeal of the area. There were so many different places to play.

The first was a set of caves, which he nearly got lost in trying to explore in the dark. They were too tantalizing not to use, and he made sure that he could find his way back to them again.

The second location was a sharp cliff looking over the side of a canyon. It had the perfect kind of ledge to dangle something or someone off of.

And the final location was a pit. The area had steep walls on every side. It was the perfect place to set an ambush. It was an area where Melvin would be able to take his time with the detective. He could savor the moment, savor the kill, and make sure there was plenty of time to make him feel every ounce of pain.

Satisfied with his scouting work, Melvin returned to his position outside of the cabin to wait until it was his moment to enact his revenge.

When Katy woke Mike up on the floor, he thought he was dreaming since it was still so dark outside. But he wasn't, and Mike did his best not to wake the others as he followed his sister outside.

"We'll need to leave here in the next thirty minutes if we want to get to town before sun-up," Katy said, walking around to the backside of the cabin. "And I'll need all the time I can get to set up the explosives."

Mike yawned and struggled to stay awake. "What time is it?"

"Four-thirty," Katy answered.

"Jesus." Mike slapped his cheeks as they rounded the back corner of the cabin, and Katy crouched at a cellar door which had a padlock over it. She inserted a key and then twisted the lock off and heaved open the doors. He glanced to the chicken coop and saw the birds still sleeping. "Do you always wake up this early?"

"Only when I have to kill people," Katy answered, and then smiled as she looked back to her brother.

"That's not funny," Mike said. "You do know that I'm still a cop, right?"

Katy chuckled to herself on the way down, and then struck a match and lit a lantern that hung near the bottom of the stairwell. A yellow glow penetrated the darkness and exposed the caches of supplies hidden beneath their feet.

"Where the hell did you get all of this stuff?" Mike stepped off the last step of the staircase then wandered around the basement, picking a can off the nearest shelf.

Katy walked over to him and snatched the can out of his hand, then returned it to the shelf. "Don't touch anything unless I tell you to touch it. This way."

The cellar was surprisingly big as Mike followed Katy. "Does this go all way beneath the cabin?"

"Yup," Katy answered. "Carved it out myself. Took me a year to do it properly." She smacked one of the nearby foundation poles. "Didn't want to have my floor give way on me."

"This is incredible," Mike said.

"Back here is what we want." Katy walked over to a cluster of long, rectangular-shaped storage boxes. He stood next to her while she used another key to undo the lock.

"You don't think that it's a little overkill?" Mike asked.

"You won't say that when you see what's inside," Katy answered.

And when Katy opened the box's lid and Mike peered over her shoulder, she was right. "Wow."

The box was filled with weapons. Rifles, pistols, spare magazines. There were enough weapons inside to arm an entire platoon of soldiers.

"Ammunition is in that box," Katy said, pointing to the one next to it. "And the explosives are in the next one. You'll need to wake everybody up and set up stations to load the magazines." Katy tossed Mike the keys to unlock the box and left him the lantern as she headed back toward the cellar's exit.

"Where are you going?" Mike asked.

"To make sure that I don't blow myself up."

* * *

KATY LEFT her brother to deal with something that she knew he could handle. He was a good shooter, and he knew his way around weapons. They used to visit the range together all the time, and it was Mike who had been the first person to really teach her how to shoot.

But times had changed, and Katy had far surpassed her brother in combat skills, and she knew that she would need all of them if they were going to win this thing.

The explosives in the last box in the cellar were remote bombs. She kept the radio detonator in a secondary location, locked away safely in a Faraday Cage.

Because of the uncertainty of an EMP detonation, experts varied on their ideas of just how wide-reaching the effects of a blast would be and what kind of electronics would be affected.

It was due to that uncertainty that Katy had constructed a Faraday Cage. It was a unique metal box that protected electronics against an EMP's destructive power.

Katy entered the house and walked back to her room, weaving around the people that were still passed out on the floor. She would let Mike wake them.

Katy returned to her room and then moved to her closet, removing the box from back behind her winter clothes. It wasn't very large, but Katy didn't have that many items that required the use of a Faraday Cage. Aside from the radio device used for the bombs, she also kept a radio and a very small personal laptop, which held some information that she wasn't sure she even needed anymore, but couldn't bring herself to get rid of. Maybe she could soon, but now wasn't the time to dwell on the past. Her focus needed to be on the present, so they could secure a future.

The detonator in hand, Katy returned the box to the closet and then rejoined her brother in the basement, who had already started loading magazines.

"What's that?" Mike asked.

"For our distraction," Katy answered, and then used her key to unlock the lid.

"I talked to Mom last night," Mike said, blurting out the words.

Katy froze. Between getting ready for this morning and thinking about the fight ahead, she had nearly forgotten all about the conversation that she had with her brother the night before.

"I'm sorry that happened," Mike said. "I didn't expect us to talk, but I needed to know what she knew."

Katy looked back at her brother, half of his face illuminated by the lantern on the ground, the other half cast in shadow. "And did she tell you?"

Mike nodded. "She didn't know what happened until after you were gone."

"Taking her side?" Katy asked.

"No," Mike answered. "I'm on your side. All the way. But she's not doing too well. And before we leave, I think that you should—"

"We don't have time for this, Mike," Katy said, returning to her work. "We have a lot to get done."

She had thought that Mike would still keep talking, but she was glad for his silence. She needed to focus on one terrible thing at a time, and having the kind of conversation with her mother that she needed to wasn't going to help her right now. She needed to stay angry. She needed to stay focused.

* * *

WAKING everyone up before dawn didn't go over well, and it took at least an hour before the kids managed to wake up and help. And they needed all hands on deck.

If the plan was to arm the people in the town to fight back against the enemy that had overpowered them, then they would need to make sure all of Katy's weapons were loaded. It would take all of them.

Mike had seen the enemy up close. They were soldiers, fighters, and they knew how to handle themselves when it came to killing. The average person didn't know how to do those things, so Mike and Katy were both hoping that the sheer size of their armed forces would overwhelm the terrorists.

But both Mike and Katy understood that in the end, they would have to kill. Mike hoped that Katy was still a good shot with that rifle, because if any of the terrorist group managed to escape from their grasp, then they ran the risk of having them run off and tell their friends about what they saw, and that would only bring more of them back.

The threat needed to be eradicated, and it needed to happen soon.

Katy returned from her work and was glad at the

progress everyone had made. "Nothing like getting a jump-start before breakfast."

"Dad, I'm hungry," Casey said. "When will we eat?"

"I'll fix you something when we're done," Lisa answered, her tired mind struggling to finish the mundane tasks of loading magazines.

Mike knew everyone was exhausted. The long day yesterday, coupled with a rough night on a hard floor and an early morning, had made for very slow and tired workers. And if Mike and Katy couldn't pull this off, then things were only going to get worse.

"Hey," Katy said, leaning closer to Mike. "We need to go."

"They're not finished," Mike said.

"We'll take what we have," Katy said. "If this fight drags out, then we've already failed."

Mike knew that she was right, but he didn't want to leave. "Mom is up. I checked on her a little bit ago." He studied Katy's reaction, hoping that she might have changed her mind, but she only walked away. She really was as stubborn as their father.

Mike called time on loading the ammunition, and the kids were dismissed from the table, all of them heading to the sink to wash the dirt and metal from their fingertips. It had been odd watching the children load ammunition.

The old world had died and been replaced by one where his children were forced to wake up before dawn to load ammunition for war, and just two days ago they had been arguing over breakfast about who they thought was the strongest superhero in the Marvel comics.

The people that detonated the EMP did more than just erase their way of life, they had also stolen the innocence of youth. How many children had seen people die in cities all across the country? How many other lives had been altered just by what they had witnessed?

Even if the world returned to the point of normalcy a year from now, the things people will have done and seen in that amount of time would have changed them. The power might come back on, but that wasn't going to erase what happened.

Once everything was collected and piled into Katy's Jeep, Mike said his goodbyes to his family. He kissed his wife, hugged his children, and prayed that he would be able to make it back to them in one piece. He walked over to Nasir and shook his hand. "If something happens to us—"

"I'll make sure that they are safe," Nasir said. "You have my word."

Mike nodded. "Thank you." He kissed his wife one last time before he joined Katy at the Jeep. "Do you want to say goodbye to anyone?"

"No," Katy said, then looked at him. "Now, are you ready for this? Because the only way this is going to work is if both of us are on our A-game. And it's going to be important the fighting is over quickly because while I'll have a good bead on the town from my position, I will also be exposed. The longer it takes for us to end this, the more time the terrorists have to track me down."

Mike had never heard his sister speak like this before. Her entire demeanor had changed, even the features on her face. She looked sharper, angrier, harder. He imagined this was how she looked when she had to go out on a mission in the war.

"I'm ready," Mike said. "I'll be down there until it's done."

"Good," Katy said. "Now hang on. It's going to be bumpy."

25

The Jeep made this trip down the mountain much faster than the day before. They still had to ditch the vehicle a mile away, but it was better than hiking the entire way down with all of their gear.

Mike was afraid that the long day and his short sleep would have made it harder for him to stay alert, but knowing who he was about to face caused a rush of adrenaline and endorphins to flood through him.

When the pair neared the town, it was time for them to go their separate ways, and they paused to go over the plan one last time.

"You're sure that you'll be able to handle this?" Katy said. "Because there is no guarantee the explosions will pull all of the guards away. And remember to find Mark Thompson if people don't want to fight. Hopefully he's still alive." Katy hesitated, studying her brother. Mike could tell she wanted to say something else.

"What?" Mike asked.

"Just know if things get really bad, it's okay to run. Get

back to the cabin and make sure everyone stays safe. The odds of those bastards actually finding you are very, very slim. But I don't want to give them any tips, you know?"

Mike nodded. "Yeah. Be safe."

For a brief moment, Mike saw the hardened face of the soldier disappear, and the return of the young girl Mike remembered playing within their backyard. But it was fleeting, and she returned to her mission expression before she disappeared into the woods without a word.

It hurt him to think that she couldn't be her old self, but Mike knew that what she experienced was far beyond his comprehension or understanding. Katy was a different person now, and that was just something that he needed to accept.

Mike departed on his path and made sure he moved quietly, which was difficult with the number of weapons that he was carrying with him. He felt like Rambo running with all of that hardware.

The sky had lightened up a little when they parked the Jeep, but by the time that Mike put himself into position behind the library in town, it had brightened to morning. Nearly all of the grey sky had been burned away, and the blue was shining through beautifully.

Mike was also close enough to listen to the sounds of the men as they woke up and started their day, and it sickened his stomach when he heard them laugh. There was nothing for those men to laugh about, and Mike's anger boiled. He wanted to annihilate them.

Mike moved as close as he dared without emerging from the cover of the woods, taking note of the pair of guards on constant patrol around the buildings. He hoped Katy's distraction worked because even though he knew he was capable of killing those men, he also knew the enemy wasn't above using the defenseless as human shields.

The day grew hot quickly as Mike waited. He had no watch, and without being able to track the passage of time, it ticked by incredibly slowly. But while he waited, he imagined his route into the building and what he would do.

The back door was his first choice. If that were locked, then he would shoot it down. If that didn't work, then his last resort would be to emerge into the front of the building and onto the town's main street. That wasn't ideal because he didn't want to expose himself.

Once he was inside, he would find Mark Thompson, who Katy said, if he were still alive, would be the man that could rally the troops. From there he would pass out the weapons, making sure that he provided guns to those that could actually shoot first, and then they would join the fight, and if everything went according to plan, then they would win.

Mike was in the middle of going through the plan for the ninth time when the first explosion sounded. It was very loud, very close, and powerful enough to rattle his bones. Gunfire sounded a few seconds later. The fight had begun.

Mike looked to the pair of guards around the library and saw only one of them had gone to join the fighting. He had told his sister that he was ready, and now it was time to prove it.

Mike set the guns aside and then raised one of the rifles to his shoulder. He flicked off the safety, then peered through the three-pronged sight, squinting his left eye shut.

Mike lined up his shot, placed his finger on the trigger, and then exhaled. But the moment he squeezed the trigger, another explosion rocked the area and knocked Mike off-balance, sending his bullet to the left of his target and into the side of the building.

The terrorist immediately glanced toward the woods where Mike had been lying in the shrubs and opened fire.

Mike ducked and then rolled left, bullets zipping past. He reached for the rifle and aimed for the terrorist moving steadily toward him.

Relentless gunfire raining over him, Mike forced his hands steady and brought the shooter into his crosshairs, and then pulled the trigger.

This time the bullet was a direct hit, and Mike's target dropped to the ground. The terrorist's finger still held down the trigger of his rifle and fired a few more spurts into the grass and dirt.

Mike rested his forehead on the cool dirt, taking a moment to collect his thoughts. But he didn't linger on the ground for long, as the sound of more gunfire pulled his attention to the building. Two more gunmen sprinted down either side of the building's alleys. They spied their comrade on the ground, but Mike already had one of them lined up in his sights before they got close and pulled the trigger again, dropping the man on the left. He then quickly pivoted his aim, needing three shots to bring down the man on the right.

Mike lingered on the ground for a moment, catching his breath, but unlike the kills Mike had made before, he noticed his hand was now steadying. It seemed he was getting used to killing.

* * *

KATY SET the explosives all around the northern entrance of the town, knowing that the library was on the south side, in hopes of drawing those forces away from the library and giving Mike the needed buffer to get in and get everyone out.

Katy had positioned herself on the same ridge that she had used to show Mike the town the first day he arrived. The only downside was its exposure. She knew that she would be safe from any rifle or pistol fire, but she would be screwed the moment they used any heavy artillery.

Hopefully, it wouldn't come to that, and the altercation would be over quickly. Once Katy had laid the devices and fortified her position, she reached for the first detonator and pressed the button.

Less than a second later, a plume of dirt and debris erupted from behind Larry's general store, and the alarm sounded. She did her best to make sure that she planted the explosives close enough to cause the enemy concern, but far enough away that she didn't cause any damage to the town itself. If they were going to set all of those people free, then she needed to make sure they all had a place to live. The cabin was crowded enough as it was.

The first explosion worked like a charm, and the cattle came running to inspect the explosion. Katy lined up her first shot and bagged her first casualty, followed quickly by her second and third.

The angle Katy had on the town was good, but it still allowed the insurgents below to duck into the buildings for cover. And while her rifle was powerful, she didn't have enough heavy-caliber of a weapon to penetrate the buildings from this distance. Good thing she had more tricks up her sleeve.

Katy reached for the next detonator and then pressed the button. Again, the device exploded without any interference, but this time there were far fewer insurgents that made their way across the road than before, and Katy only managed to shoot one.

With only one explosive device left, she knew that she wasn't going to have enough to keep them coming. And with the insurgents in the buildings, they had begun to smash the windows and fire at the ridge. Katy ducked, bullets ricocheting off the rocks around her, forcing her back down for the moment. They were too far away to hit her, but now that they knew her location, it wouldn't be long before fighters were sent up the mountain to dispose of her.

"C'mon, Mikey," Katy said. "What the hell is taking so long?"

MIKE REACHED the back door to the library, the bag of guns slung over his shoulder, and he didn't break stride as he shoulder-checked the door. His entire body stiffened from the contact. It was locked. He aimed one of the pistols at the handle and fired.

Three bullets and the lock fell to the wayside, and Mike burst into the room. The inside of the room was pitch black, but there was enough light shining through the open door that he was able to make out a few huddled faces in the darkness.

"It's okay!" Mike shouted, not realizing that he was so loud. The gunfire had made him deaf. "I'm police! I'm here to help!" He lugged the weapons inside, gun still in hand, and the door swung shut behind him, sealing him back into darkness. "Does anyone have a light?"

A few murmurs echoed through the darkness, and then there was a glow from someone's lighter, and Mike got his first good look at the faces inside. It was a mixture of young and old, but all of them wore expressions of fatigue and angst.

"I need to talk to Mark Thompson," Mike said. "Is he here?"

Heads turned toward the front of the building. The shadowy figures parted, and a man emerged from the darkness. He was slightly older than Mike, but his face was marked by a lifetime of work outside. He had short hair, stubble on his face, and his shirt was still tucked in around his jeans. He wore a pair of cowboy boots.

"I'm Mark," he said. "Who the hell are you?"

Mike tossed the bag of guns down onto the floor, the weapons clanging together. "My sister is Katy Thorton. We came to get you out of here. She's the one causing the distraction right now, and we need to relieve her before she's overrun." He glanced to the faces in the darkness, wondering why none of them were jumping at the chance to try and fight back. "We need to hurry!"

"Son," Mark said, his voice calm. "Do you know what they're doing here?"

"It's a supply station," Mike answered. "For the terrorist groups."

Mark shook his head. "This ain't no supply depot. This is a training ground. New recruits are coming in here every day."

Mike shook his head. "No, my sister—"

"Your sister doesn't have the whole story," Mark said. "They probably have another one hundred fighters waiting to come down from the hills and tear us apart. The only reason we're still alive is that they need us for work."

Mike couldn't believe what he was hearing. The people

had given up and accepted their fate, willing to roll over and let this become their new reality. "Are you serious? My sister is on that ridge taking gunfire, and you're just willing to sit back and let her die because you're too scared to fight?" He marched closer to Mark. "You want to be a coward?" He glanced around to everyone else. "All of you want to lie down? Fine." He faced Mark once more. "I'm not going to lie down. I'm not going to let my sister take on this alone." He stepped back over to the circle of guns and picked up his rifle, loading a fresh magazine.

Mike's heart rate had accelerated, brought on by the anger that he felt toward these people, toward the ones that he believed would help them fight. But he was wrong. His sister was wrong too.

"We have families," a woman said. "Children to think of."

"So do I," Mike said. "And that's why I'm doing this. For them."

Mike had hoped the last words stung because he knew that the likelihood of them being able to combat this enemy in the future was close to zero if he couldn't get everyone to band together now, especially if the threat about those recruits were true. They would be overrun. But if they banded together and established a foothold here in the city, then they stood a chance of actually surviving all of this. But they were dead in the water if they didn't act now.

"He's right," Mark said, his voice booming through the crowd. "If we don't take a stand, it's only going to get worse for us, and everyone in the surrounding communities." He walked to the pile of weapons and then picked up a rifle, tucking the stock tight against his shoulder. "We need to fight!"

Mike watched and waited as the others in the crowd

glanced at one another. People were still hesitant, and if that man couldn't get them to buy in, they were done.

But then, one of the members broke from the crowd and picked up one of the rifles. Then another, and then two more, and soon all of the guns Mike had brought were in the hands of the people who needed to carry them.

"We fight!" Mark raised his rifle into the air, igniting a cheer that rivaled the gunfire and screams outside of the library walls. With the power of twenty armed fighters at his back, Mike led the charge into the streets.

As Katy expected, the bulk of the forces had retreated into the buildings, firing from the windows up to the mountainside. Mike couldn't see Katy from his current position, but he heard her. She was still shooting. Still fighting back. Still alive.

Mike glanced behind him, emboldened by the sheer number of people that had joined him. But only time would tell if they would continue to fight once the bullets started flying in their direction. And when they made it halfway down Main Street, the group received their first taste of violence as they entered the fray.

Bullets skipped across the concrete and shattered the windows of the storefronts they passed, and Mike heard a scream as he ducked for cover behind a nearby truck. He looked back and saw one of the men on the pavement, clutching his leg where he'd been shot. And just as Mike feared, the moment that one of their own went down, several stopped in their tracks and retreated to the library.

But a few pressed on, and Mike knew that it was enough to take control of the town. This was still a fight that they could win.

Mark was still with him, and Mike suspected that man

was the only reason that everyone hadn't turned tail and run. He crouched next to Mike behind the truck.

"Can you see where the shooter is?" Mark asked.

Mike duck-walked toward the front of the truck and peered around the grill, scanning the storefronts, but the shooter spotted him, and the front headlight shattered next to his head. Mike veered away and then slunk back by Mark's side.

"I only saw him for a second," Mike said, shouting over the gunfire that was now peppering the truck and slowly transforming it into Swiss Cheese. "But it looked like he was three buildings down on the left."

"What color was the building?" Mark asked.

"Green," Mike answered.

Mark turned to the others. "The shooter's over in Patty's store across the street." He turned to face Mike again. "She has two back doors to her place."

"Do either of them go straight through to the front of the store?" Mike asked.

"One of them is a storage room, but it opens up into the rest of the store through a second door," Mark answered. "The other one is a hallway that leads straight up to the front."

Mike wasn't a fan of the hallway. With the untrained people behind him, it would be a killing alley if the shooter found them. At least with the closet, they would have better cover from the walls and a quicker retreat if necessary. "I need two of the best shooters with me."

Mark and another man volunteered. Mike didn't bother to catch his name.

"Everyone else will lay down cover fire for us when we sprint across the street," Mike said, still shouting above the noise of gunfire. "Stay low and move quickly, and do not stop, no matter what. If someone goes down, we don't have time to go back and get them."

It was a harsh policy, but Mike knew that the longer this dragged out, the more the situation would favor the terrorists.

Mike gathered Mark and their other volunteer near the truck's tailgate and then positioned the other fighters up by the engine. Mike waited to catch their attention, and then counted down from three, two, one— "Now!"

Everyone opened fire, shooting wildly at the front of Patty's store, and while none of them came close to hitting the shooter, they provided the necessary cover fire for Mike and his two volunteers to arrive safely across the street.

Mike slowed once they were down an alley between two buildings, out of harm's way. "Everyone all right?"

Both of them nodded.

"Good," Mike said. "We need to move quickly."

Mike led the trio across the back of the buildings, the bulk of his attention focused on the green-colored building while also being mindful of his peripheral, knowing that a shooter could appear out of thin air.

Mike moved quickly but deliberately, only stopping when he reached the back door to Patty's store. "I go in first, clear the right. Mark, you come in immediately after and clear the left. Then you follow next. Move through the room quickly. Focus your eyes to what you can see at the end of the barrel. If you try to look at everything, you'll miss something. Do not hesitate to shoot. Understand?"

Both men nodded, but Mike sensed their nerves. He didn't blame them. He was nervous too. One mistake was all it took to put you in the ground. And Mike desperately wanted to stay alive.

Mike grabbed hold of the door's handle and then swung it open, moving toward the right quickly, finding no signs of the enemy.

Careful not to knock anything over in the darkness, Mike positioned himself near the second door, listening for the shooter.

With the amount of gunfire that was exchanged and Mike's hearing shot for shit, he struggled to identify whether or not their perp was still in the building. But he knew the longer that they waited in the dark supply room, the worse their odds were of actually catching their guy.

Mike only hoped that the men he'd brought were up to the task and didn't accidentally shoot him in the back.

"Go," Mike said, then ripped open the door, sticking to the same protocol, clearing the right as before. The door opened to behind the counter, and sunlight from the front windows made it easier to see, and Mike spied the shooter moving toward the back of the store.

Mike opened fire, but the quick motion cost him his accuracy, and his two companions were too slow on the trigger. The terrorist was quick to return fire, sending all three of them for cover behind the counter.

Mike remained crouched, waiting for a lull in gunfire. When the lull finally happened, he popped up from behind the counter and saw the figure dart down the hallway, which led to the second exit. "Shit!"

Mike sprinted back through the supply closet, the world transforming from light to dark to light again as he burst onto the browned grass behind the building, which backed up into the woods where he saw the terrorist disappear.

All Mike could think about was that if even one of them got away, then they were all screwed. He turned back to Patty's store just as Mark and the other man emerged from it. "Keep pressing forward and move the others up toward the building. We need to catch them all! No one gets away!"

Mike didn't wait for a response as he darted into the woods, tree branches and leaves swatting and scratching his face. The scratches stung, but he kept his attention focused on the blurred figure to his left, moving quickly down the hillside.

Twice Mike raised the rifle to fire, and twice he missed. His target was moving too quickly, and there was too much foliage blocking his line of sight. He needed a clear path to kill the man.

The hill leveled out, and Mike saw his chance as a stretch of land flattened out for a shallow creek.

The terrorist reached the bottom first and never broke stride as he splashed through the water, lifting his knees high in the middle of river.

The terrorist was out of the water by the time that Mike reached the bottom of the hill, and it was here that he decided to plant his feet and take a shot. He knew that if he missed that he wouldn't be able to catch the guy. But with the clearing ahead, he might have a chance.

Mike took a breath and steadied his aim. The terrorist never stopped running, and Mike pegged the distance at sixty yards and growing, but he took his time, waiting for his shot.

Mike cleared his mind and relaxed his muscles. He watched as the man fell right between the crosshairs, and he squeezed the trigger.

The gunshot rang out for a long time, and everything

slowed down so much that Mike first thought that he had missed.

But then the man's arms spread wide, and he sprawled forward over the dirt and hard gravel, his body skidding forward a half foot before coming to his final resting place.

Mike lowered the scope and then crossed the river. He kept his eyes on the man the entire time, making sure that he wasn't playing dead. But when Mike stood over the terrorist, whose left side of his face was exposed, he knew the man was dead.

Mike had seen enough bodies during his time as a homicide detective to know a dead man when he saw one. And he had seen more than his fair share of death over the past two days, more than he had ever seen during his entire career on the force.

And now Mike was a killer too. He had become the very thing that he had spent his life trying to stop, and it made him feel as though the terrorists had already won.

Mike left the dead man and then jogged back up the hill, listening to the random pops of gunfire. When he finally emerged from the woods, he had to take a moment to get his guard up again. He had suddenly grown tired, and he didn't want to be ambushed.

Mike moved carefully through the alley between the buildings and onto the main street, where he was glad to see that the bulk of the forces had congregated.

But as Mike moved down the sidewalk to join them, he noticed the seven bodies he passed in the streets. Seven civilians. Seven people that had followed Mike and done what he'd asked them to do, and now they were gone.

Mike tried to push the images of their fallen bodies out of his mind once he was past them, but it was hard. And he had a feeling those wouldn't be the last people who died on his orders.

He reached the front back of the group, most of the people with guns huddled safely away from the rest of the pack. Mike figured that most of them had probably hung back during the fighting too. But he said nothing about their cowardice. He pushed his way to the front where Mark stood, looking up to the mountain.

"What happened?" Mike asked.

"We got most of them," Mark answered. "But one of them fired a missile up to those rocks, and then two of them took off after it."

"What?" Mike grabbed Mark's shoulder hard. "How long have they been gone?"

"A few minutes, I guess—Where are you going?"

Mike didn't turn around to explain. If they fired an RPG at his sister, then she might already be dead. And if she weren't, and was either hurt or unconscious, the terrorists would finish her off, unless Mike got to her first.

KATY BREATHED relief when she saw the cavalry sprint down Main Street. She knew that Mike would be able to get them going. He had a way about him. He had been a leader since the day he was born. It was one of the reasons she respected him so much.

For a while, it seemed that it was only a matter of time before the enemy was vanquished, and Katy continued to do her part to keep the enemy pinned down while the others wiped them out from the rear.

But as she was focused on shooting, she missed the RPG

that had been aimed at her. Luckily, it wasn't aimed well. If the projectile had been just a little higher, then the rocks that she ducked behind would have provided zero protection for the following explosion.

The ground rumbled, and dust and debris flew over the top. A sizable chunk of rock landed square on her leg, leaving a nasty gash.

Blood oozed up through the hole in her pants when she took a closer look, and while she didn't think the bone was broken, it might have been bruised. She tried to stand, but the moment she put any pressure on it, her knees buckled, and she collapsed to the ground.

Katy gritted her teeth from the impact. It was like thousands of pieces of glass all scraped the inside of her leg at the same time. It was a crippling, burning pain, and she knew she wouldn't be able to get away fast enough if those bastards decided to charge the hill. So the best thing she could do was continue to shoot.

Katy repositioned herself over the rock ledge, ready to fire when she saw two men sprinting up the hill to her left. They were coming for her.

She quickly set up her rifle, pushing past the pain in her leg, which begged her to stop and just lie still. But she refused to lay down.

Katy tracked the terrorists up the woods, but the trees and shrubbery were thick, giving the enemy good cover. Despite the obstacles that blocked her line of sight, she fired.

The bullet cracked into the base of a tree, protecting the enemy behind it, and both men continued their charge, moving closer.

Katy knew that if the pair of shooters got the high ground on her, then she was as good as dead. She continued to trail the fighters running up the mountainside, and she fired three more shots. All of them missed.

Anger and desperation only worsened her aim, and before she knew it, the gunmen had arrived at the boulders near her, and Katy heard the click of her firing pin.

With only seconds until the gunmen were directly on top of her, Katy ejected her empty magazine and reloaded, the slide racking forward. She then swung the rifle around from where she had it positioned on the rocks and aimed it toward the boulders nearby.

If they were smart, and Katy suspected that they were, one would come high, and the other would come around. The separation would guarantee that at least one of them would get the kill shot because she wouldn't have enough time to realign her weapon to kill the second shooter.

Katy then remembered the grenade that she had kept on her person and realized that if she could get them close enough, then even after she died, she might be able to take them out. It would be her one last act of defiance.

She reached for the grenade on her left side and managed to remove it from her belt with one hand, keeping the other on the trigger finger and her attention on the boulders. She could hear them getting closer, talking to one another, figuring out the best way to kill her. But while they were deliberating, she was using her thumb to remove the pin from the grenade as she squeezed the lever down tightly.

Katy had always wondered how she would die. For a long time, she assumed that it would be from some random accident since she lived alone in the middle of nowhere. But she had hoped that when she died, she would be able to give her life for a purpose. It was what attracted her to join the military. And while that part of her life was over, she found

solace in the fact she would be able to kill the enemy terrorizing the home and country that she loved. If she was going
to die, then this was the way that she wanted it to happen.

The voices grew louder beyond the rocks as the enemy
moved closer. Katy tensed, her muscles humming from the
adrenaline. Her breathing quickened and shortened, but she
kept her wits about her.

Because after they killed her and her strength disappeared, they would come down to inspect the body, only to
be blown apart.

When Katy saw the first terrorist at the top of the boulder, she immediately fired, screaming as she did. The bullet
connected with his shoulder and the man went down. She
tried to pivot toward the next target which emerged at the
same time, but just as she expected, she was too slow on the
draw, and then gunfire rang out.

Katy winced when the gunshot thundered from the
rocks, and she braced for the hot searing pain from the
bullet. But after a few seconds passed and she felt nothing,
she realized that she hadn't been shot, and the terrorist that
had rounded the boulder was dead on the ground.

Katy frowned, still squeezing the lever of the grenade
down tightly, squeezing so hard that her hands hurt.

"Katy?" Mike called out and then appeared from behind
the side of the boulder where the dead terrorist lay. "Are you
all right?"

Katy could only stare at Mike, unable to speak, unable to
move, but then he saw the blood on her leg, and he rushed to
her side.

"You're hurt," Mike said, setting his rifle down and exam-
ining the wound. "Were you shot—"

Katy looked at him as he paused and then followed his

line of sight, and she saw his eyes were locked onto the grenade that was still clutched in her hand.

Katy wasn't sure what he would say, but she hoped that he wouldn't make a bigger deal about it than what it was. And she was glad that he said nothing as he located the pin and carefully placed it back into the grenade, and then peeled Katy's fingers off and set the explosive aside.

Once that was finished, Mike shifted back to the wound on her leg. "Can you stand on it?"

"Not on my own," Katy said.

Carefully, and still, incredibly painfully, Mike helped his sister up to her feet, Mike holding up the bulk of her weight.

"Did we win?" Katy asked.

Mike was quiet for a moment, considering the answer. "Today. Tomorrow is another story."

26

$\mathcal{N}$asir rubbed his eyes as he stepped back inside the cabin after Mike and his sister had gone. The night spent on the floor didn't provide much rest, but he made a point not to complain. He knew how lucky he and his girls were to be taken in by Mike and his family.

If Lisa hadn't shown up when she did and saved him, then Nasir had no doubts that he would be dead, and his girls would be in even worse condition.

The children went back to sleep after the adults left, and Nasir headed to Martha's room to check on the old woman, unsure if she had survived the night. While he had been a good doctor, he wasn't a surgeon, and the woman was old enough to have one foot in the grave.

But Nasir's assumptions were wrong. Martha, like the rest of Mike's family, was a fighter. He changed the bandage on the woman's stitching, checking to make sure that there were no signs of infection, and then replaced her empty IV with a new one.

Once Nasir finished with Martha, he walked into the

kitchen where Lisa was heating the potbelly stove with wood.

"Do you need any help?" Nasir asked.

Lisa kept her back to him as she worked. "No. I'm fine."

English was Nasir's second language, and while he still had an accent from his home country, he spoke the language very well. But he didn't need to understand Lisa's words to understand her tone.

The woman was worried about her husband.

"They're going to be fine," Nasir said. "Both of them are more than capable of handling themselves. Mike went into the city and came back alive, didn't he?"

Lisa set a cast-iron skillet on the small heating space that acted as the stovetop and turned around. "He came back bloodied and exhausted, and I thought we were coming to this place to get away from the enemy." She frowned. "And now we have to fight them? When does it end? When do we get a break?" She spun back around and plucked one of the eggs that had been gathered this morning from the chicken coop.

Nasir was quiet for a moment, unsure of how much he should pry. But Lisa had done him kindness when it was at risk to her own safety. Now it was his turn to repay the favor in whatever small way he could.

"What's happened is unprecedented," Nasir said, remaining calm. "And while the future has always been hard to predict, there is no playbook for what happens next. The best thing we can do is keep an open mind and stay adaptable to our situation. Because all that matters now is to survive, no matter what we have to do to make that happen. But our chances of survival drop when we're distracted. We need to have clear minds."

Lisa didn't crack the egg; instead she kept it in her hands and looked up at Nasir. "It's hard to have a clear head when your husband is heading into a war zone."

"You're a fighter, Lisa," Nasir said. "Fight what you're feeling now and stay strong for everyone else. Because that's what your family needs right now."

The comment about her family softened her stern expression, and Nasir was glad to see that his words reached her heart.

"I'll try," Lisa said.

Nasir smiled and then placed a hand on her shoulder. "That's all any of us can do."

"Daddy?"

Nasir turned to the kitchen's entrance where Khatera and Maisara stood, rubbing the sleep from their eyes, their jet-black hair piled high and messy on their heads.

"We can't sleep anymore."

Nasir smiled. "Well, then I suppose it's time to start our day." He looked at Lisa. "What can we do to help?"

"Well, we'll need more eggs," Lisa answered. "And firewood for the stove."

"We're on it," Nasir said. "C'mon, girls."

Nasir held out his hands and his girls grabbed hold of them. He walked out the back door of the cabin and the sky outside lightened from a pitch black to the dull grey just before dawn. The girls continued to yawn as they walked back to the coop.

Nasir's family had chickens growing up when he was very little, so he knew his way around a coop. But his girls had never seen anything like this before, and he smiled as he watched them giggle as they were afraid to stick their hands into the coop.

"They won't hurt you," Nasir said.

Unable to conquer their fears of the clucking and fluttering hens, Nasir did the work himself but had the girls set the eggs down gently in the basket.

"They're warm," Khatera said.

"That's because they've just been laid this morning," Nasir answered. "And these are good hens. When I was a little boy in Pakistan, our family was lucky if our chickens laid three a day."

"You had chickens, Papa?" Khatera asked, her eyes wide with shock.

Nasir smiled. "I did. And I had to wake up every morning and collect the eggs just like this."

The girls exchanged a look, and then Khatera stepped forward. "Let me try and grab them one more time."

Nasir stepped aside as his oldest daughter walked up to the next cage. She was slow about her work, but steady. And while she winced as she wrapped her fingers around the egg beneath the chicken, she finished the job and pulled it all the way out.

"Very good, Khatera," Nasir said.

Khatera turned to her younger sister, acting as though nothing about the process had ever bothered her before. "See, Maisara? It's not scary."

Maisara plucked the egg from her sister's hand and examined the evidence, unsure if she believed her older sister. Of the two, Maisara was always the more skeptical, and looking at her now, she was more adult than six years old. "I don't know."

Nasir smiled, and he was about to tell his youngest girl that there was nothing to be afraid of when a scream echoed through the cabin, turning his attention toward it.

Both of his girls immediately clung to his legs, Maisara dropping the egg. It splattered on the ground.

Nasir's first instinct was to run inside, but he knew that if there was trouble there, then he couldn't bring his girls into it. He quickly squatted and grabbed both of them, looking them in the eyes. "I want you to run and hide in the woods, do you understand?"

The girls nodded, and Nasir placed their hands together.

"You hide, and you stay hidden until I come and get you or until everyone in the cabin is gone, do you understand?" Again the girls nodded, and Nasir spun them around and pushed them toward the woods. "Go!"

Nasir watched them disappear into the foliage and another scream pierced through the cabin, this one followed by a harsh thud. Nasir shuddered. He turned around, looking for anything that he could use as a weapon, and realized that all of the guns were inside.

The only thing that he found was the logs of wood that had been stacked for the stove, so he picked one up as he sprinted back into the cabin. For a moment he was blinded by the darkness inside and the sheer rush of adrenaline that was coursing through his body, but when he reached the living room, his vision had finally adjusted, and he froze in his tracks.

A man was in the living room, and Lisa was unconscious on the floor. The man had a gun in his hand, and he was aiming it at Lisa's children.

"Hello there," the man said, his voice eerily calm and unsettling. "You must be Nasir. I heard quite a bit about you back in the neighborhood."

Nasir couldn't see the man's face very well since the lighting was bad in the room, but there was something strange about him that he couldn't place. It was almost as if he had seen the man before. "What do you want?"

The man arched his eyebrows and smiled. "What do I want? Interesting." He stepped closer to the kids, who were clutching one another in the corner of the room, the older girl protecting her brother. "Not who am I? Wouldn't that be more pertinent to the situation?"

"Depends on what you want," Nasir answered.

The man laughed, his voice surprisingly playful, even though he had just knocked a woman unconscious and was currently holding two children hostage.

"You're smart," he said. "I can see why those rednecks didn't like you."

Nasir frowned. "You were at our home?"

"The detective's home," he answered. "Looking for him and his family. I came a very long way to find him. And now I'm finally here."

Nasir shook his head, confused. "What do you want with Mike and his family?" He thought that maybe this was a man Mike had wronged when he was in the city. But it seemed strange for a man to track someone down over something that happened in the heat of the moment.

"You keep staring at me like you know me," the man said.

It was true. Nasir hadn't been able to take his eyes off the man, but he thought that maybe it was more than just something petty. To come here like this... it was bigger.

"I've always had one of those faces," the man said, enjoying the fact that he was able to keep Nasir off-balance. "It was one of the reasons I was so hard to catch."

And then the realization went off in Nasir's mind like a lightbulb, and he pointed at the intruder. "You're Melvin Harris. You're the man who murdered all of those people."

Melvin smiled and spread his arms wide. "The one and only. And I have to say that I'm impressed that you've figured it out. I can't tell you how many people I killed along the way that thought I was an actual detective." He glanced down to the badge still clipped onto his belt. "The law goes a long way when people are in trouble."

Nasir glanced back down to Lisa. He couldn't tell if she was breathing or not, but he saw the blood on her scalp where she'd been hit. "You should let me help her."

"No," Melvin said. "That's not what I want you to do." He kept the gun aimed at the kids but walked closer to Nasir. "What I want you to do is call your girls in from the back."

Nasir's body hollowed out. "I don't have any girls."

Melvin shook his head, clucking his tongue in that tsk-tsk manner Nasir remembered his teachers doing in grammar school. "I've been watching you for the past twelve hours. I know everyone in this house. So why don't you save us all some trouble, and go and bring them inside."

Nasir froze. He knew that he couldn't bring his girls in here and expose them to this mad man, but he knew that if he didn't get them, then he would die, and he had no idea if there would be anyone left to help them after he was gone.

"Nasir," Melvin said. "You're wasting time. And I don't like to waste my time."

"I don't know what you saw," Nasir said. "But these children are the only people here. And Mike will be coming back with more people."

"More people?" Melvin raised his eyebrows in surprise, then glanced around the inside of the cabin. "I don't think you have the room for more people. You want to know what I think?" He stepped closer, and Nasir saw that Melvin's finger was on the pistol's trigger. "I think that the detective and his sister went down to that town to try and save people. And in doing so, he left the people that he cares about most in this world vulnerable to attack." He smiled, and it was all teeth. "And do you know what I excel at, Nasir? Exploiting those vulnerabilities. There is no one better than me at getting to the heart of what people love, and then turning it against them." He gave Nasir a hard look from head to toe and then locked his piercing gaze with Nasir's eyes. "But I don't need you to complete my plan. And if you want to leave your girls out in the wilderness to die, then so be it. Because after I'm finished having my fun with the detective's family, I'm going to hunt down your little girls and have my fun with them."

Nasir lunged for the weapon in Melvin's hand, and he saw the surprise in Melvin's eyes from the sudden act of aggression. The man hadn't expected it, and Nasir hadn't planned on it, but hearing that monster talk about what he would do to his daughters triggered a reaction.

The pair grappled for the gun, and despite Nasir having the height advantage, Melvin was surprisingly strong for a smaller man.

"Run, kids!" Nasir yelled to Kelly and Casey, and Kelly quickly led her younger brother outside.

"No!" Melvin screamed, baring his teeth like a rabid dog, and then focused all that anger on turning the weapon in their hands back to him. And no matter how hard that Nasir tried to resist, he felt his strength leaving him.

But despite how frightened Nasir was of his life ending, he found solace that his final thoughts were of his daughters. He could see their smiling faces and hear their joyful laughter, and he prayed that even though he had failed, they would survive.

Those thoughts filled his mind until Melvin pressed the barrel of the pistol against Nasir's stomach and pulled the trigger.

* * *

THE GUN JOLTED VIOLENTLY in Melvin's hand, but the moment it fired Nasir's resistance ended, and he dropped to the floor, gasping and shaking the way every person did when their life was about to end.

And while Melvin always enjoyed savoring his kills, he chased after the detective's children. He couldn't believe he had let his guard down like that, and he couldn't believe he had misread the brown bastard's intentions. Melvin had always prided himself on being able to see everything before it actually happened.

It was the fatigue from the night before, that was all. He was just a little tired. But now he was wired and ready to reclaim what he had lost.

Melvin burst out of the front door and then paused to survey the area. He caught his breath and then tried to put himself in the shoes of the children that had sprinted away from him. He walked down the front porch steps, scanning the trees that surrounded the cabin.

The sun was getting higher in the sky, and Melvin knew that the longer it took him to find the little runts, the less time he would have to put together his game for the detective.

The porch steps groaned as Melvin walked down them, his eyes locked onto the forest. He needed to find the children quickly. But where would they go?

Heading down to the town to find their father perhaps?

No. If they were the detective's children, then they would want to stay close, keep an eye on their mother. Would they split up? Also unlikely. They would stay together, so they could take care of one another.

Melvin stopped when he reached the bottom of the stairs, squinting as he tried to narrow down the children's options. "Where oh where would I be if I was trying to still help my mother?" He took three steps forward out onto the dirt and grass and then stopped again, listening as much as he was looking, and then paused when he heard the snap of a twig on his right.

Melvin smiled as he slowly turned toward the noise. It had come from behind a cluster of bushes, and the moment he started moving toward them, they rustled, and he fired his gun, freezing the children in place before they managed to escape.

"That'll be far enough if you don't want me to put a bullet through your mother's skull!" Melvin shouted and then watched as the children turned to look at him. The threat had worked. "Now, why don't you two be the good little children that I know you are and come back over here to me." Melvin used the gun to wave them to him.

The young boy clung to his older sister's leg, and she led the pair of them toward Melvin. They looked like scared little dogs, but the older girl had that unabashed bravery that only someone who didn't understand the gravity of their situation could hold. But that would change soon enough.

Once both the boy and the girl were directly in front of Melvin, each of them within arm's reach, he smiled.

"Good," Melvin said. "Now, isn't this better?"

The older sibling, the girl that possessed that unabashed courage, snarled. "My father is coming back. Soon. And he'll be bringing my aunt, and she was in the military, and she knows how to kill people."

"A commonalty your aunt and I share." Melvin chuckled. "You really are like your father, aren't you. But you have your mother's looks. I imagine you're starting to get some attention from the boys at school."

The girl blushed and then finally broke eye contact with him.

"It's nothing to be ashamed about," Melvin said, then used the barrel of the pistol to gently push back some of the hair that blocked her face. "Girls dream about that kind of attention." He sighed and then lifted her chin with the tip of the pistol's barrel. "And today you're going to have my attention." He looked down to the boy. "And yours as well." He removed the pistol from her face, and then stepped backward, still aiming the weapon at her. "As for your father and your aunt coming back, that works fine with me. Because we're all going to play a game together. You won't find it very fun. But I will. I will enjoy it very, very much."

27

*W*hen the body count was finished, Mike confirmed all of the terrorists were dead. None of them escaped to alert any of their comrades. They piled their bodies off to the side of the street and then set them on fire, standing upwind of the smoke.

The smell was bad, but no one wanted to waste time and exertion to bury the enemy, and the easiest way to get rid of the bodies was by fire. The only person opposed to the plan had been Katy because she knew that a fire would attract attention.

But what Katy failed to realize was that even though people could be dangerous, they could also be a resource. And they had gained several valuable resources through the rescue of the town.

Three of the townsfolk had farms, all of whom agreed to continue to work the land and help feed the community. Two more were engineers. Another was a soldier. And they had several folks with trade skills that would be important in getting the town back up and running again.

"Thank you again for your help," Mark said, shaking Mike's hand.

"Fight's not over," Katy said, joining the conversation from the back of the truck tailgate, where a nurse was helping to fix up her leg. Far as they could tell the bone wasn't broken, but the cut needed stitches. "Those recruits that the terrorists were training will be coming back any day now. And they won't like what you've done with the place."

"She's right," Mike said. "You'll need to fortify your defenses and put those guns to good use."

Mark raised his eyebrows. "You're letting us keep them?"

"Consider it a loan." Katy winced when the nurse threaded the needle through the skin.

"The best thing for you to do right now is set up guards," Mike said. "Twenty-four-hour patrols. You don't want to be caught with your pants down. We might be able to help you set up some alert devices for you to throw the enemy off-guard. But I need to get my sister back up to the cabin for that. And I was hoping to ask for a few volunteers to help me get her back up there."

"I don't need help—GAH!" Katy bared her teeth and then leaned back as the nurse continued her stitch work.

"Let her finish, Katy," Mike said. "And stop squirming. She's doing you a favor."

The nurse kept her attention focused on Katy, but didn't mince words when she finally spoke up. "I'll consider us even after this."

Mike turned to Mark. "Once we return to the cabin and rest, we'll return for a formal meeting."

"I think that's a good idea," Mark said, and then lowered his voice so that Katy couldn't hear. "Do you mind if I talk to you in private for a moment?"

Mike didn't object and followed Mark to the front lobby of the hardware store, which had taken the brunt force of the fighting.

"Mike, I don't think there is anyone in this town that doesn't appreciate what you and your sister did today," Mark said. "Without those weapons, and without your sister's distraction, we wouldn't have survived for much longer."

Mike crossed his arms over his chest. "I'm sensing a 'but' coming."

Mark looked out the window to where Katy was still stationed on the truck bed. "It's just that we've known your sister for a long time. And while she was helpful today, that hasn't always been the case."

"What do you mean?" Mike asked.

"More than a few altercations have occurred between her and some of the townsfolk that have, by mistake, wandered onto her property," Mark answered. "She even put one man in the hospital."

"When did that happen?" Mike asked.

"A few months ago," Mark replied. "He ended up being fine, but it definitely put a sour taste in everyone's mouth about her. And while I believe what she did today went a very long way to help erase some people's doubts about her, I don't know if everyone is convinced she's turned over a new leaf."

Mike considered his response. The last thing he wanted to do was alienate a man who was considered a leader amongst the townspeople and whose sway he needed if things were going to work out long-term. But he also didn't want to roll over at the first sign of trouble.

"I can understand those concerns," Mike said. "But if you're telling me that people can't handle getting their feelings hurt after breaking the law, and trespassing is breaking the law, then I don't have a problem taking back those guns."

Mark held up his hands. "Don't shoot the messenger."

"I'm not," Mike said. "But I hope that messenger can get everyone else in this town on board with working together. Because if this place really was a training ground and the enemy comes back, we're going to need everyone to fight."

It was his first taste of politics and Mike didn't enjoy it, but based off of Mark's complicit reaction, he thought he performed the job well enough.

"I'll spread the good word," Mark said.

The conversation ended when the pair shook hands, and then they rejoined everyone in the street. The nurse had finished Katy's stitches, and two men agreed to help carry Katy back up the mountain. And while she put up a fight at first, Mike was able to convince her to accept help from at least one of the men.

After a few more goodbyes, the trio departed and started their long trek up the mountain. Katy was quiet along the way, but Mike knew he would need to address the elephant in the room about Katy's relationship with the rest of the town. It wouldn't be a pleasant conversation, but it was necessary. However, until they reached the cabin, Mike was going to enjoy the victory because he wasn't sure how many they would have in the coming days.

28

*G*rowing up, Melvin had always heard people say that crime was the easy way out, but after making a career of killing people, he would have to respectfully disagree. Because after he incapacitated the detective's family, he then had to drag each of them into the woods to his desired location, and then restrain them.

It was five very long trips over terrain that wasn't easy to navigate alone, let alone carrying another person. But he managed to put everyone in their place, and he saved the wife for last.

Melvin returned to the pit with its high walls, dropping Lisa in the dirt. She hit the ground hard, and she stirred a little bit, but Melvin didn't care if she woke up, she was bound and gagged.

The woman could squirm and scream to her heart's content, but she was going to stay exactly where she was.

"Good morning, Mrs. Thorton," Melvin said, staring down at the dried blood on her head from where he struck her. It was just a flesh wound, one that she would recover from. "We didn't formally meet earlier."

Melvin purposefully stuck out his hand and then laughed as he withdrew it. "Sorry. I forgot about your hands being stuck behind your back."

The detective's wife grew very still the longer that she stared at Melvin, and he became completely giddy when she looked at him.

"I know that look," Melvin said, wagging his finger at her as if she had done something naughty. "I saw it earlier today when I killed Nasir."

Lisa whimpered.

"Now, now, now," Melvin said as he knelt by Lisa's side. "I know that you're worried about your family. You're a good mother. And a good mother worries." The smile melted from his face, his expression going slack. "My mother wasn't a good mother." He glanced off into the woods, briefly lost in the memories of his youth.

But when Melvin returned his gaze to Lisa, he suddenly realized that he had never spoken to anyone about his upbringing. All of the lawyers and experts that interviewed him after he was caught had tried to get him to open up, but he wasn't interested in talking to them.

Most of them were nothing more than academics who had never done any real work in their entire lives. But Melvin had done what most people only study in books and photographs. And if Melvin had one weakness, it was his affinity to attempt to connect to people that he never had in his own life. Such as a good mother. But he had one here and now, right in front of him, and it seemed a shame to let it go to waste.

Melvin sat down, sitting cross-legged style, and grabbed

hold of his ankles. "When I was a little boy, my mother never seemed to care about what I did. She would just let me wander off. In fact, the only times that she actually spoke to me were when she needed me to head down to the gas station to get her more smokes." He laughed, but Lisa only stared at him with the same look of horror that she had worn from earlier. "I bet you never made your children do something like that. I bet your children knew exactly how much you loved them." He smiled and then brushed her hair back behind her ear, and he felt her shudder from his touch. "Oh, I know that you might be worried about what I might have done to your children, but I can tell you that I didn't hit them too hard, just enough to make sure they stayed asleep until I needed to get them where I wanted them."

Again Lisa whimpered into the gag.

"I understand it's hard for a good mother not to worry," Melvin said. "But if your husband is half the man that I think he is, then we should have quite a fun day ahead for ourselves."

Melvin continued to brush his fingers through her hair. "I can see why he loves you so fiercely, your husband. I've never been the kind to engage in our more primal instincts." He winked at her, then chuckled. "It just never really interested me. But killing?" He nodded. "Oh, that had me hooked from an early age. Do you know the first thing I killed? My neighbor's dog. It was a monstrous beast. The damn thing kept barking all hours of the night, making our entire family even more irritable than normal. But as annoying as it was, that wasn't the reason why I killed it. I killed it because I thought it would make my mother happy. I thought that maybe, just maybe, if the dog stopped barking, she might take a look at me, say something nice." He frowned. "But she didn't even notice. She was too drunk to notice. Just like she was too drunk to notice me or the fact that she was in a terrible relationship." He sighed and shook his head. "Anyway. What I wanted to ask you was this—" He paused and leaned closer, almost pressing his nose against Lisa's. "If you could give your life to save your children? Would you?"

Lisa couldn't stop shaking, and with the gag in her mouth, she couldn't speak, but she slowly nodded.

"Look at that," Melvin said. "A good woman, good mother, good wife. You know, a lot of people think that I might not have turned out this way if I would have had a mother like you, and a father like the detective. But do you want to know the sad truth?" Again he leaned closer, but there was no smile on his face, and his eyes darkened as he moved closer. "I would have gutted the both of you while you slept, let your blood mix together and congeal on the bed. And then I would have stood there and smiled until you finally bled out, saying absolutely nothing as you wondered why your sweet son would have done such a thing."

Lisa started to cry now, and her trembling became uncontrollable.

"Because killing is who I am down to my very core," Melvin said. "And when your husband caught me, he did something I never thought was possible. He made me feel mortal. And now that's what I'm going to do to him. By leaving a trail of bodies comprised of his family until they're all gone, and he's as alone as I am." He smiled. "We're going to have a wonderful time."

29

By the time they neared Katy's cabin at the top of the ridge, Katy had insisted she make the rest of the trip alone. She didn't want to give away the exact location of her cabin and turned their helper back down the mountain. While she managed to walk on her own, she still had a limp.

"You're too stubborn for your own good," Mike said.

"Stubborn has kept me alive more times than it's tried to kill me," Katy replied. "I'll stick with stubborn for the foreseeable future."

Mike reached for his sister's arm and forced her to stop. He made sure to look her in the eye when he spoke because he wanted this message to resonate with her. "I know that you've made it on your own for a long time, but things have changed. If we're going to survive, we'll need to make alliances with people who we might normally not speak with, because people are going to be just as valuable a resource as food and water."

"I know that you think I don't need people, Mike," Katy

said. "I've crafted an image around it. But I understand what you want. I understand what else is out there and that my world is getting bigger, whether I like it or not. That was inevitable the moment that you showed up with your family."

Mike studied his sister carefully, unsure of where she was heading with her thoughts.

"And I don't have a problem playing nice," Katy said. "If we need to make a few compromises to ensure that our lives are a little more comfortable, then so be it." Katy stepped forward, and this time Mike noticed the intensity in her eyes. "But everyone always has some ulterior motive. And when push comes to shove, even with all of the new friends we're making, I can tell you that it's always going to come down to us. We can only trust each other. And I want to make sure that you understand that."

"I do," Mike said. "And we'll cross that bridge when we come to it. But for the time being, we extend a little bit of trust and faith to the people outside of our own circle. Deal?"

Katy considered it a moment longer than Mike would have liked, but she finally agreed. "I'll follow your lead on that one."

The rest of the trip to the cabin was made in silence, both of them tired from the fight and the journey up and down the mountain.

But when they approached the clearing to the cabin, Katy held up her hand for Mike to stop. He saw the concern on her face and was immediately worried.

"What?" Mike asked, speaking quietly.

"Listen," Katy answered.

Mike tried to concentrate, listening for whatever Katy had heard. "I don't hear anything."

"I know," Katy said. "I don't either."

The pair exchanged a glance, and both of them drew their weapons. Katy paused at the edge of the clearing and studied the cabin. Mike took a knee right next to her and then waited.

"What is it?" Mike asked.

"I don't know yet," Katy answered. "But something's wrong. The front door is wide open, and I don't see anyone."

Mike stepped from the cover of the forest, gun up, and moved swiftly toward the cabin. Katy reached to stop him, but she missed, and then joined her brother's advance.

Mike quickly ascended the porch steps and entered the cabin without hesitation where he saw Nasir on the floor, surrounded by a puddle of his own blood.

Mike knew that the man was dead, and he didn't stop to check as he moved past him and into the bedrooms, which were all empty. Even his mother was gone.

With the cabin cleared, Mike rushed past his sister and stumbled back outside. The sun, the situation, the heat, his own exhaustion, all of it had combined to overwhelm him, and Mike couldn't prevent his knees from buckling as he landed hard in the dirt.

How did this happen? They had killed all of the terrorists in town, they had made sure of that. Were there others Katy didn't know about?

Mike sat there in the dirt, unable to find answers until Katy placed a hand on his shoulder. He flinched from her touch. He shut his eyes and tried to think.

"Only one body," Mike said, then opened his eyes. "Whoever attacked the cabin must have killed Nasir and taken the others."

Mike stood, then turned to his sister. "Search the woods.

See if you can find any trails of where they might have gone and how many people might have been here."

Katy nodded. "What are you going to do?"

Mike glanced to the cabin. "Work the crime scene."

The pair separated, and Mike returned to the living room where Nasir lay slaughtered and forced himself to think like a detective. But Mike had never been so attached to a case like this before. This was new territory, and he wasn't sure how it would affect him. Mike drew three deep breaths and then examined Nasir's body.

Cause of death was a gunshot wound to the stomach. Mike searched for a shell casing and found it nearby. It wasn't necessary, but Mike still picked up the casing with a piece of cloth so his fingerprints wouldn't be on it. He knew that he wouldn't have forensics backing him up. There was no lab to send evidence to. No DNA match. No hair fiber or blood splatter analysis. All he had to go off on was the small bits of crumbs that had been left behind.

Mike stood and then stepped back for a moment, trying to get a look at the bigger picture. He studied the area in grids, searching for anything that the killer might have left behind, searching for any other sign of struggle.

Mike found a few drops of blood that were separate and far enough away from where Nasir lay that it suggested that it was from another person. But whether it was from his own family or from the perp, he couldn't be sure.

But the small amounts of blood suggested that the wound was small, and could have been the cause of blunt force trauma. He studied the floor more closely and saw drag marks through the dust and dirt along the cabin floor, leading to the front door.

Mike walked to the bedroom where his mother had been

sleeping. The sheets were messy and ruffled, but again he found no blood. Her IV and medications had been left behind.

Mike glanced down at the shell casing in his hand and stared at the small piece of brass. There was something familiar about it, and then he realized it was a .45 ACP round. The same caliber pistol used by most detectives.

Unsure of why Mike thought that information important, he left the bedroom and returned to the living room. He stood there, staring at Nasir's fallen body, and then looked to the open door. Someone had been in a hurry to get everyone out. And if Nasir put up a fight, the children might have had time to make a run for it. Maybe even got away.

Mike stepped out of the cabin, walked down the steps to the grass, and studied the tree line which circled the cabin. If someone had sprinted from the cabin to escape trouble, then they would have run straight ahead.

Mike walked the path that he believed someone would have taken under the duress of a life-or-death situation, and he studied the ground, searching for any more clues. He found nothing until he reached the tree line and found more drops of blood on leaves.

The amount was small and looked like it could have only come from scrapes or bruises. Mike noticed that the brush around the area had been trampled down, almost as if someone fell, or had been pushed. He studied the ground a little closer and saw the digs in the dirt made from heels and a few more droplets of blood, the amounts matching the same kind of blunt-force style trauma as the drops he saw inside.

"Who would have done something like this?" Mike

asked, speaking aloud to himself. The forest remained silent, his only witness to the crime. And that's what this was, a crime.

Something about that fact bothered him, and he couldn't quite place why it did. He glanced down to the shell casing still in his hand and found that it was the same kind of question that was bothering him here too.

A cop's gun. A murderer. Struggle. Fear. This was a premeditated crime. It wasn't born out of some reaction. Someone had watched the cabin. This had been planned. It was the only way that someone would have been able to keep that number of people contained without killing every last one of them.

Up until now, all of the crime that Mike had witnessed had come from a purely impulsive nature. It had come from panic and desperation. But the way that his family had been hunted down and clubbed and then dragged away revealed the outlines of a plan.

But a plan to do what?

"Mike!" Katy shouted, her voice coming from somewhere behind the cabin. "Mike, get over here!"

Mike sprinted away, following his sister's voice to the back of the cabin. He spied her through the trees. She was standing up, looking down at something on the ground, and his heart skipped a beat as he passed the chicken coop and then weaved around the trees.

All Mike could think of was that Katy had found Casey or Kelly, or Lisa, dead on the ground, shot and killed like Nasir had been. But he slowed when he saw what she had found. It was Nasir's daughters. And they were alive.

The girls were holding onto one another, both of them covered in leaves and dirt, and they had tucked themselves into a small hole barely big enough to keep both of them together.

"They have been silent as church mice," Katy said.

Mike knelt and extended his hand to Nasir's oldest daughter. "It's okay, girls. You're safe now."

Khatera, the oldest, regarded Mike with skeptical eyes, but she eventually reached for his hand, and both girls came out of their tiny hole. They remained close to one another, never letting go of each other's hands as they stood before Mike, staring at the ground.

"Girls," Mike said, doing his best to keep his voice steady. "Did you see what happened?"

Neither spoke, but then after a stretch of silence, it was Khatera who finally shook her head.

Mike exhaled. If they didn't see who came, then there was a chance that they didn't see what happened to their father. "How did you get outside?"

"We were helping Father with the chickens," Khatera answered. "And then we heard a scream, and Father told us to run into the woods and hide."

Mike was careful not to push for more answers too quickly. He knew that both of them were still frightened. "Did your father tell you anything else? Did you try to go into the cabin to look for him?"

They shook their heads.

Mike stood, relieved that they hadn't found their father in a pool of his own blood, and then motioned for Katy to step away. Once they were out of earshot from the kids, Mike spoke.

"We need to get the body out of the cabin," Mike said. "Bury him, cover him up, just something to make sure that the girls don't see him."

"Right," Katy said.

"Did you find anything else?" Mike asked.

"There were at least three other trails I found, each of them breaking off into a different direction of the woods. The one I found leading here was the first one where I actually found someone. So we could be dealing with multiple individuals."

Mike frowned. "I don't think so."

"Why would you say that?"

"Because the crime scene was too neat," Mike said. "If there were more than one person involved in this, then the scene would have looked more like an ambush. There was time for some of them to try and get away. I think this was the work of one person."

"All right," Katy said. "So we get rid of the body in the cabin and then head out to find the others."

"No, not we, just me," Mike said.

"Mike, you can't track worth shit," Katy said.

Mike knew that she was right. If he wandered out into the woods alone, then he'd only get lost or worse. He couldn't find his family without her. "We can't leave the girls here alone."

"I might have a solution for that." Katy led him and Nasir's daughters into the cellar. Mike hadn't noticed anything peculiar on his previous visit down there, so at first, he thought that she was just going to dump them in the cellar, but then she led him back to where the weapons room was located and moved to the far right wall.

The walls inside the cellar had been coated over with wood paneling. Mike watched as Katy carefully felt along the end of one of the pieces of wood and then pulled back. Only a section of the wood broke away, and it revealed a door handle. She inserted a key, unlocked it, and then pulled the door open, exposing an entire section of the wall.

Inside was a concrete room with more supplies, a bed, and other small items and a few battery-powered lights. Katy looked back at her brother, the girls standing next to him. "They'll be safe in there. It's soundproof, so even if they make some noise, no one will be able to hear them. And if we don't make it back, there is a release valve so they can let themselves out."

Mike nodded and then looked at the girls. Both of them looked scared to enter, but he coaxed them in and then had them take a seat on the edge of the cot. "My sister and I are going to leave, but we're going to come right back."

"What about Dad?" Khatera asked.

Mike knew that he would have to tell the girls the truth eventually, but he didn't think it was best to let them be so terrified about it now. "We'll talk about your dad when I get back, okay?"

The girls simply lowered their gazes and stared at the tips of their shoes. Mike showed them the food and water that they could eat, and the small bucket toilet in case they needed to go to the bathroom. Neither of them said a word.

And as Katy shut the door to the safe room and then locked both of them inside, Mike couldn't help but feel that this was a mistake. But he had entered a world where there were no easy choices, and he needed to find his family before they ended up like Nasir, covered by a tarp on the side of the cabin.

30

*U*nsure of how long they would be gone, Katy made sure that both she and Mike packed enough supplies to keep them alive for at least seventy-two hours should they go missing or become incapacitated. Mike loaded more magazines with ammunition.

Once they were both geared up, Katy took some medicine to help manage the pain in her leg, and they departed for the northernmost trail Katy had found.

Mike had gone on manhunts before, but this was his first time without wearing a badge. His shield had always given him purpose and rules. But the rules had changed, and as difficult as it was for him to admit it, he needed to change too.

"You're awfully quiet," Katy said.

"I thought the point of hunting was to make as little noise as possible."

"Usually. But right now we're alone." Katy glanced behind her. "Are you all right?"

"Tired, but other than that, I'm fine."

Katy stopped and turned around, holding most of her weight on her good leg. "You never were a good liar, brother."

Mike's voice hardened. "It's nothing."

Katy placed her hand on his shoulder, her touch comforting and strong. "I'm sorry, Mike. I am. I don't know what you're going through, but I do know that if you can't keep a cool head through all of this, then it might be best if you head back to the cabin and look after the girls."

It was the first time in their sibling relationship where Mike felt like the younger kid. He was the one who was supposed to be the person that people leaned on. It was a role that he had adopted at a very young age, and it was something that he always believed was his duty to uphold. But he always told his kids to never be afraid to ask for help. And right now, he needed help.

"I don't know what I'll do if something happens to them —" Mike's voice cracked and he bowed his head and wiped at the sweat and tears that stung his eyes. "But I have to do this. No matter what."

Katy leaned closer, setting her weapon aside, and then brought her brother in her arms. The pair stayed like that for a moment, Mike thankful for what family remained to him.

"We'll find them," Katy said. "We will bring them home. All of them."

Mike nodded and then took another deep breath as he pulled back from his sister. His face was red and wet, his eyes glassy. But he felt better. He had been keeping so many things bottled up for so long that he didn't realize how much he needed a release.

"Thank you," Mike said. "For being here. For helping."

"You're my brother," Katy said. "You're the only one that

I've ever been able to count on. It's about time that I returned the favor."

Mike watched as Katy followed the trail, tracking them through the middle of the forest. He was amazed at what she was able to notice because it was just the smallest of details that gave away a break in a trail and veered them into a new direction.

The farther north they walked, the rockier the terrain became, and Katy finally stopped.

"What's wrong?" Mike asked.

"Trail's breaking up," Katy answered, and then pointed ahead. "I know of some cave systems up here. They might be inside, along with some other things."

"Animals?" Mike asked.

"Could be," Katy answered. "Bears, mountain lions."

Mike glanced ahead, studying the terrain. Between the massive rocks and sharp turns and the fact that they would have low ground, it was the perfect place for an ambush. "Any possibility we took a wrong turn?"

"Nope," Katy answered, still studying the ground. "The tracks don't double back. Whoever was brought up here decided to stay." She adjusted the weapon in her hand, readying herself for an attack. "We take it slow. Keep it quiet."

Mike followed his sister up the rockier terrain, careful where he placed his boots. The ground was precariously uneven, and one slip or wrong move here and he would most certainly break bones.

The movement was slower up the rocks, and it was interesting for Mike to see how his sister reacted in the field. She had gone full military mode, and Mike was glad to have her on his side because while he had been in tense situations before and he was no stranger to life-or-death scenarios, this was new terrain.

Katy neared the mouth of the cave and then held up her hand for Mike to stop. She crouched low, gun aimed into the darkness, and waited.

The sun burned hot against the blue sky, the heat beating down on both of them. Mike and Katy remained silent and still for a long time, and just when Mike's legs were starting to cramp up from the crouched position, Katy squat-walked in reverse until she was right next to him.

"I think someone is inside," Katy said.

Mike frowned, staring deeper into the darkness. If that was true, and it was an enemy, there wasn't any reason for them not to come out firing and shooting them as quickly as possible. "Are you sure?"

Katy tilted her head from side to side. "Fifty percent."

Mike paused to consider the situation for a moment. "Are they alive?"

Katy froze. "I don't know."

"So what do we do?"

Katy considered the question for a moment, and then finally nodded. "We go in. I'll take the lead, you watch my six, make sure no one sneaks up from behind us and tries to bite us in the ass. I don't think that'll happen, but you never know for sure."

Mike nodded. "Lights?" He knew that the flashlights would grant them better vision inside, but it would also alert any threat to their presence.

"If we go deep enough," Katy answered. "Just follow my lead. Mine goes on, then yours goes on."

"Got it," Mike said.

Katy moved forward first, and then Mike followed,

staying on her tail like a shadow. They stepped over the crest of the cave and then entered the darkness. The sunlight, so bright and so hot, vanished the moment they penetrated the cave.

The dark cavern was cool, and Katy only made it a dozen steps before she finally flicked on her light, and Mike followed her lead. Their beams penetrated the darkness, exposing the rough cavern walls and low ceilings.

Both of them had to hunch forward as they moved deeper through the caves, but the farther they traveled and found nothing, the more Mike worried they had entered a dead end. Still, he kept quiet, knowing that his voice would echo all through the caverns, giving away their position.

Finally, Katy held up her hand, forcing Mike to stop, and then shone her light on the rocky ground. A footprint. Clear as day. Someone was inside.

They continued forward, the caves veering left and right, growing smaller, and then opening up into larger spaces where they could stand fully upright. With all of the twist and turns, Mike wasn't sure he would be able to find his way back, but he was confident Katy could lead them out.

When they entered another large chamber of the cave system, they heard a crash of rocks to their left, and both Katy and Mike swung their weapons and lights in the direction, finding nothing. The pair remained frozen and quiet for a few moments, waiting for another sign of movement, but none came. At least until they moved again.

"Of all the caves in all the world, you had to walk into mine." The voice echoed through the cavernous space, bouncing in all directions, creating an omnipresence, made more ominous by the laughter that followed.

But despite the voice's distortion from the echo, Mike knew that it was male, and... familiar.

"Did I make you worry about your family, Detective?" The man's voice again rang clearly through the cave, causing Mike to spin. "Well, worry no further, because I'm going to give you the chance to save them. But you have to play my game."

Mike froze. He had heard those words before. He had seen numerous crime scenes where the victims had been tortured before they were killed. This was the mark of a mad man. Somehow, Melvin Harris had found Mike. And now, Melvin Harris had his family.

"If you haven't figured it out by now, Detective, then I'm disappointed," Melvin said.

Mike realized the man was waiting for a response, and he knew Melvin well enough to know that the longer you resisted playing the game, the worse it would be. "I didn't realize you missed your flight to Quantico, Melvin."

Melvin laughed harder. "I knew you wouldn't disappoint me, Detective. You're the only person who understands. We're going to have some serious fun."

"My family is alive?" Mike asked.

"Of course they're alive," Melvin answered. "For now, at least. It did take you slightly longer than I anticipated to find me here. But since you have your wonderful sister to help you, I'm sure you'll be able to make up for lost time."

"This only ends one way for you, Melvin," Mike answered. "There are no more jails. No more courts. I find you, and I get to put you down myself."

Melvin clapped, slow and methodical. "Very good, Detective. Very good. I was wondering how long you would keep wearing that badge you're so proud of. But it seems that you're finally understanding this new world. I must admit, even I had some trouble adjusting to it. I mean, people are just so trusting when it comes to someone who can provide answers and help in a time of crisis."

"I'm sure you've killed plenty of people since you've gotten out," Mike said, and then he had one question on the tip of his tongue that didn't revolve around his family. "My partner?"

"Oh, he did his best," Melvin answered, then sighed. "Sadly, he just wasn't up to par."

Mike closed his eyes. Kevin was a good man.

"I'm sure your sister will find the other trails," Melvin said. "I made the others easier to follow. I hope I didn't give you too much of a handicap. I was just so excited to get everything started!" He laughed again, but this time Mike noticed Katy had turned off her light, and he saw her moving in the darkness, slowly, toward the left side of the cave.

Mike thought she had a bead on Melvin. If they could find the bastard now, then Mike might be able to get him to talk.

"You didn't leave any mementos behind at the crime scene," Mike said. "Changing your MO?"

"Oh no, Detective," Melvin answered. "I left them for you hear instead. Take a look at the center of the cavern."

Mike repositioned his flashlight, and then he lost his sister in his peripheral. It took a few sweeps of his light, but Mike finally saw the little treasures Melvin had left behind.

"A little something from each of them," Melvin said. "For Kelly. Casey. Mother dearest. And your lovely wife, who I must say holds a very high opinion of you. I hope you don't let her down."

Mike walked over to the items, which were locks of hair

from each of his family members. The same kind of tokens that Melvin kept of all his victims.

"I'll be waiting for you, Detective." Melvin's voice faded. "Best of luck."

Mike picked up the lock of his wife's hair. It was quiet for a long time, and Mike grew lost in his own thoughts. Thoughts of what Melvin might have done to his family, and of what the psychopath would do if he couldn't find them in time.

Lost in all of his own terrible thoughts, Mike jumped when Katy touched him, and he looked up to find her face cloaked in darkness.

"I lost him in the caves," Katy said. "The echo made it too hard to get a read on where he might have been hiding. But once we get back into the woods, I'll pick up the trail."

Mike nodded and then picked up the rest of the items that Melvin had left behind. Once they were secure, he cleared his throat and then turned to his sister. "Let's go."

Once they were out of the cave, Katy picked the trail back up, and it led them deeper into the wilderness.

Mike told Katy what he knew about Melvin and the serial killer's behavior. "He was the most ruthless criminal I ever saw. He would lure all of his victims to him under the pretense that he needed help, and then trap them and torture them until they died."

"Sounds more like an animal to me," Katy said.

"No, he's not an animal," Mike replied. "Animals kill and hunt, but they aren't cruel. They don't feed people little pieces of hope before they kill. Melvin is something different. He's intelligent, manipulative, cunning, and the most dangerous man that I've ever known in my entire life. He's evil incarnate."

"How long did it take you to catch this guy?" Katy asked.

"Eight months after he killed his first victim," Mike answered.

And even though Mike explained Melvin, he knew that

his sister wasn't ever really going to understand the kind of person he was. It was impossible to accurately describe Melvin. You needed to meet him in person. You needed to look evil in the eye to understand what drove him.

Katy moved a little quicker through the woods once Mike was done talking, but Melvin's nagging voice plagued Mike's thoughts. He wasn't even sure if his family was still alive. It wouldn't have been unheard of for the man to have already killed them. He had done that in his early days, and Mike imagined that Melvin would find it very thrilling for Mike to follow the breadcrumbs to his family members only to discover their dead bodies.

It was sick and demented, and right up Melvin's alley.

As Mike grew more worried about what he was going to find, Katy stopped, and he bumped into her back.

Mike immediately stepped back and scanned the woods, searching for whatever Katy had seen. But he saw nothing but trees, rocks, and bushes. Then, a breeze blew from the west, and it carried voices with it.

Both Mike and Katy sprinted toward the voices at the same time. But as fast as he ran, he didn't overtake his sister, who was more surefooted on the rough terrain than he was.

"Wait!" Mike reached for Katy and brought them both to a stop. He panted, catching his breath, able to hear the voices more clearly now even without the wind.

"What are you doing?" Katy asked. "We can hear them."

"I know," Mike said, frowning, and then studied the ground. "If Melvin's game is built around me trying to find my kids, then he wouldn't have made it so easy for me to just hear them crying out for help." He shook his head. "He wants me to run into this headfirst."

Katy narrowed her eyes as she slowly caught on. "He set a trap."

"Yes," Mike said, his heart aching from the cries of help from his children.

Mike and Kate moved carefully but deliberately over the remaining terrain between themselves and the kids. After a few minutes of finding nothing, Mike began to think that maybe he was getting in his own head, but that disappeared when Katy called out to him.

"Mike, freeze!" Katy thrust out her arm when she spoke, and Mike did as he was told. "Do not move. I'm coming to you."

Mike remained completely still. He wanted to look left or right but was afraid that anything that he might do would end his life. It wasn't until he felt Katy's hands on his shoulders that he finally relaxed.

"Tripwire," Katy said. "Down by your ankle."

Mike glanced down to his feet. It took him a moment to find the fine thread of fishing line that ran along the ground, but when he did, he slowly inched his foot back, the sole of his boot scraping along the dirt and rocks.

Katy knelt down and examined the wire, following it to a nearby cluster of rocks where it ended, and she found a small grenade. She glanced back to Mike. "Does this guy normally work with explosives?"

"No," Mike answered.

"Great." Katy stood and left the device where it lay.

"Help!" The voice was stronger this time, and it pulled both Mike and Katy one step toward it.

"That was Kelly," Mike said, his voice a whisper.

"He's probably set more traps along the path," Katy said. "But we might be able to speed this process up a little bit."

She retrieved the grenade, very carefully, then squeezed down the lever to make sure that there wasn't any chance of it going off until she was ready. "If he's never set up explosives before, then he probably stacked the grid, putting a bunch of them in a row in the direction he knew that we'd follow." She pointed toward Kelly's voice.

Mike nodded and then glanced along the ground. "How many do you think he put down?"

"Hard to tell," Katy said. "Fish wire is practically translucent, but he did a shit job with keeping the line secure for pressure. It's too loose. You're also lucky you didn't just blow yourself sky-high to kingdom come."

"What do we do?" Mike asked.

Katy gestured to the grenade. "We trip the wires." She swung her arm back like she was about to go bowling with the grenade and then flung it over the ground, sending it rolling over rocks and twigs and dirt.

The first explosion was only a dozen feet ahead of them, followed by several more, the percussive blasts causing Mike's bones to vibrate. The explosions continued to go off for several more minutes, and by the time that it was finished, Mike had collapsed to his knees on the ground, eyes shut.

A steady din filled Mike's ears, and when he finally opened his eyes, his vision was overwhelmed by the light. He blinked a few times and then managed to stand back up and saw the destruction left behind by the several traps triggered by the rolling grenade.

"Jesus," Mike said, taking a step forward before quickly stopping himself.

The ground was upheaved in several places, but Mike

wasn't sure if the grenade managed to trigger all of the trip-wires that Melvin had set up.

"Damn," Katy said. "Where the hell did he pick up all that stuff?"

"I don't know—"

Another scream caught their attention, this one more blood-curdling than the one before, and Mike took one step before Katy stopped him.

"We can move quicker, but we still pay attention to the ground, all right?" Katy asked. "And you step where I step."

Mike nodded, but only to make the situation move more quickly.

The closer Katy and Mike moved through the forest, the louder Kelly's screams became, and eventually, Katy broke out into a sprint, and Mike matched her step for step. The forest foliage thickened, making it difficult to walk, but they pushed into a clearing which ended at the edge of a cliff.

But there was no sign of his kids.

"Kelly!" Mike stepped past Katy, panic taking over. "*Kelly*!"

"Dad!" The scream was close, but Mike still couldn't see her. Until Katy grabbed his arm and pulled him back toward her and pointed to a nearby tree.

A piece of rope had been tied around it, and it was taut. Mike followed the rope and saw that it went over the cliff.

"Oh my god." Mike sprinted toward the cliff's ledge, skidding to his knees, numb to the pain and only focused on his daughter. He peered over the side of the ledge and found both of his children. "Kelly! Casey!"

Kelly and Casey were tied together, twirling precariously through the air with jagged rocks several hundred feet below them. If they fell, then they would die on impact.

"Dad, get us out of this!" Kelly cried out.

"Hang on!" Mike noticed that Casey wasn't responding. "Is your brother all right?" And just before Kelly answered, Mike had this terrible vision that Kelly was trapped with her dead brother, suspended from the air.

"He got knocked in the head," Kelly said. "But he's still breathing."

Mike exhaled with relief. "We'll get you up!" Mike saw Katy already trying to get the rope properly anchored, and he rushed over to help. "What's the matter?"

"It's slowly giving way, but I don't have any slack to retie it without it dropping both of them. Do you think you can hold it?"

Combined, Mike's kids tipped the scale at over two hundred pounds. It was a deceptive amount of dead weight. "I can do it."

Katy handed Mike a pair of gloves. They were too small to fit his hands, but he placed the grip between his palm and the rope to give him better hold. He pulled back with all of his strength, his muscles burning and the pressure in his head building so high that he thought he was going to explode.

But despite the intense pressure, Mike was able to keep pulling, and he managed to give enough slack for Katy to retie the knot properly.

"Just hold it right there, Mike!" Katy shouted.

Mike's hands ached, and even though he pressed all of his weight down into his heels, the soles of his boots inched forward. "Hurry!"

"Just a little bit longer!" Katy said.

Mike shut his eyes, focusing every ounce of his strength and concentration on not letting go, but he felt his grip slipping.

When his fingers numbed, Mike opened his eyes, afraid that since he couldn't feel the rope, then he might let go, and saw that two of his fingers had already slipped off from his right hand. "I can't hold it for much longer!"

"Almost done!" Katy shouted, then she murmured something inaudible beneath her breath.

Mike grunted, his breaths labored. He had maybe two more seconds before the grip was gone. But he had to hold on. He wasn't going to lose his kids now, not when he was so close to them.

And the moment the rope slipped out of Mike's hands, his heart skipped a beat, and he lunged for the rope again, but instead of feeling the slack pull him forward and drag him across rocks until his flesh peeled off, the rope grew taut again.

"Done!" Katy yelled, and then slapped Mike on the back. "C'mon, let's pull them up."

Mike stared down at his red, trembling hands and almost broke down in tears. Without saying another word, he wrapped his sister in a firm hug and kissed the top of her head. "Thank you."

When he let go, Katy smiled at him, and then pulled him toward the ledge. "C'mon."

It was slow going, but between Mike and Katy, the pair slowly pulled Kelly and Casey toward the ledge. When they neared the top, Kelly helped pull her brother over the edge, and then once both of his kids were on firm ground, Mike dropped the rope and scooped both of them in his arms and squeezed them tight.

But the relief and reunion were short-lived when Mike realized that Casey was still unconscious. He checked his boy for injury and saw the bloodstain on the top of his skull where he'd been hit, but he couldn't tell if any bone had been broken. But he was still breathing, still alive.

"Do you remember what happened?" Mike asked, turning to his daughter.

"A man came into the cabin and knocked out Mom," Kelly said, her voice matching the same trembling motion as her body. "He had a gun and pointed it at Casey and me, and then Mr. Nasir came running inside, and he fought him. Then I took Casey and ran outside, but he caught up with us. He knocked Casey out and threatened to shoot him if I didn't carry him into the woods."

Kelly's speech pattern eventually dissolved into nothing but whimpers and tears, and she collapsed forward into Mike's arms.

All Mike wanted to do at that moment was hold his daughter, tell her that she was safe now and that she didn't have anything to worry about. But he didn't have time for that, and neither did Casey.

Mike gently sat Kelly upright, making sure that his daughter understood what was at stake. "Listen, I need you to carry your brother back to the cabin."

"I—I don't think I can." Kelly sniffled and then bunched her face up again like she was going to cry.

But Mike gave her a gentle shake, and she stopped. "You have to, okay? You need to take your brother back to the cabin and get him into a bed, and then clean up the wound on his head. Do you remember how to do that?"

Mike had made both of his kids take a standard first aid class a few years ago. He wanted to make sure that they could take care of themselves in case of an emergency. Like now.

"Yes," Kelly said, finding some strength in her voice. "Yes, I remember."

"Good," Mike said. "I'm going to give you a compass, and I need you to head due southeast. If you stay on that heading, it should take you back to the cabin. Your Aunt Katy and I are going to find your mother and grandmother." He paused, hoping for a miracle. "Did you see where the man took them?"

Kelly shook her head. "No. He took us out first and left us over that cliff." Her voice grew very quiet. "Are Mom and Grandma still alive?"

Mike didn't answer the question. Instead, he simply lifted Kelly to her feet and held her upright until she could stand on her own. "Can you carry him?"

While Kelly hesitated before, she didn't do it this time, and Mike was glad to hear the strength in her voice. "Yes. I can."

Mike kissed her forehead, and then Katy gave her the compass. Mike then helped place his son in Kelly's arms and kissed his son's forehead too, then he held them both. "I love you. I love both of you. And I'm going to come back as soon as I can, okay?"

"Okay," Kelly answered. "I love you too."

Mike watched her leave, struggling a little with her brother's body, but she didn't quit. Mike waited until he couldn't see her anymore and then Katy walked over to him.

"If he brought them out one at a time, then he probably kept the others nearby," Katy said. "He wouldn't have had time to go any farther than this and make three trips."

Mike nodded, hoping that his sister was right. But even if his mother and wife were close, Mike knew that he was running out of time.

*M*ike did his best to keep his attention focused on the task at hand, but his mind was in three different places. One part was with Kelly and Casey, worrying about their return to the cabin. Another part was with his mother, unsure if she would even survive the trip into the woods. She had been so weak and tired. And the final part was with his wife, praying he would be able to deliver the good news that their children were safe.

But he could die out in these woods. The man lurking in these woods could think of ways to kill someone no other person could fathom.

Katy stopped, and Mike stood next to her as she studied the surrounding ground. "The trail gets all turned up here." She frowned, kneeling to touch the earth. "It's almost like..."

Mike bent over, trying to see what she saw. "What?"

Katy stood and then walked forward a few steps, her eyes still locked on the ground. Mike waited, watching her from a distance.

A branch snapped somewhere in the woods, and it triggered both Katy and Mike into a state of alertness. Neither of them spoke, both of them ready to engage whatever was waiting for them in the trees. But after a few minutes of quiet, there was nothing else.

"Could have been a deer or any of other hundreds of animals that live out here," Katy said. "Hell, it could have been the wind." She dismissed the noise and returned to studying the ground.

But Mike didn't take his eyes off of the trees and rocks because he knew what was waiting for him. Melvin's shadow of death was all over these woods.

Katy continued along the path, and she started to call out what she saw. "It looks like there was some kind of struggle out here. Someone was fighting back."

Mike finally looked at his sister.

"No, wait." Katy stopped and shook her head. "No, someone was being dragged."

Mike joined Katy, studying the same ground, but he saw nothing in the patterns. "How can you tell?"

Katy pointed to a pair of lines in the dirt. "Heels. Two of them. The person was carried by their arms, like a fireman carry. It's the easiest way to move someone if you're too tired or too weak to pick them up."

Melvin wasn't a strong man, but neither his wife or mother were big women. He could have managed to carry them.

Katy pointed to the lines, continuing to follow them. "And then the body is dropped here." Katy stopped, pointing to a large imprint in the ground. It didn't look like a human shape, but Mike could tell that something had definitely flattened the leaves and grass among the dirt. "And then..." Katy stepped forward, following the tracks in the ground, and then stopped. "And then the body was moved here."

Mike frowned and then looked at his sister. "So where is it?"

Katy glanced around the rest of the earth and shook her head. "It doesn't make any sense. It's like the person stopped dragging the body back there and then picked it up again." She glanced up toward the hills. "But why would they decide to carry it up the hill?"

Mike walked over to join his sister, but on his way, his foot kicked something on the ground. He glanced down, not giving it much thought. It was probably a rock or a stick, but it was neither. Instead he found a small piece of pipe sticking up through the ground. "Katy, look at this." He bent down to inspect the item and gave it a little tug.

The pipe was wedged firmly into the ground. Katy joined him and then frowned, taking a closer look at the earth, and suddenly she gasped.

"Oh my god," Katy said. "He buried her. He buried someone in the ground!"

Katy immediately set her gun aside and started digging. Mike was frozen for a moment, but after Katy scooped a few mounds of earth to the side, he set his own weapon down and then raked his fingers across the earth, scooping dirt around the piece of pipe that was protruding from the earth.

Katy reached the box first, and then Mike started to help clear the top off to find the edges when gunfire surprised them from the rear.

Both of them ducked, but it was Katy who reached her weapon first, and she returned fire. Mike continued to unearthing the box, clearing the edges.

"He has the high ground!" Katy shouted back to Mike. "If he moves closer, we're in trouble."

Mike heard her voice, but he didn't move. All of his concentration was on rescuing whoever was inside the box. And as much as he loved his mother, he hoped it was Lisa because he wanted to at least have his wife and kids be safe. "I've almost got it open!"

Mike managed to get his fingers under the edges of the lid, and he pulled with all of his strength. The box creaked, and then wood splintered, and Mike was flung backward, a piece of the lid in his hand. He quickly lunged forward, keeping low from the gunfire that was still being exchanged between Melvin and his sister, and saw his mother inside the box.

Martha was still and calm, dirt sprinkled over her face and body, the dark pieces of black peppering the white puff of her hair. Mike immediately reached down into the box to check her pulse, and he felt nothing. But he knew that his hand was shaking and his senses were overwhelmed by the moment, so he forced himself to reset.

Mike took a breath and then felt for a pulse again, keeping his hand steady. He turned around toward his sister. "It's Mom! And she's alive!"

"Get her out!" Katy shouted, her attention still focused on Melvin. "I'll provide cover fire! Go!"

Mike scooped his mother in his arms, as quickly and as carefully as he could. Once Martha was secure, Mike moved toward the nearest cluster of trees, but along the way, a flash of sharp, hot pain stung near his lower left back, and his right knee buckled and then banged into the dirt.

But Mike managed to stay upright and pushed through the pain. He continued until he brought his mother behind safe cover and gently laid her down. He checked her pulse one more time, and once he felt it again, he rejoined his sister in the fight.

Katy had secured herself behind a cluster of low-lying rocks and even pushed her way forward a few feet, gaining precious ground against Melvin. When Mike joined her, she pointed to the crest of the hill. "You see him? He's right between those rocks. He keeps retreating after every round of gunfire. I've got his pattern down."

Mike peered through the sights of his own rifle, searching, and then eventually found the same target. "I've got him."

"When he runs again, we'll unload," Katy said. "I don't think he's even aiming anymore."

"Should we bum-rush him?" Mike asked. "Head up the hill and end this now?"

"Depends on how good of a shot you think he is," Katy said. "And if we get closer, he'll still have the advantage of the high ground."

Mike nodded and then discarded his idea.

"C'mon, you bastard," Katy said. "Run. I know you want to."

Finally, Melvin emerged. He fired a few rounds in their general direction, but Katy and Mike were prepared and unleashed hell on the man, bullets chasing him on his run up the hill.

Katy stopped firing first and then cursed under her breath. "I missed."

Mike rolled to his side. "Me too." He glanced back to where he left their mother, and then they both stood, Katy still covering them on their retreat, and returned to Martha, who was still unconscious where Mike had placed her.

"She has a pulse, and she's breathing," Mike said, updating

275

Katy when they were out of danger, at least for the moment. "You need to take her back."

"And leave you out here alone?" Katy asked. "No way. Plus, you can't track worth shit. You take Mom back, and I'll finish this."

"I won't be able to find my way back as fast as you," Mike said, then placed a hand on his sister's shoulder. "I need you to do this."

"All right," Katy said. "But the moment I put Mom back in the cabin, I'm coming back to help you."

"Good," Mike said, then smiled. "You know I'll need it."

Katy lunged forward, hugging him tightly. "Stay alive. Promise me."

It wasn't a promise he could keep, because if it came down to saving his wife's life or giving up his own, he wouldn't hesitate. But Katy didn't want to hear that. She wanted to know he was going to be all right. She wanted to hear that he was going to be safe and careful. And so he lied. "I promise."

Katy nodded and then wiped away the tears that had collected in her eyes. "Good. Because if you don't, then I'll bring you back to life just so I can kill you again." Katy took a breath and then glanced down to their mother. "Do you think she'll make it?"

There was a genuine worry in her voice, and Mike was glad to see some of the wall Katy had built around herself crumble and expose the girl he remembered.

"She'll make it," Mike said. "But you need to hurry before that killer decides to make a victory lap."

Katy nodded, then hugged Mike once more. She scooped Martha up in her arms with the same care and gentle nature that Mike had done. "I'll be as fast as I can."

Mike watched Katy leave, carrying their mother through the trees. He waited until he couldn't see them anymore, and his smile faded as he looked up toward the hill where Melvin had been waiting for them. He didn't want to climb that mountain, because he had already caught Melvin Harris once. The first time, Mike had an army of law enforcement at his back. Now, he was alone.

Mike winced and then reached for the spot on his lower left back that had stung from earlier. The moment his fingers touched the warm goo, he examined his fingertips and the blood on them.

Mike wasn't sure how bad the gunshot was since he didn't have a mirror to examine it, but for now the pain was manageable and the blood loss limited. He might have just been grazed. Or the bullet might have gone all the way and he was just in shock, but he knew that whatever the scenario, he was going to find Melvin. And when he did, Mike would finish this for good.

*K*aty moved quickly but made sure not to push herself too hard too fast. The last thing she needed was to take a spill, sending both herself and her mom skidding over the dirt and rocks. And based off of her mother's condition, Katy was afraid that even a simple fall might kill her.

It was surprising to feel how light her mother felt in her arms. The frail, shriveled woman that she now held was a far cry from the strong independent warrior that she remembered from her youth.

When Katy was younger, she had loved her mother, fiercely. But all of that changed after the incident between Katy and her dad.

Katy had done a good job of cutting out the people in her life. She had perfected the art of living alone and avoiding creating any new attachments.

But now Katy was carrying her dying mother through the woods, who had just been buried alive after surviving a gunshot wound, returning to the cabin where her niece and nephew waited anxiously for their parents to return. Katy understood she had gone too far.

Anger had made her bitter and cold, and it had taken her family being torn apart to finally see it. But it wasn't too late to make things right. She only needed a little more time. She needed to believe in hope again.

The trek back to the cabin was longer than Katy had anticipated, but she didn't stop, remembering all of the times her mother had carried her as a child. She refused to fail.

And Katy's perseverance paid off when she saw the cabin. She sprinted the last stretch, and was then aided by Kelly who had arrived safely home.

"Where's my dad?" Kelly asked, following Katy into the bedroom where Katy set her mother down over the covers. "Did you find my mom?"

"He's still looking for her," Katy answered, and then quickly cleaned the crook of her mother's arm and reinstated the IV, again checking her pulse. It was faint, but it was there.

"What's going on?" Kelly asked.

Katy knew the girl wanted answers. She turned around and placed both hands on her niece's shoulders. She looked more like Lisa than Mike.

"Is Casey all right?" Katy asked.

"Yeah, he's still breathing, and I cleaned his wound, but he still hasn't woken up," Kelly said, and then the last bit of strength broke in her voice. "What's going on?"

"Your father is still searching for your mother," Katy answered. "I'm going back into the woods to help." She reached for her sidearm. "Have you ever used one of these before?"

Kelly stared at the gun. "My dad has taken me to the range a few times."

"This is a standard Glock 9mm." Katy went through the motions of the weapon: slide, magazine, trigger. "It has internal safeties, so the weapon is always ready to fire. Got it?"

Kelly nodded, staring at the weapon.

Katy took a step for the door then stopped. "Nasir's daughters are in the cellar." She tossed Kelly the keys. "It's a hidden door all the way in the back. Feel along with the wooden panels until you feel a loose one and pull. That key will let you inside. Make sure they're okay, and if things get really bad, take your brother and hide in there with them. It's soundproof, so people won't be able to hear you."

"What about Grandma?" Kelly asked, looking to the old woman on the cot.

"Bring her if you have time, but if you don't—" Katy saw the shock in Kelly's eyes and realized how harsh and cold all of this sounded, and she changed her tack. "Hopefully it won't come to that."

Without another word, Kelly moved toward Katy and then flung her arms around her aunt. "I'm scared."

Katy didn't know how to react at first, but then she gently stroked Kelly's hair. "Me too. But we need to brave. For our family. Okay?"

Kelly pulled back and nodded. She adjusted her grip on the pistol and then took a breath. She was so young, and Katy knew she was being forced to handle a situation most girls her age couldn't. She was forced to grow up quickly now. The world no longer spared kids their childhood.

"Go and get Nasir's daughters," Katy said.

Kelly nodded and then left. Katy turned back around to her mother. The old woman was so still, she didn't even look like she was breathing. But if she stared long enough, she was able to see the small rise of her chest when she inhaled, and the tiny divot when she exhaled.

Katy hoped they both survived. Because Katy wanted to make things right between them again. She needed to make amends.

34

*M*ike was slow but deliberate on his trek up the hill. He didn't think that Melvin would finish the job here, not before Mike saw whatever he had planned for Lisa. Melvin always hated when his prey didn't survive to see his grand finale.

Mike crested the top of the hill and was relieved when he saw the land flatten out. He reached back behind him to touch the source of the gunshot and found a little bit of blood had soaked through the bandage he had wrapped around himself.

Mike had attempted to clean up the wound with the supplies in his pack the best he could, but the job had been rushed and sloppy.

When the terrain flattened, Mike picked up his pace, but he struggled to find Melvin's tracks. And what was worse, his vision was starting to blur. The blood loss, combined with his fatigue and injury, was beginning to wear him down.

Mike leaned against a tree trunk and closed his eyes. He took in a few deep breaths, the top of his ribs pinching on the deepest portion of his inhale. But when Mike opened his eyes, his vision had cleared, and some of his strength returned.

Unsure of how long it would last, Mike pushed himself off the trunk and charged forward. He knew time was running out, and every second counted.

More alert, Mike was able to move through the woods faster, making up time from his slow shamble from earlier. He wasn't sure what he was looking for, only that he would know it when he saw it.

While Mike traversed the woods alone, he couldn't shake the feeling of a pair of eyes watching him from somewhere between trees. He tried to convince himself it was only in his head and Melvin wasn't nearby, but the irrational portion of his mind wouldn't stay quiet.

It was because Mike knew Melvin. He had seen firsthand how the psychopath worked. It was possible Melvin had a bead on him at this very moment, and he was just waiting until the right time before he ambushed him.

But Mike couldn't control what he couldn't see, so he kept all of his focus and attention on reining in his own hysteria. No sense in making his situation worse in his mind than it was in reality.

The combination of the sun, the terrain, and Mike's injury made the rest of the journey hell. But he pressed on. He had no other choice.

Another hundred yards and Mike neared the edge of a pit, and his heart flooded with hope at the sight of his wife.

Mike took one step toward the edge, but then stopped himself. Just like with the kids, Melvin was trying to lure him in, and Mike saw why.

The pit walls were steep and high. If Mike ventured down

by himself and Melvin showed up (and Mike was positive that the man was hiding nearby), then both he and his wife would be in the kill zone.

Mike tried to get a better look at Lisa, checking to see if she had any injuries. He could tell she was bound and gagged, and her clothes were torn and dirtied, but that was all he could see from his current vantage point.

"Lisa!" Mike whispered softly and as loud as he could. He glanced around to see if his voice triggered any movement from Melvin. When he saw nothing, he tried to call her again. "Lisa!"

Lisa stirred, lifting her head. She glanced around for a moment, almost like she was drugged, but when her eyes found Mike at the top of the heap, she came alive again.

Aside from the restraints and the gag, Lisa seemed unharmed. Mike held his finger up to his lips. The best thing would be to toss a rope down to Lisa and pull her up. But with her hands bound, Mike would have to throw the rope lasso-style, something he had never done before.

Mike turned around and then slowly and carefully circled the pit, searching for any other signs of Melvin or his traps. But when he made it all the way around without finding anything, and with no timeline on when Katy would return, Mike knew he had to try and get her out now.

Mike pressed his foot on the pit's wall, testing the earth. When he applied some of his weight, the dirt loosened and triggered a small landslide.

And just when Mike took that first big leap down the side, something hard pushed him forward, and he was flung into the air for a few feet, tumbling downward until his arms connected with the walls and sent him rolling down over the dirt and rocks until he landed with an abrupt stop at the very bottom.

Disoriented from the fall, Mike rolled to his hands and knees. He shook off the dizziness and spotted his weapon a few feet away in the dirt. He crawled to reach for it when a gunshot fired, the bullet kicking up the dirt between Mike and the rifle.

"Not so fast, Detective," Melvin said.

Mike slowly raised his eyes from the rifle on the ground and to the man standing at the top of the pit. Melvin wore a broad and winning smile, and he kept his rifle aimed not at Mike, but at Lisa.

"I knew you'd be able to find her sooner or later," Melvin said.

Mike didn't move, unsure of how happy Melvin's trigger finger was at the moment. "And I did."

Melvin laughed. "I can't believe I actually have you down there! I had high hopes that you would make it this far, and look at how well you've done! Saved your children, saved your mother, at least for the time being. I almost felt that putting her in the ground the way I did was a better service than keeping her alive. But I suppose my views on motherhood are more skewed than your own."

Mike studied Melvin, and while his vision began to blur again, he saw the rifle Melvin had. It was the same AK-47 the terrorists had been armed with. He also noticed something shiny on Melvin's belt.

Melvin gestured down to the shiny object on his belt and smiled. "Do you like it? I thought it was beautifully poetic that I wear your partner's badge. And you wouldn't believe how much I got away with by wearing one of these!" He laughed again, still keeping the gun aimed at Lisa.

"I know what you want, Melvin," Mike said, slowly getting to his knees, and then standing. "But I'm not going to let you hurt my wife."

"Detective," Melvin said, his tone slightly playful. "Do you really think that you're in a position to be bargaining with me right now? I mean just look at yourself for Christ sakes. You've stumbled all the way down into the most basic of all traps, and I have the high ground." The smile slackened, and even though it was in the middle of the day, the sun shining through the trees, Melvin's face darkened. "I can do whatever I want to you or your wife. And there is nothing that you can do to stop me."

* * *

KATY RETRACED her steps through the woods, moving with the same kind of purpose and drive that she had learned during her stint in the military. Despite the one terrible, horrible thing that happened to her during her time overseas, she had learned much from the military. It had taken her a long time to distinguish between the rape and the rest of the military, because for years after she lumped it all into the same category.

And while she had felt betrayed by the members of her team and a few of the superior officers in her chain of command, she also received support from many people. And those were the individuals that she chose to remember. Those were the people that she knew were the core of the military and had done their duty to serve and protect.

Katy had finally healed from her encounter all of those years ago, and now that she had her family here, she wanted the opportunity to heal with them. But that wasn't going to happen unless she stopped the predator from hunting all of them down.

MELVIN CIRCLED the rim of the pit slowly, his rifle aimed at Lisa the entire time. Mike hadn't tried to make a move for his own rifle, because he had seen enough of Melvin's crime scene photos to know that he was a decent shot. The man had even bragged about bringing down one of his victims with a pistol from twenty-five yards while the victim was on the run.

But Melvin liked to embellish the truth. It was his Achilles heel, a way for him to build his own superiority. And Mike hoped to exploit that weakness now.

"You just weren't good enough this time, huh, Melvin?" Mike asked.

Melvin frowned. "What are you talking about?"

"I mean with the rest of my family," Mike answered. "I saved my children and my mother."

"And you think I was just going to let them get away once I had you here?" Melvin laughed, shaking his head. "Oh, Detective. And people always told me I was the delusional one. While there is still your sister to deal with, how long do you think she'll last before she throws down her weapon when she sees the gun that I have pressed against the back of your skull?"

Mike shrugged. "We've had our differences over the years. She might not care."

"That's true," Melvin said. "I did read her letter. It was how I found out about this secret location. But you'd be surprised at how quickly people have a change of heart when the harsh realities of a situation finally hit them. Probably like they're hitting you now."

Mike slowly turned with Melvin, watching him every step of the way. All he needed to do was keep him talking, keep his attention focused on him.

"You're stuck in a pit with your wife, who has been tied up and gagged, and at the top of the pit is one of the most brilliant serial killers this country has ever seen," Melvin said. "You should really be flattered, Detective. It's rare that an individual such as myself personally selects someone like you. But you impressed me the moment I met you."

"I impressed you because I was the one who caught you," Mike said.

Melvin laughed again. "Yes, I suppose there was that too. And for a long time I thought maybe, just maybe, you weren't the man I had built up in my head. But you delivered."

Mike knew Melvin was laying it on thick only to stroke his own ego. Mike was a good cop, yes, but the truth was Melvin had made mistakes. He was just too arrogant to admit them.

"So, what we're going to do now is have a family reunion," Melvin said. "I'll need you to pick up your wife, keeping the restraints around her wrists and ankles of course, and carry her out of that pit so we can make our way back to the cabin. And I'm very, very glad that you made it this far, Detective, because I honestly don't think I could carry her out of there. If you hadn't shown up, then I would have just had to shoot her and leave her! And that wouldn't be any way to treat the wife of Detective Mike Thorton—"

The bullet struck the tree to the left of Melvin's head, missing the man by only inches. But it was enough to startle him, and he quickly fired blindly in the direction of Katy, and then fired twice into the pit before he sprinted away.

Mike dove for his wife, removing her from the line of fire. He carried her to the far edge of the pit, positioning his body between Lisa and Melvin, holding onto her tight.

"Are you all right?" Mike asked, feeling along her body for any injuries and removing her gag.

"I'm fine," Lisa answered, her voice hoarse.

"Mike!" Katy shouted from the top of the pit. "Are you all right?"

"I'm fine! Go!" Mike shouted.

Katy nodded and then sprinted after Melvin.

It was a struggle for both of them to escape the pit, but once they reached the top they dropped to their knees and embraced.

But when Lisa pulled back and saw the blood from the wound on Mike's back, she started to shake again. "Oh my god, what happened?" Lisa stared at the blood on her palm, moving her fingers back and forth, which caused the sunlight to brighten the red.

Mike covered her palm and his blood with his own hand. "I'm fine."

Lisa squeezed Mike's palm and nodded. "And the kids and your mother?"

"They're all back at the cabin," Mike answered.

Lisa started to sob and then collapsed forward in his arms. Mike held her until another gunshot made her jump, and she opened her eyes wide with terror. "He's still out there."

Mike stared into the direction of the gunshot and nodded, but then looked back to his wife once she dug her fingers into his arm.

"You have to go, don't you?" Lisa asked.

"If we don't bring him down now, then he's never going to stop hunting us," Mike said. "My sister needs my help."

Lisa had tears in her eyes, and as much as Mike knew that she wanted to tell him to stay, she nodded. "Go."

Mike kissed her and then handed her the pistol that he had brought. "In case you need it. Just stay here, and Katy and I will find our way back to you."

"I love you," Lisa said.

"I love you too."

35

*M*ike hurried as fast as his legs would carry him through the woods, chasing the random pops of gunfire that echoed through the hot air. Even though life had changed so much, Mike couldn't help but be transported to the original manhunt when he had first captured Melvin Harris. It had been in a wooded area similar to this.

It was nighttime then, and Mike still remembered the unusual spring chill in the air and the dozens of flashlights that pierced the darkness. The hum of helicopter blades swirled overhead. Never before had there been so many resources dedicated to the capture of a single man.

Hundreds of law enforcement officers were present at the time, and the woods were filled with them and the K-9 units that had been brought in to sniff him out.

But this time Mike didn't have any K-9 or air support. He didn't have hundreds of trained and armed law enforcement officers at his back. This time he had a gunshot wound on his lower back, the rifle in his hand, and his sister who was currently engaging the monster on her own. Two against one still sounded like good odds, but Mike knew that it would be foolish to underestimate Melvin, especially now that he was on the run.

The gunshots grew louder and Mike slowed a little bit, not wanting to rush into anything with same foolhardy arrogance that Melvin had. He needed to outthink his opponent, he needed to be smarter than the highly-intelligent killer he was chasing.

Finally, Mike spied his sister by a tree, but she was busy reloading her weapon, and Mike didn't want to vocally make himself known to both her and Melvin. Instead he moved nearby, then tossed a rock at her shoe.

Mike had hoped that her reaction time would be good enough so she wouldn't shoot him, but he was still nervous when she finally turned the weapon on him. He breathed a sigh of relief though when she didn't pull the trigger.

Katy started to use hand signals that she had used in the military, but then stopped herself when she realized who she was speaking with. Mike didn't know the signals. Instead, she pointed back in the general direction where Melvin was shooting from.

Mike nodded and then mapped out a path between himself and Melvin. If he took a long, curving right, he would be able to stay out of Melvin's line of sight long enough to stop the man before he managed to get a lucky shot off on Katy.

Mike saw enough trees and rocks and medium-tall shrubs to do the job, and he tossed his sister a thumbs-up before he started the trek.

Melvin was tucked behind a cluster of boulders that looked out of place amongst the trees, but the closer that

Mike moved toward his target, he saw that it was the beginnings of a small mountain ridge that rose above the trees.

Gunfire continued to be exchanged between Melvin and his sister, but when he reached the halfway point of his journey, the shooting became one-sided.

Mike paused for a moment and tried to look back at his sister. He couldn't physically see her, but he could still hear the gunfire coming from her position.

It was Melvin who had stopped firing, which Mike didn't like. Either the man had run out of ammunition, he was injured, or he had something else planned.

Mike remained frozen halfway between Melvin and his sister. A part of Mike tried to reason with himself over the fact that there was probably nothing wrong. But then there was another part of him, a part that knew Melvin couldn't be trusted to do what normal people would do, that frightened him to his very core.

Mike broke from his covert mission, sprinting through the open back to his sister because that was the quickest way back to her. At the very least Mike thought that he would be able to draw Melvin out, make the bastard hurt him instead of his sister.

Mike's back injury slowed his pace, and while he was running as fast as he could, it was little more than a shambled limp. But on the way, Mike raised his rifle, and when he no longer heard his sister's gunfire, he screamed. "Katy!"

Mike skidded to a stop, his boots sliding over the dirt and the twigs, and discovered why the gunfire had stopped.

"Not another step, Detective." Melvin stood behind Katy, the automatic rifle pressed against the back of her skull. "I did say that this was going to end with my gun against the back of your head, but I suppose that your sister will have to do."

Katy was looking up at MIke, not with fear, but with regret. In her darkest moment, she was more worried about Mike's approval than saving her own life. She thought that she had failed him.

"Nothing more challenging than trying to get everything right the first time, Mike," Melvin said. "And while I always aimed for perfection, I fell short a few times. But it's all about being adaptable." He panted between words. He was tired, fatigued, just like they were.

"Let her go, Melvin," Mike said, but he didn't drop the weapon from his hands. Not yet. He wanted Melvin to show his hand, and he thought that the man was desperate enough to do it. "I know it's me that you want. And I'll let you have me. But you're a fool if you think that putting a bullet in her won't make me put a bullet in you."

Melvin smiled. "And what would be wrong with that? I think killing the sister that you finally reconnected with after all of these years would be a nice wound for you. I imagine that there are worse ways I could leave this earth than killing a family member of my arch-nemesis."

"One family member," Mike said. "But that's not what you wanted, remember? You said you wanted to make my entire family suffer, Melvin. That's what you said. I didn't realize that you were a fucking liar."

Melvin laughed. "Detective, I'm surprised by you. I never took you for a big psychology man, but trying to change my mind here won't help you. I've read every trick in the book. I've measured all of the outcomes. And I know that the only way for me to hurt you at any point in this juncture now would be to blow the top of your sister's head off and let the crows pick at her brains. Then you'll mow me down, and this will be over for me, but just beginning with you. Because her death will haunt you long after my shadows have stopped chasing you. Because that's all death is. It's remembering. Without remembering, death serves no purpose."

Mike nodded. "I suppose that has some truth to it. But I wasn't trying to change your mind, Melvin." Mike kept his eyes locked on the serial killer's.

"You weren't?" Melvin asked, tilting his head to the side, maintaining his arrogant tone even though he knew he wasn't going to walk out of this alive. "Then tell me, Detective. What was your plan?"

Katy slowly moved her hand down to her shoe, keeping her movements hidden from Melvin. She carefully removed the small blade on the side of her boot and then looked to her brother. It would happen quickly.

"Speak up, Detective!" Melvin shouted, and he grew angrier. "Don't keep all of your thoughts to yourself! Share it with the class."

"It's nothing really," Mike said, waiting for Katy to make her move. "I was just thinking about what we're going to do with your body."

Melvin frowned. "We?"

Katy moved left and swung the knife into Melvin's leg, avoiding the bullet he fired from the stabbing. The blast of the gunfire was directly adjacent to the left side of Katy's face. She cried out in pain from the blast, but it was more from the noise than any contact from the barrel or the bullets.

Mike fired his weapon a second later, shooting Melvin twice in the chest. He then immediately charged Melvin, knocking the rifle out of his reach. "It's over, Melvin. You're done."

Melvin placed one shaky hand over the gruesome wound on his chest and then opened his mouth where a hiss escaped in place of any cry of pain. He narrowed his eyes as blood filled his mouth and stared at Mike.

"You're right, Detective," Melvin said, then coughed up some blood that speckled his chin and neck with crimson drops. "I'm done. But you're not, are you? You're the new law of the land. A man who doesn't answer to any courts or Internal Affairs. You've never had that kind of power or authority before, and it makes me wonder how you'll use it." Melvin smiled and then rested his head back, unable to hold it up any longer. "I wonder if you'll stay as righteous as you did when you were on the police force. Or maybe, just maybe, a little bit of my violence slipped into you. Maybe you become a little more like me?"

Mike tightened his grip on the rifle, the composite and plastic creaking under pressure. "I will never be like you, Melvin. Not on my worst day."

Melvin laughed, but it was cut short by another cough, this one more gurgling and painful than the one that came before it. "I wouldn't be so sure, Detective. You'd be surprised what the wild forces a domestic animal to do. I wasn't sure if you had it in you to survive. But now I see it. Now I... see... me... in... you..."

One last hiss escaped Melvin's mouth, and then he lay still. With the killer dead, Mike turned his attention to his sister, who was staring down at Melvin with a mixture of disgust and fear. Mike helped her up and then took a closer look at her ear.

"It's ringing loud," Katy said. "Not sure if it'll come back or not."

Mike made sure to speak on her right side. "Time will tell. You all right beside the ear?"

Katy nodded, then looked down at Melvin again. "He's a bastard, but he's right, you know." She looked at her brother. "The world has changed, and people are going to change with it. People will do whatever they can to survive. It's in our nature."

Mike nodded. "That's true. But we also have good things in our nature. We just have to make sure that the good outweighs the evil."

"And how do we do that?" Katy asked.

"By finding people like you and me, and people like Nasir, people who are willing to put their lives on the line to help others," Mike answered. "Because the only way people like Melvin win are when good people stop taking care of others. It's when selfish desire takes over that society truly collapses. And that's not us."

Katy hesitated for a moment and then shook her head. "I don't know, Mikey."

"I do," Mike said, and then placed his hand on his sister's shoulder. "And we'll help remind each other every day."

36

THE NEXT MORNING

$\mathcal{M}$ike had gone to bed early the night before. He had fallen asleep between his wife and son, Casey, who had yet to wake up from the injury to his head. Unable to do anything other than feeding him fluids through an IV, the best that they could hope for was that he was able to heal himself and wake up in a day or two.

The injury to Mike's back wasn't as severe as he originally thought. It was only a scrape, and after a pair of butterfly stitches the bleeding stopped. But Jim didn't feel better until son finally woke up.

Casey was groggy and tired, but he was alive and conscious. Katy helped perform some field tests on the boy, making sure that all of his motor functions were still working properly, and the final diagnosis was a concussion. They would have to keep an eye on him over the next few days, but he should recover just fine.

Once Casey had woken up, all the attention turned to Martha, who was still fast asleep on the cot. Her pulse had grown a little stronger overnight, and her body was still taking fluids, but the old woman was very unresponsive.

Katy had stayed with her most of the night, and Mike saw the hurt and worry on his sister's face. There were things that Katy needed to say, and there were things that she needed to hear. And after everything that his sister had gone through, all of the pain and loss that she experienced, Mike hoped that she would be able to find peace.

And three hours after the sun rose, Katy finally got her chance.

"Mother?" Katy asked, reaching for Martha's hand as she stirred awake. "Mom? Can you hear me?"

Martha Thorton blinked a few times and then stared up at the ceiling. For a moment, she looked like she didn't know where she was, and considering what she had gone through over the past two days, it was understandable.

Mike remained by the door, watching as Martha turned and saw Katy holding her hand.

"Katherine?" Martha asked. "Is that you?"

Katy nodded, tears filling up her eyes. "Yeah, Mom, it's me." She wiped the tears away and then sniffled. "How are you feeling?"

"Tired," Martha answered. "Very tired."

Katy nodded again, remaining quiet, her sinuses filled with phlegm. "Mommy, I'm sorry for what happened. I'm sorry that I left, and that I blamed so much on you and—"

"Shhh, sweetheart," Martha said. "It wasn't your fault. And I never blamed you for leaving." She smiled weakly. "I only wish that I could have reached you before you left. What your father did was unforgivable. But he didn't blame you for leaving either. Not at the end. The burden that you're feeling, whatever guilt that you still might be harboring. Let it go. I beg you." Martha teared up, and then with what little strength she had, she reached for her daughter's hand. "Just let it go."

Katy dropped to her knees and then wrapped her arms around their frail mother, gently holding the old woman, who did her best to hold back. They stayed like that for a long time, and then Mike walked out of the room, glad for what he had seen. Glad that both his mother and his sister had been able to break free from the pain that had plagued them.

Mike walked out onto the front porch and saw Nasir's girls in the yard, both of them holding hands and staring at the space where Mike and Katy had buried him.

"We'll take care of them." Lisa snuck up behind him and gently placed her arm around the fresh bandage on his back.

The physical wounds would heal. But Mike wasn't sure how about everything else.

"It's not going to get any easier," Mike said, watching Nasir's girls. "We've got a long way to go before we return to any sense of normalcy. And I don't know how—"

Lisa cupped her palm over his mouth, and he stopped talking. "Whatever happens. Whatever we face. We'll beat it. Together." She lowered her hand and then Mike kissed it.

"You're right," Mike said. "We will. Because we can."

Made in United States
Troutdale, OR
09/24/2024

23096745R00169